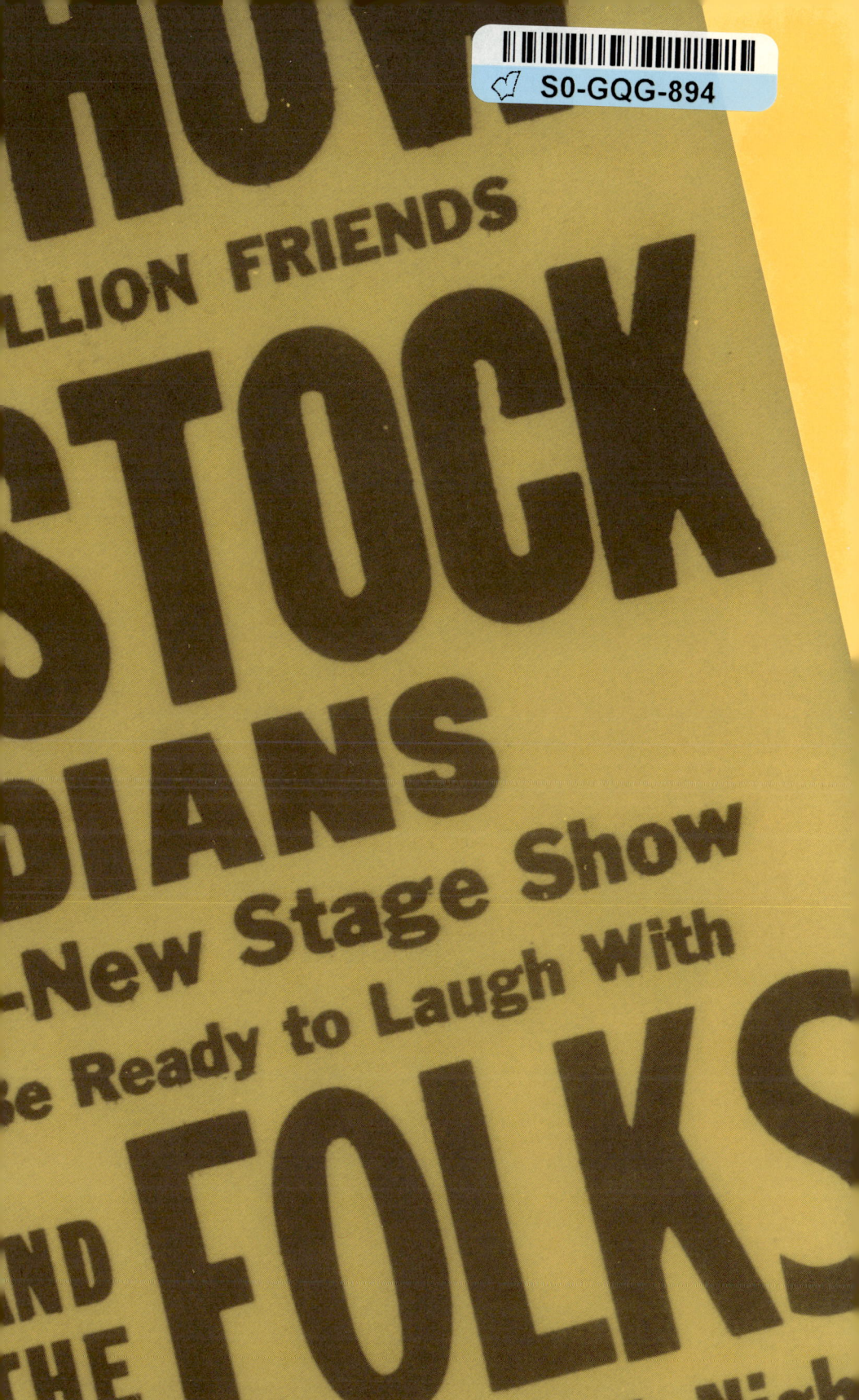

The History of the Haverstock Tent Show

The History of the Haverstock Tent Show

"The Show with a Million Friends"

Robert Lee Wyatt III
With a Foreword by
Peggy Haverstock

Southern Illinois University Press
Carbondale and Edwardsville

Copyright © 1997 by the Board of Trustees,
Southern Illinois University
All rights reserved
Printed in the United States of America
00 99 98 97   4 3 2 1

Library of Congress Cataloging-in-Publication Data

Wyatt, Robert Lee, 1940–
The history of the Haverstock Tent Show : the show with a million friends / Robert Lee Wyatt, III.
p. cm.
Includes bibliographical references and index.
1. Haverstock Comedians Company—History.
2. Repertory theater—Southwestern states—History—20th century.
3. Haverstock, Harvey, 1886–1970. 4. Haverstock, Carlotta, d. 1954.
I. Title.
PN2297.H38W93   1997
792'.0979'09041—dc21   96-29917 CIP
ISBN 0-8093-2140-8 (cloth : alk. paper)
ISBN 0-8093-2141-6 (paper : alk. paper)

The paper used in this publication meets the minimum requirements of American National Standard for Information Sciences—Permanence of Paper for Printed Library Materials, ANSI Z39.48-1984. ♾

With love to Fran and Mart, who said:
"This story must be written!"

For Peggy, Louise, Melly and Bob, and Melba

Contents

Illustrations ix
Foreword by Peggy Haverstock xi
Preface xiii
Acknowledgments xxi

1. Tent Repertoire's Place in Rural American Culture 1

2. Harvey and Carlotta Haverstock Before Tent Repertoire 14

3. Haverstocks Found Their Tent Show 28

4. The Early Years, 1911–1919 40

5. The Good Years, 1920–1929 56

6. The Lean Years, 1930–1939 90

7. The War Years, 1939–1945 107

8. The Years of Decline, 1946–1954 117

Notes 133
Glossary 143
Bibliography 147
Index 151

Illustrations

Following page 60

Rolland, Lotta, and Harvey Haverstock
The F. G. Perry Uncle Tom's Cabin Company
The front entrance to the King-Haverstock Company's tent
The Haverstock Comedians' tent in Bluford, Illinois
Rolland, Harvey, and Lotta Haverstock, ca. 1917
The Haverstock Comedians' stage front with advertising signs
Harvey Haverstock in his first Toby costume
Harvey Haverstock in his 1930s Toby costume
Lotta and Harvey Haverstock in their Susie and Toby costumes
Lotta and Harvey Haverstock as Toby and Susie playing a song
Susie Haverstock (Lotta) and Toby Haverstock (Harvey) in the early 1950s
Portrait of Lotta and Harvey Haverstock
Rolland and Peggy Haverstock
Rolland, Lotta, and Harvey Haverstock before their fleet of cars
Peggy with her accordion helps Rolland and Lotta perform magic
The Haverstock Theatre Company's first railroad car
Lotta Haverstock
Some of the cast
The Haverstock tent ready for use
The Haverstocks' automobile trailer
Lotta Haverstock in a glamour pose
The Olney Hayseed Band

Foreword

How good it is to have someone care enough to remember!

Bob has taken some scattered facts and material, and with a good deal of thought, and even more work, has told the story of the Haverstock Tent Show. The story up to 1930 is essentially from Haver's memoirs, diaries, route books, and photograph and clipping albums. I know little about those times other than the stories I remember Haver and Lotta telling. I became a Haverstock in 1933. Rolland had a sketchy memory of those years prior to 1933, too. He spent summer vacations with the tent show, but only after graduation from high school in 1927 did he become a full-fledged member of a theatrical troupe.

But Bob tells the story, and he does it with love. He, Rolland, and I spent many enjoyable hours of sharing, as if we were all three members of the Haverstock family, since the first time we met in the early 1970s.

Whether or not our story is valuable historically may be debatable, but it has stirred at least one person, me, to laughter and to tears. I hope that you enjoy our story. We lived it with love and devotion to the theater crafts and for our many friends along the route. The friends we had and gathered were foremost to us. I think that is why we were called the "Show with a Million Friends."

Peggy Haverstock

Preface

The story of Tent Repertoire has not been adequately told. Though uniquely American, it lies heavily among the neglected facets of American dramatic history. Little has been written to share the way itinerant show people took drama to the rural areas of the nation, giving those who lived away from Broadway a chance to enjoy live theater. A rich treasure in the history of many dozens of such Tent Repertoire companies lies buried just below the surface waiting to be uncovered by researchers and shared with interested readers.

One such treasure is the story of the Haverstock Comedians. They made a contribution to this forgotten saga of facing the frontier to help bring one form of culture to the hinterlands, and their story is an exciting one. In my nearly twenty years of studying this group of players and their tent drama and comedy presentations, I visited with Rolland Haverstock dozens of times before his death. He was the son of Harvey (Haver) and Carlotta (Lotta) Haverstock, founders of the pioneer dramatic Tent Repertoire company that began on the prairie of Oklahoma in 1911 and performed continuously until 1954. Rolland played the leading man in the company for more than thirty of its forty-three years, and his memory of those times was vivid and unimpaired. We became as close as if we were both Haverstocks.

Until very recently, I still visited regularly with my dear friend, Peggy Haverstock, Rolland's widow, to pick her brain for her memories of the tent show days. She acted in the Haverstock company from 1933 until the show closed. She had her own vast store of exciting vignettes about life on the circuit. Though some of the events occurred as many as sixty years ago, her memories were as clear as if they happened only yesterday. With just a little encouragement, she would recite a passage from a former role,

Preface

play a ditty on the accordion she used in the olio acts, or even sing "White Horse," a highly favored comedy song she used to capture audiences for many of the years she performed with the company.[1]

Rolland and Peggy allowed me to photocopy and study the family letters, Haver's memoirs and diaries, their route books, record books, and scrapbooks. They gave me copies of their scripts, many of which are handwritten in pencil and bound with oilcloth covers to protect them after years of use. They gave me a selection of hundreds of photographs of their family and other show people. These pieces of memorabilia added an authenticity to the personal recollections of both of them and the dozens of people I have since interviewed about the Haverstock shows.

Occasionally, I have come upon someone who had worked for the Haverstock show and who could hardly talk rapidly enough to tell me wonderful vignettes of life on the road, which revitalized my efforts to complete my writing of their story. The more stories I heard about the Haverstocks, the more I searched for histories of other tent show companies. When those searches came up empty, I became convinced that the story of the Haverstock troupe had to be added to the annals of theatrical history. A full story of American dramatic history could not be complete without an explanation of the role of people such as the Haverstocks and their Tent Repertoire experiences in that history. The Haverstocks began their show among the earliest of Tent Repertoire entrepreneurs, and they continued long after all but a few had darkened their tent stages. The Haverstock Comedians' theatrical run lasted nearly half a century, and they played to many, many audiences, earning their title and show motto, the "Show with a Million Friends."[2]

Not once have I talked with any person who knew or worked with the Haverstocks who could find anything negative to say about the show, its cast, its working conditions, or its owners. If those interviewed were former employees of the company, they would get twinkles in their eyes as they told about Haver's withholding system to save them from the winter hardships or about Haver's and Lotta's love and care of the company and it members. They all related how the Haverstock troupe was a working *family*.

Barney McDaniels was one of those players whom I interviewed. He traveled with the company for several years, and in all those years, he told that he had never heard a cross or unkind remark. He recalled:

Preface

> Lotta was such a wonderful actress. She would be furious if an actor didn't deliver accurate cue lines, but most of her anger was directed at Haver. Honestly, Haver ad-libbed most of his lines. He loved to see the expressions of those on stage who had waited for a perfect cue from him. He especially tantalized Lotta, his straight person to whom he delivered most of his comedic lines. Occasionally, someone on stage would get out of character and grin at Haver's miscue, or at times, even laugh with the audiences who sensed the bad line, but Lotta never got out of character. She was always the professional who stayed in her character to the fullest possible extent.[3]

McDaniels worked for the Haverstock troupe during the 1930s when many troupes folded because of the Great Depression. He added about those days:

> I worked for them when times were hard, and if the Haverstocks were ever going to have been hard to get along with, it would have been during the 1930s. The Haverstocks just didn't get out of sorts. They loved their work, and when people love their work, they don't have to have dissension. I wish all my theatrical employers had been so great to work for.[4]

Local promoters and businessmen happily welcomed the Haverstock troupe. When the Haverstock tent show came to town, business boomed for everyone. People came to see the show, and while in town for the show, they also shopped. The only businesspeople who might have had room for complaint while the stage was lighted were the local motion picture house owners. With almost everyone in the entire community attending the tent show performances, movie theaters didn't sell many tickets. Haver respected those movie house businesspeople, too, and made a point to visit with them soon after arriving in a town, seeing to it that they had free passes to his show. Those free tickets didn't replace their lost earnings, but they appreciated his effort to keep them mollified. He always tried to jot a personal letter to all the motion picture house owners on his route well in advance of his show's coming to town so that they would not book an expensive road show engagement or exhibition type film. For the most part, he wouldn't have had to worry because most of the cities the Haverstocks played were small, rural towns in Oklahoma, Texas, and Illinois. Generally, movies brought to those towns were not first-run or road show engagements, so owners of the movie houses often closed their

PREFACE

movie houses and just joined their neighbors in attending the tent show and cheering Toby and Susie on to their victories over evil conditions and villainous men.[5]

Occasionally, unscrupulous male actors gave a bad name to their art by trifling with the affections of young female towners. Such activities gave the Tent Repertoire owners severe problems in preserving their reputations. Haver always was very careful to choose only respectable singles and happily married couples for his troupe. In all his journals, he never cites a reputation problem with the towners. While other itinerant acting companies suffered such a stigma, Haver and his troupe received openly warm welcomes from even the most discerning critics of traveling show people. The Haverstocks had very conservative religious convictions, and they applied that same conservatism when hiring their troupers, deleting, or at least repairing, questionable language that might appear in a script, and even altering stage blocking that might suggest impropriety on stage. At one time, Haver received a letter from a reformed alcoholic actor who applied for a job with the Haverstocks asking for a new chance, but Haver, ordinarily wanting to help down-and-outers decided not to take a chance at sullying his reputation. He did not hire that applicant.[6] He did nothing that could possibly tarnish the clean image he and Lotta had striven so hard to maintain.

People respected Haver for standing by his convictions. Dale Madden, a company member after the death of Lotta, said of his time with the Haverstock company:

> Everyone in the business knew that Haver tolerated nothing less than the best in attitudes, language, habits, and manners. When my wife and I went to work for the show after Lotta died, we would have seen Haver at one of his worst times, but there was not a moment when he allowed his feelings to dampen the spirits of the cast or the towners we met with the show. We loved working with the Haverstocks, and they treated us the way a man treats his family.[7]

Howard King, now of Okeene, Oklahoma, whose mother, Katherine King, ran a boardinghouse in Olustee, Oklahoma, told of his memories of the Haverstock show's coming to their town:

> Whenever the Haverstock Comedians came to town, the troupers took rooms in my mother's boardinghouse. We had many roomers from the time Mom opened for business, but we loved having the

PREFACE

Haverstock troupers stay with us. They told stories; they sang songs. It was as if they were on stage all the time. But they were good people. Sometimes other traveling people who stayed in our boardinghouse warned Mom with stories of actors skipping out on their rooming bills, but that never happened at Mom's place with the Haverstock troupe. While the Haverstocks were in town, it was just as if they lived in the town. People respected them because they were involved with the community. They attended church and other community functions while they were in the community. My folks and my friends and I always got free passes to the show. Of course, my friends and I had to pass out fliers advertising the show or had to help set up the tent and chairs for our tickets, but Haver made us think he couldn't put on the show without that help. It gave us kids a little pride in getting free tickets for the show, too.[8]

Such stories, always pointing out the good, would cause a reader to think that I have written merely a monumental history. On the contrary, I have tried to use a reporter's delving to get at the truth, but the Haverstocks, from all that I have been able to find in my research, were something of an exceptional group and deserve this kind of history. They surely had faults, but none of those individuals whom I have found still living have anything but praise for them, and I have talked with members of their audiences, their competitors, their employees, and their family members, as well as several Tent Repertoire historians.[9]

Caroline Schaffner, founder of the Tent Repertoire Museum and former co-owner of the famous Schaffner Players, one of the world's most renowned Tent Repertoire companies, told me:

I didn't know the Haverstocks personally, but we all knew each other by reputation. We knew good companies and good owners, and I have never heard a bad word about the Haverstocks. Tent Rep people knew the bad. Word got around about those who treated the towners or their employees badly. I would know of a bad reputation. I saw their advertisements in *Billboard* and in *Bill Bruno's Bulletin*, and since Tent Reppers were all like a vast family, I knew them even though I had never actually met them. When any Tent Repertoire family members died, I responded with a card of sympathy or a spray of flowers. All the Tent Rep people did that. I remember responding in such a way when both Haver and Lotta Haverstock died. When their show closed its final season, I felt the pain of another loss to the industry and to theatrical history. We don't have much on the Haverstocks in our museum and library in Mount Pleasant, Iowa, but I know their memorabilia is housed at Texas Tech University in Lub-

Preface

bock, Texas. I am so delighted to know that their history is being written and will be preserved.[10]

The Haverstocks enjoyed the life of the traveling show. Life was never too difficult for a people who lived their lives as they wanted to live them. The Haverstocks loved visiting the towns on their routes and knowing the locals in each place. They didn't call the towners on their routes by derogatory names such as rubes or hicks because those local people were their friends, who, by their attendance at the shows, produced the livelihood for the show folks.

When I asked Peggy how the troupers kept busy during the daytime hours of their season, she responded:

> There was never time for us to be bored. We were always getting up on our lines for the night's play. We prepared other olio acts for our between-the-acts activities. We used our days pressing costumes, running lines, getting our concessions ready for the night's crowd. We were just too busy to be bored. Our work was so varied; there was certainly no way that one could possibly think of it as being tedious or boring.[11]

Peggy also recalled that every day brought a new adventure. Each week the Haverstock show was in at least one new town with one different three-act show each night in that given town and perhaps even an added concert show (different from the regular shows and usually shorter) after the first performance if there was enough interest from the audience so that the company could earn more money. Occasionally, they tried out a new script. To get it ready for production, there were rehearsals and new scenery and costumes to prepare. They worked up new routines for the olio between the acts as often as they could come up with a new idea. Occasionally, they got to drive to a nearby town to buy some new clothing for their wardrobes or to see a movie or a concert. Rarely, when some other Rep show was nearby and played when their stage was dark, the Haverstocks would even attend one of the competitor's shows. Generally, they were happy with life on the road, and there was rarely a time for them to think about being otherwise.

Peggy told of their lives in their trailer homes:

> Once we got our own small trailer homes, there was a place where we could go to get out of the tent. We could visit, nap, read, or do

PREFACE

just whatever we wanted. We didn't cook in our trailer homes, but we did bring in a plate lunch or some sandwiches so we could enjoy a private meal once in a while.[12]

Tent Repertoire offers many stories, most of which have disappeared with this all-but-forgotten form of theater. Occasionally, someone discovers a script and revives it for a nostalgic moment in a seminar dealing with popular culture, or occasionally, someone will set up a display in a theatrical museum. On very rare occasions, a Toby show will appear in a re-created version performed by a community theater group or a college drama class where a drama history teacher mentions Toby or Tent Repertoire. Both were an integral part of America's growing up, and as such, must not be forgotten.

My efforts to show the Haverstocks and their company makes just a slight inroad into that vast number of stories that surely exist in the memories and files of those who saw or worked on the more than seven hundred Tent Repertoire troupes who traversed rural America during the early and middle decades of this century. I hope someone will try to tell some of those other stories, and I hope that they will turn out as memorial histories dedicated to people who perhaps sacrificed a great deal in fame and fortune to bring a touch of culture to the hinterlands of America.

Acknowledgments

In no way can I hope to name all who have helped me in gathering material and putting together my thoughts in this nearly twenty-year effort. I owe untold thanks to my favorite critics and proofers who volunteered over and again to praise, to criticize, and to mark the rewrites of this book and who helped me put the words into the various typewriters and processors we have used: Louise, Melanie, and Bob. I am especially indebted to Melanie for the last transfer to a format that my computer could read. I could not have completed the task without that bonus; I think I would have given up.

A very special thanks to my dear friend, Dr. Sandra Ransel of Las Vegas, for her many hours of laborious reading and editing of a recent copy. I really needed her extra assurance that the book was worthwhile. Thanks to Denny, Hugh, and Chris for the hours they gave Sandy to me on the telephone for consultation and in reading time.

Thanks to Martha Mills and Frances Dunham for their early critique and structural suggestions. They encouraged with rigor and red ink, tempering their criticisms with love and respect for both the Haverstock history and me.

Thanks to Caroline Schaffner for the visit in the summer of 1992 and again for a second visit at the 1993 Tent Repertory meeting in Mount Pleasant, Iowa. She said, "History and research needs this volume so much. Please share it with us."

Thanks to the many librarians who have helped me search out and order microfilms, articles, journals, and books to help me to complete the effort. Thanks especially to the Grandfield Public Library (Athlea Mundkowski and Patty Watson), to the University of Oklahoma Library, and to the East Central University Library.

Acknowledgments

Thanks to those who worked with me on the Toby shows at Harvest Theater in Grandfield. That list is long and spans several years, but Loretta Avant; Lee and June Platner; Margaret and Charles Witt; David and Jerry Asbery; Jody Read; Billy and Yvonne Allen; Gilford and Minrosa Miracle and family; Louise, Melanie, and Bobby Wyatt; Gary Palmer; James and Janet MacWilliams; Frenchie Tisdale; members of my high school drama classes for work on the Haverstock re-creations; Elton and Wilma McClurkan and Pam; and Elmo and Thelma Maxey have to be mentioned. They gave special insight into the comedic and dramatic characters the Haverstocks played over the years. I also need to mention the Grandfield audiences and their counterparts in twenty-nine cities in Oklahoma and Texas who came to see Harvest Theater's renditions of the Haverstock shows as we billed ourselves The New Haverstock Comedians; their special interests and questions at receptions following our productions helped to assure me of the need for collecting this historical data.

Thanks to those who lived the adventures and loved the Haverstocks, then shared their memories with me as I collected stories. A special thanks to them for being among the show's million friends who want to read the Haverstocks' history in printed form.

The History of the
Haverstock Tent Show

I
Tent Repertoire's Place in Rural American Culture

For many years, the backbone of American life was the small, rural town. For the most part, people living in these rural communities kept a busy, hardworking schedule. These pioneers had to break new ground, build new buildings, learn new ways of living. They had little time for entertainment. They could hardly worry about adding culture to their already too-busy lives. They appreciated the simple pleasures. They enjoyed talking across their newly built fences as they rested from plowing their fields. They shared the news brought by traveling salesmen. They displayed their pride by assuring straight rows in their plowed fields or by showing off their clotheslines hanging with laundry made bright by lye-soap prepared from lard drippings and the ashes from their stoves. They talked of weather and crops on their days of quilting bees or barn raisings or hog butcherings or weddings or funerals. After they had time to erect their schools, they began to have an occasional school program or a box social or a weekly church service in the school building, but still, they could not really justify time for outside cultural entertainment.

As the prairie country towns grew more progressive and larger, these pioneers began to have more leisure time, especially after they harvested their crops and laid by their ground. During these lulls in their busy lives, they began to feel the need for some kind of culture. Before long, some enterprising entrepreneur added an opera house to the town. During the last thirty years of the nineteenth century, the opera house grew into a prominent part of virtually every community in America.

Usually nothing more than a rude hall filled with backless benches, the opera house generally had a flat floor with a small, slightly raised stage area at one end or the other of the room. The hall often occupied the second story of a large building, sitting above a more functional lower-floor business place. Visiting stars or dramatic ensembles, who happened to be coming through town anyway, stopped off to perform a solo presentation or a highly touted Shakespearean play so they could earn a bit more money to help them get to the next town or just to add stature to their names. The opera house owners kept a steady flow of vaudeville troupes stopping in for one-night stands of song, dance, and comedic routines as well. Whatever the entertainment, the opera house boasted of itself as the center of community culture. Eventually, local groups aspiring to the dramatic arts began performing much-practiced theatricals or terpsichoreans.[1]

If a rural community had a rail line going through it, a touring actor could easily stop over in that place for a show. Railroad towns more quickly added opera houses because they had immediate access to acting troupes traveling by train. Many larger rail centers even had more than one show house. Prominent players on Broadway often traveled across the country for various reasons. Often, in order to make the money necessary to continue their journeys, many would stop over in the rural centers for brief engagements. Route towns treated those who had the most prominent names as if they were visiting royalty, perhaps because the performers almost thought themselves to be such.

Some actors enjoyed the special treatment too well. Some abused the power they had. Often nothing more than itinerant tramps with a flair for memorizing dramatic monologues and strumming an instrument, they enchanted their listeners. They sang the bawdy music of the Eastern beer halls and recited Shakespeare. Those actors would come into a town and schedule a performance at the local opera house. They would check into a local hotel or boarding house, asking the landlord to keep their expenditures on a tab until they collected their gate, or the show's receipts. They would schedule perhaps three nights of performance, and then they would skip town after the first night's gate, leaving several locals unpaid and angry at all traveling actors.[2]

The more the itinerant tramps desecrated the name "actor," the more there appeared to be a need to have theatrical booking agencies to help keep down the haphazard, fly-by-night impostors. Theatrical act managers organized tours for their legitimate companies. Actors soon became tolerated again, even if they were not fully accepted. With these booking agencies, eventually only the most remote, provincial communities, well

TENT REPERTOIRE'S PLACE

off the beaten path, fell prey to the unscrupulous, ne'er-do-well, derelict actors and their disreputable troupes.

Enterprising agents could fill an entire itinerary across the country with one- or two-night stands in the rail-connected communities. With the widespread use of the telegraph and the telephone by the end of the century, agents could secure confirmed bookings for their clients. However, those same communication devices did a service to the opera house owners, too. Troupes who failed to make bookings or those who were late for their curtains could be reported down the line to other opera houses. Local managers of theatrical houses began to check with managers in other cities to determine the reliability and the quality of their prospective acts. The house managers had a responsibility to see that their patrons saw a good show, and in the remotest rural areas, that they saw a good, clean, family-oriented show.

Before too many years had passed, the problem of poor shows or unsuitable acts began to be solved. Some houses still had to deal with delays of cast arrival due to inexact train schedules. Many of the enterprising house managers began booking two shows for the same time slots so as to assure a performance. This double booking was no less ethical than an actor's showing up at the theater intoxicated pretending to be able to do a Shakespearean scene. Then the manager would have to turn away the extra booked troupe who often relied on the money they expected to earn from the night's performance. The opera house began to have a reputation that caused performing companies to contact other performing troupes for proof of that house's reliability and quality.

The opera houses had other problems, too. Comfort could never be guaranteed. The houses were often too hot or too cold. Before long, the opera house declined as the desirable place to meet the entertainment needs of the small community. With the disappointing inconsistencies in the rural theater, some changes had to occur. Actors demanded fairer treatment so they could maintain a decent livelihood. House managers had to offer better security for the actors and theatrical companies. A repertory company seemed to resolve the problems and later paved the way for the Tent Repertoire (they preferred it spelled this way to separate tent companies from legitimate repertory) groups.

Repertory companies flourished as a popular entertainment form in the more urban East. The groups, formed by a reputable owner or manager, himself usually one of the stock actors in the company, prepared five to ten plays suitable for the audiences their casts would encounter along their short circuit tours. By committing that many plays to memory, the troupes could move from town to town across the circuit or even across the country. It would be no problem to follow a previous troupe into a town, for with a repertory of scripts, they would not have to repeat a play given just previously by the earlier visiting troupe. Another advantage of having several memorized scripts ready to perform was that the troupe could stay in a town for more than one night with the same audience returning to the show as often as the script changed assured that it would see no play repeated.

Companies would select bills that offered the same number of characters and the same scenic demands.[3] Ironically, most companies even chose the same scripts other companies chose because popular shows drew crowds wherever actors played them. Popular early repertory plays included *East Lynne, Lena Rivers*, and invariably, *Uncle Tom's Cabin*. All troupes had standard handbills printed. Painting on a date and a location for the play kept the preprinted handbills current. Most even had printed in advance on the handbills, "Appearing at the Local Opera House," which necessitated only the addition of a date and hour of performance.[4] If a previous troupe had played all the shows in a company's list, the company manager would merely do the same plays. He would generally use new names for the characters and would give the play a new title to draw an audience, but rarely did he fool the audience. Most did not even mind seeing repeated shows; they were still getting to enjoy a night of entertainment.

The number of repertory groups grew so rapidly in the last years of the nineteenth century that companies began appearing in the rural areas, as well as in the most populated centers. Those companies that had names and scenery to command places in the city houses were well staffed and outfitted. Those performing mainly in the hinterlands had a small staff, with actors often playing more than one role, and they were ill equipped in the scenery pieces, lights, and other stage accouterments. According to William Slout in his book, *Theater in a Tent*, those who traversed the middle section of the United States, from Ohio to Kansas, were called "prairie actors."[5] These prairie actors were the forerunners of the Tent Repertoire groups.

Entire family groups made up many of these companies of prairie actors. Each member of the family played roles usually suitable to the specific age that an actor happened to be at the time of the production. In the event that a part did not happen to be suitable in age, however, the manager of the company merely improvised about the character's age, and sometimes even the character's gender, so he could use the actor he had available to play the role. By the turn of the century, nearly 350 repertory troupes toured the United States. But because of an overabundance of such improvised troupes, that number had dwindled to fewer than 50 by 1920.[6] The use of the opera house also declined. The houses themselves were ill-kept and uncomfortable, especially considering that they were usually up a flight of stairs and that they were too cold in winter or too hot in summer.

Some visionaries moved their stages from the opera house stage to a walled but unroofed building called an airdome. The seats were usually built into dirt mounded up inside the walls, using unbacked planks for benches, stairstepped into the mounds, amphitheater style. That innovation proved an enticement to the audiences in the summer months, but in locales with no hills to help hide a setting sun, the hour for a show to begin was usually far too late for people to keep their children out. Another difficulty was the rains. Because patrons would not sit out in the rain, such weather brought on a loss of revenue to the airdome owner and to the show people who depended on their percentages of the gate to pay their expenses.

Another problem, mainly facing only the actors, besides the rain storms, was the wind. It usually howled on the prairie, causing line projection difficulty. With people sitting on the dikes around the walls, there was little from which actors could bounce lines. The airdome would later prove to be very effective for watching visuals, such as silent films, but it never worked well for acting companies who had lines that their audiences had to hear.

Film had come into the world of entertainment near the turn of the century. Opera house managers and airdome proprietors could see that this form of entertainment offered them quicker profits and only demanded a small rental fee and the purchase of some operating equipment. They could charge lower admission prices for film than for a "live" company performance. Their profits at the ten, twenty, and thirty-cent admissions were far greater when they did not have to share them with an acting troupe.

Slout also notes that pirated scripts caused real financial problems for reputable company owners who felt obligated to pay royalties for scripts they produced. Those companies could not afford to pay the normal royalties and still charge such nominal admission prices to see their plays. Many publishing houses published only pirated scripts, stealing the royalties from authors. The publisher would send stenographers to a hit play to have the script, as well as the intricate stage directions, copied and then transcribed to be printed. With smaller, one-time royalties that they could then offer for the pirated scripts, companies could charge as little as ten cents per person, give away a door prize, and still realize a good profit. Even the low ten cent charge did not guarantee a crowd for the visiting show people because a motion picture show at the local nickelodeon cost a patron only a nickel. Repertory companies began leaving the ranks rapidly as their profit margin levels decreased.[7] The demise of the uncomfortable opera houses and weather-inappropriate airdomes perhaps helped to generate the theatrical tent—the traveling "canvas opera house," the "rag op'ry."

Circus tents, white-topped behemoths, had been used for more than fifty years before the turn of the century. In 1893, Ringling Brothers' Circus boasted of a tent measuring 180 feet by 430 feet. It required some ten acres for a comfortable set up.

The brown-topped Chautauqua tent, also popular by the 1890s, was a place where learned lecturers, small discussion groups, or instrumentalists performed. Still popular through the 1920s, Chautauqua circuits established routes for the tent performers. People hungry for culture, such as the Chautauqua offered, would happily pay a fee to hear a noted lecturer such as William Jennings Bryan present a lecture, or a noted operatic diva perform an aria from a fabled opera. The Chautauqua was devoted to educational and cultural enhancement. Since the Chautauqua was not theatrical and offered educational stimulation, even the most fundamental religious sects did not object to its material. The Chautauqua featured only a rostrum with a glass of water and perhaps some chairs for the local dignitaries who would introduce the visiting guests. Sides of the Chautauqua tents could be rolled up so that a breeze might blow through on a hot summer's evening. The tent protected both the audience and the guest performers from the elements, and the performer's voice could easily be heard.[8]

At just about the turn of the twentieth century, someone decided that a dramatic show could also be performed in this portable opera house made of canvas. Acoustics were preferable to the airdome's, and the roll up sides offered a cooler environment for summer theater goers. Too, the show owners could own their own tents and could play their shows without being at the mercy of any unscrupulous opera house owner or inclement weather presented by using the airdome. If they should produce a pirated script, they subjected only themselves, rather than frightened opera house owners, to legal repercussions.

Some problems with performing a dramatic production in a tent such as those used by either the circus or the Chautauqua did exist. The Chautauqua speaker, who used only his voice, did not have to worry about a tent pole's standing in the center of the tent, blocking the view of the stage for some viewers. Tent poles proved useful for riggings in a circus tent. For theatrics, however, some of the acting subtleties could not be seen behind existing tent poles.

In 1910, *Billboard*, the trade newspaper published for vaudeville and other entertainment occupations, announced the invention of a new design in canvas theater. This design offered two center poles in front of, but near the outsides of the stage's proscenium. These two poles, more widely spread, would eliminate most of the viewer problems if the actors played well to the center of the stage. Walter Driver designed this first stage pole arrangement and named the design Driver's Improved Theatrical Tent. Even this tent did not fully meet the needs of a dramatic company, but its design and slight improvement over the Chautauqua tent opened the way for a new genre in theater, the Tent Repertoire.[9]

The dramatic performance in a tent had not waited on the development of Driver's tent. Drama had been given under canvas from the earliest use of circus tents. Most of the tents that did offer drama, however, usually combined its dramatic selection with circus acts. The play was generally not the main attraction in the days prior to the twentieth century. Though it is true that some dramatic tent companies did perform in the nineteenth century, only a very few were really active.[10] *Billboard* carried dramatic notices in 1903, but with little importance until after 1910.

By 1914, *Billboard* devoted a full page to dramatic companies playing in tents. Later, for a time, during the heyday of Tent Repertoire, in the 1920s, *Billboard* devoted much of its publication to the promotion of Tent Repertoire. In the 1930s, however, the trade journal limited its Rep space to four pages, and by the 1940s, the space had fallen to two pages or even fewer. By 1950, only occasional Tent Repertoire notices appeared.

Tent Repertoire as an art form developed primarily for the rural areas of the country. It flourished in the Midwest and the Southwest. At the height of the art, almost seven hundred companies performed full seasons. The tent show did depend almost entirely on the farmers and their families and the residents of small communities primarily dependent on the farm income. In the 1930s, a successful company opened in Oklahoma City, the largest city to host tent shows, and it flourished for at least one successful season.[11] But once the novelty and the attraction of low admission prices of the show wore off, the show closed. Playing large cities was a problem addressed in gatherings of tent show owners, but rarely tried again. Ashby and May (1982) noted in their book on Harley Sadler's show that: "The tent shows, Sadler's included were mainly a village phenomenon. In a letter to *Billboard*, Harley remarked that his type of entertainment was generally restricted to towns of fewer than ten thousand. No crossroads settlements were too small to attract a traveling tent company."[12]

A favorite play in the early years of the century was *Uncle Tom's Cabin*. Nearly every troupe advertised that they would play the highly moral script on at least one night of their stay in a given town. In their advance advertising, they all noted that the father of the author of that script was Henry Ward Beecher, a clergyman of note prior to the Civil War, and that the play had a religious element that would add to anyone's moral development. The play was a perfect example of the tearjerker genre, characterizing the types of show of all early-day Tent Repertoire companies. Who could keep a dry eye when Little Eva was lifted into heaven after she had touched the life of the little imp slave, Topsy? Would anyone not hate a Simon Legree type after seeing his persecution of the faithful old manservant, Uncle Tom? That play, along with the highly moral *East Lynne*, *Lena Rivers*, and *Trail of the Lonesome Pine*, would keep the audience crying at least three evenings of a week's bill of shows. The Tom shows still played successfully into the late thirties while *Billboard* ran advertisements soliciting actors to join their companies.[13] Rural people with fundamentalist religious philosophies enjoyed having a good moralistic crying session. Their early times on the prairie had been hard. They felt that they deserved a good cathartic cry, and these dramas gave them a chance to show that emotion without being looked upon as being weak. Even a man could brush away a tear, especially if he let it be known that he had probably gotten some dust in his eye!

Canvas theater achieved a great deal of dignity when the world-renowned dramatic actress, Sarah Bernhardt, toured the United States in 1905–6, her second American tour. Cornelia Otis Skinner notes in her book, *Madame Sarah*, that many opera houses closed to Bernhardt because of a disagreement between her and the syndicated owners of a large theater chain. Bernhardt solved that problem by purchasing a circus tent seating 4,500 people. She rigged it with a makeshift stage and fulfilled her tour engagement schedule. She was a big hit in the tent in Dallas, Texas, and drew large crowds in Waco, Texas. By that time, she had proved that her audience would follow her anywhere, even to a tent, so the opera house and theater owners begged her to abandon the tent and come to perform in their buildings.[14]

Bernhardt did another tent performance when she allowed her tent to be used in Chicago, where a big show was staged to benefit those who suffered in the San Francisco earthquake. She performed in the tent and enticed dozens of American performers to join her. They raised a fortune for the sufferers and further showed the value of a tent, especially because it seated such a huge crowd, something that no building in Chicago could then do. She later gave the tent itself to the city of San Francisco as a temporary theater there, since all the theater district had burned during the fires following the quake. An actress of the stature of Madame Bernhardt performing well in a tent, gave credence to tent dramatics on every level.[15]

Another event, World War I, further established Tent Repertoire. Theater offered diversion from the routine of daily living. At first, the tent could go anywhere that a train could take it; then later, it could go anywhere that a truck fleet could travel. Entertainment-hungry rural Americans, engrossed in the war effort, happily received the tent show. At the same time, they questioned the patriotism of a show carrying an apparently able-bodied, young leading man. The draft age in 1917 ranged between eighteen and forty-five. Because of their patriotism, audiences, then, expected the leading man to be at least forty-six! Acting in a show company did not give draft-exemption status, but even if it had, audiences likely would not have supported those companies using able-bodied, draft-age actors. During the Great War, audiences grew tired of weeping. They had wept through nearly ten years of Tent Repertoire tearjerkers, and the news of deaths from the battlefronts caused much more weeping for many families in rural America.

Audiences began to want comedy as a relief from sadness. They wanted something on the stage to give them something to laugh about. Comedy and farce gave them that option. Every company still did some patriotic plays. They filled the olio, vaudeville type acts played between the acts of the plays, with patriotic pieces. Many of the shows even sold war bonds at their performances. Many troupes bragged about the money they had invested in such bonds. But people needed relief, and when they demanded, owners played comedy, which became more dominant than drama in Tent Repertoire.

The principal, and perhaps the easiest, way of introducing comedy into a play was to change a straight character into a rube role. This slight change made the already memorized scripts switch from drama to comedy. The changed lines added incongruity to the plays, yet the teaching value of the drama could be kept. Neil Schaffner, a prominent tent show impresario and playwright, adapted John Fox's novel, *Trail of the Lonesome Pine*, by adding a rube named "Toby" and a soubrette named "Susie" to the book-play. The rustic viewers wanted comedy, but they still insisted that virtue, parental guidance education, and morality be maintained in their scripts. Nearly every adaptation added a Toby, his female counterpart, and usually a chin-whiskered character, referred to by Tent Reppers as a *G-String*. The female rube often called *Sis*, came from the old play, *Sis Hopkins*. The character soubrette later evolved into "Susie," the character so identified with Lotta Haverstock, co-owner of the Haverstock Comedians, and to Caroline Schaffner, of the Schaffner Players. Toby, the silly kid character, was the most popular addition. In fact, the scripts employing the Toby character became an entire new genre of theatrical literature called the Toby genre. The character who played Toby lost his own identity to the Toby name. This actor became just *Toby* to those whom he met.[16]

Though every Tent Repertoire owner from the earliest day will claim the honor of originating the Toby kid, Fred Wilson is most universally credited with being the first to be identified with the origin of the Toby part. He was said to have changed the name of one of his rube characters to "Toby" as early as 1909,[17] in the play *Out of the Fold*. Neil Schaffner tells this story of the origin of Toby in the first pages of his book, *Toby and Me*:

> In the summer of 1911, an actor named W. C. Herman wrote a new play, and it broke in the C. Charleston Guy Repertoire Company, a tent show in Indiana.... [He] titled it *Clouds and Sunshine*. He [Herman] sold it outright to Alex Byers.... In 1912, Byers sent a copy of the script to Lorin H. Guin, the director of a popular priced resident stock company at Magic Theater in Fort Dodge, Iowa, my home town. I was the juvenile light comedian in that company, and it happened that just a few days before Guin received the Herman script, he and I had been talking about the sad state of Repertoire

comedy. . . . He said, "I wish somebody would write a play that had a comedy part." . . . Toby Haxton was a minor part [in *Clouds and Sunshine*]; he and a school girl named Susie Green [were the juvenile characters].[18]

After the performance of the play, Schaffner continued:

> The week following our brief run, Guin wrote Alex Byers about how *Clouds and Sunshine* had been received . . . and commented at some length on my characterization of Toby Haxton. Byers then sent the script . . . to Horace Murphy who had two Repertoire companies playing in tents in Louisiana under the name of Murphy's Comedians. Murphy sent it on to his No. 2 unit where a red-headed actor named Fred Wilson was the comedian. . . . [He] introduced it in the middle of one week's Repertoire. . . . The second bill. . . . [had] a comedy character named Bud. . . . When Wilson [as Bud] hit the door, a small boy down in front called, . . . "It's To—bee!" . . . He [Wilson] said, "I am Toby and from now on everybody is going to call me that."[19]

Most theater historians use this same story to credit Wilson with being the first Toby. Toby Schaffner argues that he was actually the first. Toby Haverstock would say that he thought of the idea and was the first to use Toby in one of his productions. If the 1909 date is correct, neither Haverstock nor Schaffner had a position of authority as show owners or producers that would allow them to add a character change in the form of Toby to any show, so the Wilson story of the Toby addition is most likely the true story.

Whoever originated Toby, Toby had a terrific impact on Tent Repertoire theater in rural America. If Wilson, a red-head, did originate the part, that is likely the reason that Toby is usually played as a red-haired kid.[20] An overly freckled face, a brash demeanor, and a shrewd, prank-pulling character evolved. Toby hated ugliness, so he looked for good. He could find beauty in all things. He was naive, yet wise enough to deal with any problem. Toby usually saved the day!

Toby soon became a part of every script, regardless of whether a rube appeared in that script. If an audience were more sedate in a given town, Toby could be played quieter. If the audience preferred broad comedy, Toby could be played as ludicrous, loud, and terribly slapstick. Very often, as was the case with Schaffner, Haverstock, and Harley Sadler, the company manager himself played the role of Toby and did some ad-libbing to make his Toby fit the mood of the given audience. The manager, who prided himself on knowing his audience, could read the audience and could milk every Toby line and movement as much as each could be milked, often to the point of being an overdone farcical character, almost shutting out the others. Toby often broke his character and ran from the stage to carry on a conversation with someone in the audience. However objectionable some dramatists thought that kind of behavior, Toby became an integral part of rural Tent Repertoire. Most of those who attended the plays in the rural areas loved Toby and all his antics, however ludicrous they seemed.

Toby became the prominent character on the rural tent stage. But in case the audience began to tire of Toby, almost every play had his female counterpart. Her name was usually *Sis* or *Suzanne*. As Lotta Haverstock grew older and white-haired, she could no longer feel secure or believable in her ingenue leads, so she began enlarging the soubrette role. In plays with a soubrette, Lotta named her character part *Susie*, and played her as a kid much as Haver played the youthful Toby, even though as she aged, she played her youthful part white-haired. Once she established that character, wherever the Haverstock tent traveled, audiences knew the Haverstock Comedians' troupe as the "Toby and Susie Show." When people addressed her, they seldom used the name Lotta; most people knew her in her later years simply as Susie Haverstock, just as Fred Wilson was known as Toby Wilson and Harvey Haverstock was better known as Toby Haverstock. Lotta Haverstock did not originate the role of Susie, but she owned the part in every show in which she performed it. She was Susie.

Tent Repertoire companies were a prominent part of the American entertainment scene through the 1920s. As the Depression ravaged the economy in the 1930s, it was a terrible time for Tent Repertoire. People who could hardly afford food could not justify spending money on such a frivolous thing as a play. By the end of the 1930s, fewer than a hundred Tent Repertoire companies still existed. World War II, with its rationing and sorrow, further decimated Tent Repertoire ranks. By 1945, the active tent shows could be counted on the fingers of both hands, and *Billboard* begged Repertoire owners to send in their news for the Repertoire page in the magazine.[21]

Just as Toby was the savior of rural Tent Repertoire at the time when the tearjerker had grown unpleasant to those people on the circuit, Toby may also be somewhat responsible for the demise of Tent Repertoire. As the world moved into the age of television and electronic media, the sophisticated world outgrew the often overplayed, slapstick, rustic rube. Toby just did not offer the diversion he had offered in previous times. He improvised and ad-libbed away the essence of an otherwise good play. A more sophisticated story-oriented audience no longer enjoyed Toby's intrusion into their story lines. By the mid-1950s, when the Haverstock show closed, the rural audience wanted something more sophisticated. They wanted to watch television even if it was fuzzy and snowy with weak transmission signals. They just wanted to sit at home, relax, and be entertained. Over the years, they might allow a Jethro Bodine from *The Beverly Hillbillies* or an Eb from *Green Acres* or a Hooterville of *Pettycoat Junction* to come into their world. They would still allow an Abbott and Costello and a Milton Berle or a Pinky Lee, or even a red-haired Lucille Ball Lucy-type character, but such interjections were rare.

Occasionally, the Toby and Susie shows are reborn for a moment. The Schaffner Players featuring Toby shows among its productions, billed itself as the longest running continuous Tent Repertoire show, having played since the 1920s.[22] Their company, under new ownership was still a regular into the mid-1970s and runs in the 1990s in the summer months.[23] The Corn Crib Theater in Branson, Missouri, performed Toby shows similar to the old Tent Repertoire shows during tourist season, adding its humor to the rusticity of Silver Dollar City.[24] Texas Tech University, in Lubbock, under the direction of Dr. Clifford Ashby, revived the Harley Sadler Toby Show with a grant from the National Arts and Humanities Council for a Bicentennial project in 1976, actually performing their shows in a tent.[25] Grandfield, Oklahoma's, Harvest Playhouse produces a Toby and Susie play periodically in commemoration of their regard for the Haverstocks,[26] who once called Grandfield their winter storage headquarters.[27] As recently as December of 1991, Granbury Opera House in Granbury, Texas, did a special, financially successful production commemorating the Toby Show with their adaptation of *The Awakening of John Slater* and did a second Toby in their 1993 season.[28] Generally speaking, however, Toby and Susie now must be left to theater history buffs.

2
Harvey and Carlotta Haverstock Before Tent Repertoire

Harvey Haverstock prided himself in being a musician's musician. He loved playing the horn. In the late 1890s in mid-America, nearly every town, however small it might be, boasted a city band. The first thing usually constructed after the homes and the business houses had been completed was the city bandstand. If the town were built around the city square, the bandstand stood most generally on the square. If there were no city square, the bandstand graced the center of the busiest four-corner intersection in town. Sometimes it occupied a place of prominence in a city park. The prime objective of the location of the bandstand was for it to be built in a place where musicians could gather and play for large audiences. Addresses could be delivered from the bandstand by a roving evangelist, the grand mogul of a lodge, or an electioneering politician. In whatever city Harvey happened to be, he could usually be found practicing with the city band or giving some kind of solo concert to anyone willing to listen.

Harvey Claude Haverstock (known often as Haver) was born February 22, 1886, in Elkhart, Indiana. English farming families made up his ancestral stock. By the year of his birth, Indiana no longer claimed to be a part of the American frontier; its citizens had moved into an advanced part of Midwestern society.

The Haverstocks were a poor family, as most farmers still were in 1886, regardless of the era's being called the Gilded Age. Farming technology, as of that time, was still not very advanced. If a man could break out enough land to feed his family adequately and make a modest living, he thought himself lucky. The Haverstocks only farmed one hundred and sixty acres, which the family had acquired some fifty or so years earlier.

Harvey and Carlotta Haverstock

The fact that Haver's mother died at his birth and his father had remarried to a very young woman who wanted her own child caused Haver to have few good memories of early home life. Before the new marriage, Harvey's father had too much to do in caring for a baby and keeping up a farm at the same time. His father placed the child with a foster family even before bringing home his new bride. Haver did return to the Haverstock household immediately after the elder Haverstock remarried, but his stay there was short-lived. When his father saw that neither his wife nor his young son were happy, he returned Haver to the foster family.

Because of his circumstances, Harvey had to work during his childhood to help pay for his keep. While still a very young child, he had family and farm chores to prepare him to appreciate working. Berry-picking in Bristol, Indiana, was his first paying job. He often missed school during berry-picking season there. When berries were out of season, Haver cleaned and stocked shelves at a local grocery store. When he was eleven, he went to another foster family in Elkhart, Indiana. Elkhart's chief industry was the manufacture of large cardboard boxes. As he grew older, Haver worked in the box factory after school, on school holidays, and during vacation times. He must have been a precocious child because at the age of fifteen, in 1901, in spite of having missed so much school, Haver received his high school diploma.

It was while still a student in school, however, that Haver learned to play the cornet. He loved every moment of playing it. To get in more playing time, even during the time he played in the high school orchestra, he also became a volunteer member of the Elkhart Community Band. Officials chose him as a cornet soloist for a political rally for William Jennings Bryan. Haver wrote in his diary: "Bryan was the silver tongued orator from Nebraska, but he had to take a seat behind the golden throated cornet player from Indiana that day. My playing drew almost as much applause as the long-winded Mr. Bryan."[1]

Following his second marriage, Haver's father rarely saw his son. Haver loved his father in spite of the apparent neglect on his father's part. He longed to have his father share his pride in playing the horn, but the elder Haverstock never did. To a dirt farmer in that era, a boy who spent his time playing a horn was considered frivolous. After Haver had written about playing for the Bryan rally, his father wrote to Haver telling him that he should move back to the Haverstock farm to help with the farm work instead of playing "that silly horn."[2]

By this time, Haver lived under the guardianship of Mary Weaver. She and her next door neighbors, Mr. and Mrs. George A. Smith, acted as the only parents that Haver ever really had. They recognized Haver's musical ability. When the elder Haverstock demanded that Haver return to the farm to help with the work, Miss Weaver and the Smiths interceded for Haver. They asked the father to allow Haver to stay in Elkhart and continue his music work. In order to make their argument more valid, Smith told Mr. Haverstock that Haver could also have a job at Smith's cigar factory. Smith organized and led the Elkhart Community Band; therefore, he employed in his factory only musicians who would participate in his company band. If his workers in the cigar factory had a routine break from work, they would all take out their instruments and have an impromptu practice session.

Haver could also get a leave from work, usually with pay, any time he played for special occasions. On nights when the community band was not performing, Haver did cornet solos at the local skating rink. His solos paid the fare for the time he skated. Not only did his playing improve with the extra practice at the rink, but he also became an exceptional skater. Later in his life, he used not only his cornet experience, but also his skating expertise in some of the olio acts for his tent theater.

After Haver completed high school, through the connections of Mr. Smith, he got a job at the C. G. Conn Band Instrument Company. He tested cornets under the supervision of the world's greatest cornetist of that era, Jules Levy. The testers played a note on an organ, then hit the same note on the cornet. Only if the sounds were exactly correct was the horn ready to be delivered to a retail music store. Conn's reputation hinged on that kind of exactitude. Levy amazed the younger cornetist by suspending a cornet from the ceiling by a string, walking up to the hanging horn, and pressing his mouth to the mouthpiece hitting high C without ever touching the horn with any part of his body except his lips. Levy demonstrated the Conn Cornet in this manner to retail shops, proving the potential customers that the instrument was the top of the cornet line and very easy to play. Haver quickly learned to do Levy's trick, and in later years, he also incorporated that feat into his tent olio shows.

While Haver worked at the Conn plant, John Philip Sousa, the famed band leader and composer, came to the factory with his own design of a horn which he called the sousaphone. He commissioned the horn to be built by the Conn company. In its first design, it was a larger horn than the further refinements eventually made it. The first one was a B-flat bass horn. To commemorate its completion, Sousa brought his entire concert band to Elkhart to play a concert, employing the new sousaphone, which he, himself, played at the concert. It was at this special Sousa concert that Haver made a big decision concerning his own musical career. During the concert, Arthur Pryer, first chair trombonist for Sousa, played a solo selection. From that time on, Haver knew he wanted to become a professional trombonist. He bought a used brass trombone the next day and set about mastering it.[3]

Not too long after Haver's high school graduation, George Smith decided to move his cigar factory from Elkhart to North Judson, Indiana. North Judson needed a band leader, and Smith was hired. He could lead the band to earn one salary and operate the cigar factory simultaneously to earn greater income. Since the Smiths hated to be separated from Haver, whom they thought of as their own son, Smith looked for a job for Haver in North Judson. He found that a druggist needed someone to work in the pharmacy and confectionery, so Smith encouraged Haver to accept the job and move to North Judson. In that way, Haver could also join the North Judson musicians.

The druggist, who hired Haver, and his wife had organized a chamber orchestra in North Judson. He played the violin, and she played the piano. They wanted a piece of brass for their combo, so they looked to hire someone who could play brass. Whomever they hired, they reasoned, could work in and live above their pharmacy. In 1902, Haver accepted the pharmacy job and moved to North Judson. Though Harvey wrote his father about the job change, he never heard from the elder Haverstock regarding the move. While working at the pharmacy, Haver's job included cleaning, dusting, keeping the shelves straight, turning the ice-cream freezer handle, preparing the various syrups for the soda fountain, and then opening the store at 7:00 A.M. each day as its fountain operator.

As he played with the three-piece combo, the brass sounds Haver played on his own horn were too loud for the subtle chamber music played by the druggist and his wife, so the druggist ordered Haver a C clarinet to replace the brass instrument. Haver knew nothing about a woodwind instrument, but soon after its arrival, he quickly mastered it as the third instrument in the chamber music group.

In North Judson, Haver discovered another love. He joined and played on the city's baseball team. He had always wanted to play baseball, but while holding so many jobs during his school years, and striving at excellence as a student, he had not had time for games. In those days, baseball had to be played during daylight hours. With regular hours at the pharmacy, Haver tried out for the North Judson city baseball team, fell in love with the sport, and played on the team all the years he lived there, sandwiching the sport between his work and his musical performances.

Haver attended the Methodist Episcopal Church in North Judson. He played in the church orchestra. He also played trombone, cornet, and clarinet for the local dance orchestra that played each Friday and Saturday night for dances held at Schricker Hall. Mr. Schricker and his two sons also played in the dance orchestra. Later, Henry Schricker, the younger son, became lieutenant governor of Indiana for two terms, then served two terms as the state's governor. Schricker, a Democrat, became the only member of that party to hold the governor's office in Indiana up until that time.[4]

It was in 1902, at Schricker Hall, that Haver's life took a dramatic turn. While he played one night, a young square-dancer slipped and fell to the floor. Haver, seeing her embarrassment, jumped off the stage to lift her to her feet. Then he fell! At least, that is the way he phrased it in his journal. He noted that the chance meeting was the single most important moment of his entire life. The young dancer was Carlotta Mosher. He recalled in his journal that it "was love at first sight, for always, for him."[5] After the dance ended, Haver saw Carlotta home. Her sister, Daisy, who lived in North Judson, chaperoned. Haver asked Lotta if he might call on her again some evening while she and her mother visited in North Judson. He related of that experience:

> The next day at the drug store, I took no end of kidding and compliments. Most of them laughed that I was the only boy in North Judson to "fall" over a girl who fell first! They also teased me because Lotta was a "show girl" who only visited in North Judson during the off-season of the show.[6]

Haver's and Lotta's friendship continued. Haver also met Lotta's mother, Nina Mosher, and her sister Daisy, who, like Lotta, traveled with Swift Brothers' Circus and Dramatic Show. Daisy had married Jack Swift, of the father-son team, who owned the circus. Nina later married the father, Herb Swift.

In January 1903, the city band contracted to play a concert at the local lodge hall. The band leader thought of a unique advertising technique. Since the city orchestra could not afford regular uniforms, all the players were dressed in rube attire to attract attention. Mr. Smith sent his bandsmen out in pairs to the various areas of the city, equidistant from the band stand. Each pair had to begin playing and marching at a synchronized time. If the technique worked as planned, the marchers would meet at the band stand at the same time and be playing the same notes of music. Haver and his partner, a bass drum player, marched by the Swifts' house where Lotta visited. Jack Swift, Daisy's husband, happened to be at home at the time and came to the street to watch the action. Impressed with Haver's capability, he later offered Haver a job playing with his circus orchestra. The Swifts already had signed Mrs. Mosher and Lotta for parts in the dramatic group traveling with the circus. Haver decided to try the show and signed his first contract as a professional show musician with a salary of five dollars a week, plus board and transportation. Haver said later, "I would have worked for board only, especially after he told me that Lotta would be on the show."[7]

Haver immediately wrote his father to tell him of the new job with the Swifts. Before the circus left in March of 1903, Haver received a letter from his father, who wrote this time to tell his son that henceforth he did not want to hear from him ever again. The elder Haverstock wrote that he had prayed for years that his son would make something worthwhile of his life. He also stated his distasteful feeling about anyone who would take on the life of a traveling show person.[8]

The idea of final separation from his father did not deter Haver from his new goal. He liked the thought of being a full time, professional musician. When any new man joined a traveling show, the old troupers referred to him as a First-of-May.[9] This name suggested that the new man would get his fill of show business and its hardships by the first of May, shortly after the season began, and would desert the company. If he did not desert, they would recognize him as a full-fledged member of the traveling show society. All First-of-Mays had to withstand a good deal of hazing from the oldtimers on the show. The oldtimers confiscated and wore the new man's clothing, took his money, used his clean bedding, and generally made life miserable for him. These activities constituted a rite of passage for a novice to enter that unique, traveling community. Haver looked upon those problems as nothing more than exciting days, and considered the hardships of a First-of-May as merely his first "union dues" into a very elite union.[10]

Life in the circus was quite different from that which Haver had previously experienced. In his journal, Haver tells an interesting story of his first day out with the show:

> My first day on the show I learned something not to do. I was trying to make friends all around and went over to where Speed, a large white bulldog who did a high-dive fall act, was tied up, his tail wagging. I reached over and patted him. As I turned to walk away—you guessed it! He took the seat completely out of my pants, and took along with it a mouthful of me! That cured me of too quickly assuming friendships. It was a lesson that I knew I would use a great deal.[11]

The Swift Circus was a first-rate group as small circuses went. It boasted a cast and crew of fifty people, including an eighteen-piece uniformed band. They also had a comedy band for the parade bandwagon. As the parade wound through the streets on the first stop of their tour, Haver made his debut into show business, playing in both the marching parade's comedy band and later in the more serious orchestra that played prior to the opening of the show.

The Swift show had two dramatic bills, *Ten Nights in a Barroom* and *Uncle Tom's Cabin*. The orchestra, sitting to the right of the stage, played an overture just prior to the rise of the curtain. Up to that point in his life, when he was just seventeen years of age, Haver had never seen a dramatic tent show before. After the overture, the rest of the orchestra members, seasoned professionals, crawled under the flaps of the tent so they could have a smoke. Haver, the only First-of-May, enthralled by the drama, stood behind the proscenium to watch the show from the wings. Suddenly, he heard a commotion from the actors on the stage. They called for Harvey Green, a character in that particular play. One of the actors pointed to Haver, standing quietly in the wings, and said, "There's Harvey."

While his name was, indeed, Harvey, he certainly was not the character Harvey Green, whom they summoned to the stage. Haver had not even seen a rehearsal of the play. The cast had not bothered to rehearse the show because it was the one show in which all the characters were "up" on lines. They all had apparently forgotten, however, that the actor who had played the Harvey Green part had recently resigned from the company. They had filled his parts in the other bills they had rehearsed, but not the Green part in this show. The actors standing in the wings offstage began to push the First-of-May onto the stage for his real test and final hazing into his new union.

Haver nervously asked as they pushed, "What will I say?"

The main one pushing said, "Just move your mouth in pantomime. I'll read your lines offstage."

The Harvey Green character had lines on the stage for most of the rest of the show, so Harvey Haverstock made his stage debut the same day that he made his show musician and parade band debuts. Haver just moved rather awkwardly around the stage moving his mouth, later recalling that he looked much like an animated ventriloquist's dummy. Some of the movements of his mouth did not quite match up to the words being said behind the scenery, but evidently, he performed to the satisfaction of the audience. He did so well, in fact, that Swift assigned him the Harvey Green role to double in every time the group performed that bill. That first venture on stage with lines hooked Haver. From that night on, Harvey Haverstock the musician was also Harvey Haverstock the stage actor.[12]

During the 1903 season, much to Haver's disappointment, Lotta hardly traveled with the Swift Brothers after all. She had soon signed to do an acrobatic and barrel jumping act, billed as "The Maid and the Dummy," for the Majestic Vaudeville Circuit, which originated in New York City.[13] Her agent got her act accepted as one of the features of the St. Louis World's Fair. The Swifts allowed her to break her contract for this better opportunity. When Haver found that Lotta would be leaving the Swifts for the new contract, he did not want to go on the tour either. When the troupe stopped at Burlington, Illinois, Haver gave notice to Swift and joined another theatrical group, the Sollen and Neadles New South Show Boat. That job lasted only three weeks. Because Haver was so despondent about having to be away from Lotta, he decided that he had to just leave show business altogether.

Haver returned to North Judson, where he took a job as a Wells Fargo Express agent. Since the Wells Fargo office was in the same depot as the Pennsylvania Railroad office, the railroad also hired Haver as their agent for express. He felt that only by keeping himself completely busy could he keep his longings for Lotta in check. In the spring, he joined the North Judson baseball team once again. He also played for the community band, but no longer played in the chamber orchestra or at Schricker Hall. He and Lotta corresponded, but had no hope of seeing each other again until mid-1905 when her contract ended. That year and a half moved very slowly for Haver, but he and Lotta often wrote to each other of their mutual devotion.

Lotta rejoined the Swift Circus after her World's Fair stint. The Swifts scheduled North Judson on the calendar with their new bill, *The Daniel Boone Show*. Both Haver and Lotta delighted at the prospect of seeing each other again. However, Lotta got another offer at big-time vaudeville just prior to the North Judson play date. Taking the advice of her mother, she once again left the Swifts to join the Majestic Circuit with a group of young ladies who were billed as the "Gibson Girls," a song and dance group. It seemed to Haver that Fate had dealt him a terribly unjust hand by taking Lotta from him again.

He had another hand dealt him from his work. The railroad notified Haver that if he planned to keep his job with them, he would have to transfer to Logan Point, Indiana, as a regular, full-time railroad clerk. Since times were hard and jobs scarce, Haver could not afford to decline the advancement. He transferred, but all was not bad for Haver. In Logan Point, he immediately joined the local band, a fifty-piece ensemble. The band had begun rehearsals for a gigantic band concert/contest set in Terre Haute. Twenty bands would combine for the special concert. Prior to each band's being judged for its own individual playing, all of them would join together for a grand march through the downtown section of Terre Haute. All the musicians had to prepare the famous march, "Gloria," for that part of the program. Haver related the event in his journal:

> I was never so thrilled as when we started marching between those buildings. The brass resounded. I was among the trombonists at the front of the unified trombone section. There were seventy-five of us in that group alone. We led the more than nine-hundred musicians, all playing and marching to "Gloria." It was deafening. It was beautiful. My heart skipped beats as I listened and played! Tears welled in my eyes![14]

Haver's assignment with the railroad at Logan Point did not last long. Rather than just lay him off, the Pennsylvania Railroad did offer him a new position as an express messenger. The job entailed accompanying large, expensive items in a freight car to their points of delivery. Most of these special-order items carried a policy insuring delivery, and company officials wanted to assure that the items would arrive properly at their destination, avoiding costly insurance payments. They always sent along their messenger to get the delivery papers signed. The job involved constant traveling over all the Pennsylvania Railroad lines. He would not be permanently placed at any address.

This messenger job soon took Haver into New York City for his first visit there. While delivering an item to New Jersey, just across the river from New York City, Haver decided to pay the three-cent ferry charge and see the city about which Lotta had told him so much. New York City had become a special place to Lotta, not only because it was her birthplace, but also because it was a place where she had spent several years playing on the stage. Carlotta Mosher was born in Brooklyn, New York, on September 15, 1890. Her father, William Mosher, deserted his family soon after his fourth daughter was born. Lotta's three older sisters were Jessie, Elizabeth (Lizzie), and Daisy. Lotta, a child planned to save a foundering marriage, was much younger than the other girls. Even though Lotta's mother, Nina Mosher, was an actress who had her children travel with her, only two of her four children followed in her theatrical footsteps. In fact, Daisy appeared for only a few seasons in her husband's circus and dramatic company, so only Lotta became a devoted, lifelong actress.

In 1890, just prior to Lotta's birth, Nina Mosher played Eliza in the C. G. Phillips' *Uncle Tom's Cabin* touring company. In 1893, she was also cast as Eliza in the F. C. Perry Company, which toured the Tom show into Chicago and Indiana. Mrs. Mosher carried her child, Lotta, in her arms as she crossed the ice floe, escaping from Simon Legree and the bloodhounds. This role was Lotta's formal stage debut. Her theatrical career was a full one from that point on. She was reared in the theater. The 1893 company set the real stage for Lotta's later life in Tent Repertoire since Perry presented his production under a big top as a part of a circus.[15]

Lotta's father's life remains a mystery. Neither she nor her family ever spoke of him. Her ancestral background is also rather obscure. Nina's mother was a Scotswoman whom Nina left in Scotland as she fled the potato famine of the 1870s. When Lotta was born, her grandmother, M. B. Tufts, who still lived in Scotland, sent an heirloom brooch made of ivory to be her inheritance. It was a treasure Lotta kept always in her jewelry case, wherever she traveled. After Nina's death, Lotta also inherited some of her Grandmother Tufts' silver serving spoons engraved MBT. Though she never had a home from which she served meals, the spoons were prominently displayed on a wooden spoon rack by Elizabeth, Lotta's sister, in her home in St. Louis.

In 1904, when she was fourteen, Lotta had a role in the Valentine Stock Company's version of *Uncle Tom's Cabin*. The company toured out of New York City. She played opposite Gladys Smith.[16] Miss Smith went on to become "America's Sweetheart" of silent film, Mary Pickford, who first appeared in D. W. Griffith's *The Violin Maker of Cremona* in 1913.[17]

Mrs. Mosher would not consider allowing Lotta to accept a moving picture contract. She was convinced that flickering pictures were just a passing fad and that Lotta would lose her theatrical seniority by leaving the stage for film. She and Lotta decided to stay in New York. Ironically, fate soon took Lotta and her mother away from Broadway to jobs acting with a repertory company touring midwestern opera houses. By joining the touring company, Mrs. Mosher decided they could visit Lotta's newly married sister, Daisy Swift. The Swifts wintered their circus in North Judson, Indiana, where Nina would later marry Daisy's father-in-law, Herb Swift, and where Lotta would meet Haver.

While Haver visited New York City that first time in 1905, he picked up a copy of *Billboard*, a show trade publication he thereafter read religiously. He was interested in an advertisement of a position with The Batch Royal Shows of Mount Vernon, Ohio. Batch had interviews set up in the City; Haver interviewed and got the job, which paid him fifteen dollars a week plus his board and transportation. The show had contracts for the very best opera houses in larger tour cities. Tired of traveling with express items in a baggage car, Haver could not resist the prestigious job with a company that traveled in a Pullman car. He quit his railroad job, giving the company no notice. The acting troupe needed him to come to Mount Vernon as quickly as he could get there.

The Batch Royal Show never opened. The night before the date of the opening, Batch sneaked out of town. When the desolate cast broke into Batch's room in their hotel, they found everything stripped from it except a box of their letters of application and the worthless contracts each of them had signed. This event proved a tragic one. Not only had Batch fled, but he fled leaving the hotel bills, including the board he promised the actors in their contracts. That room and board bill happened to be in one of Mount Vernon's most plush hotels. By the time Batch left, each company member had already signed tab cards with the very expensive facility for a week. As collateral for his share of the bill, Haver had to pawn his trombone, his most prized and only valuable possession. All of the troupers took jobs, many in menial tasks at the hotel, to pay their debts. Haver served there as a hotel clerk for a time. While doing that duty, he met and became a quick friend of the son of the president of Milikin Glass Company, a local operation.

Before long, Milikin saw to it that Haver was offered a job with the glass company's band. Haver quickly accepted, and in that job he learned to play a new musical instrument—water-filled, hand-blown crystal goblets made by the company craftsmen. The varying levels of water in the glasses produced varying pitches when the player rubbed his dampened finger over the edge rim of the crystal containers. Haver became proficient in that art almost immediately, and the act was such a novelty that he arranged bookings in a vaudeville show in a nearby city. Haver carefully crated his forty-eight goblets in a wooden box for delivery to the theater. The dray driver unloaded the crate from his large wagon by dropping it at the stage door. When Haver opened the box of his instruments, he could not find one unbroken glass, making his musical glass-playing stage debut nothing more than a wishful thought. He decided that he preferred less fragile instruments. However, the musical goblet act was the genesis of an idea that he used later in his olio acts. He designed and had built a set of forty-eight musical cowbells, each varying in pitch because of its being just a fraction different in size. The bells were one of the most successful olio acts he and Lotta performed in their shows over the years.

In 1906, Lotta and Haver saw a chance for them finally to be able to work together. Lotta wrote in late 1905 to tell Haver that she planned to leave the Majestic Circuit. Her sister, Daisy, and Jack Swift, Daisy's husband, had decided to leave his father's circus and buy their own circus and dramatic show. They offered Lotta a job as lead actress in the company. Lotta related the information that Daisy and Jack also wanted Haver to lead their orchestra and do parts in the dramatic company. He was elated for the opportunity, not only to do what he wanted to do with his life, but that he would be traveling with Lotta. In April 1906, Haver joined the Jack Swift Show.

In October 1906, Nina urged Lotta to leave Daisy's show and rejoin Herb Swift's show in Arkansas for the winter months. The company would be playing circle stock in area opera houses. Lotta agreed to do so if they could also make a place for Haver. Both were hired, and the two journeyed to the home of Nina and Herb Swift in St. Louis, Missouri, to rehearse the scripts for the upcoming circle stock season. The troupe's first stop was to be the Clarendon Opera House in Clarendon, Arkansas.

The young actor and actress enjoyed working for Herb Swift. In April 1907, they made a decision to stay on with the company. By then, Nina had married Herb, and they were expecting their first child. This presented some real health questions for Nina as she was already well into her forties. It also presented an opportune time for Lotta to suggest to her mother that it was a good thing for a woman to have children early in life, subtly planting the seed for her next question. She and Haver asked Nina if they could have her blessing to marry. Mrs. Swift, perhaps too ill to arrange for Lotta to get a new vaudeville circuit booking, her previously used ploy to keep the young couple apart, reluctantly gave her permission. On April 17, 1907, between the acts of a show playing in Evening Shade, Arkansas, Carlotta Mosher became Mrs. Harvey Claude Haverstock.[18]

Even though they had the wedding ceremony carefully planned to coincide with the olio acts presented during the intermission, when they arrived at the church, the minister found the doors to the chapel locked. He had not brought along his key. Haver had to jimmy the window and crawl through to open the door for the others in the wedding party. They rushed the ceremony, and they made it back under the tent flaps just in time for the show's second act curtain.

In 1907, when they closed the regular season of Herb Swift's show, Haver read in the newspapers of a big oil boom going on in nearby Robinson, Illinois. Haver visited the city, thinking it would be a profitable place to winter so that he and Herb could go into painting signs for businesses. Because of the booming population, Haver reasoned that the Swift troupe might be able to play nightly all winter at the local opera house with the chance of a different crowd at each performance. However, when he arrived in Robinson, Haver saw that no opera house even existed. All he saw were just hundreds and hundreds of people milling about. George Root, a local entrepreneur, talked with Haver, and based on Haver's enthusiasm for the idea, decided to build a combination hotel, opera house, skating rink, and motion picture house all under the same roof. Haver convinced Root to sign contracts for not only for the Swift show to perform in the new building, but also that he and Herb be contracted to paint all the scenery pieces for the new opera house. He made a further agreement with Root that Nina and Lotta would be hired to sew all the costumes that would become stock costumes for the opera house. Haver also contracted to form and lead an orchestra for the opera house, noting that the group could also play at the skating rink when the opera house was dark.

While in Robinson supervising the construction project, Haver learned that Lotta also expected a child. Nina and Herb had just become the proud parents of a healthy son, Herbie Swift, Jr., and Nina was in St. Louis, so that her daughter, Elizabeth, could help care for her and the baby during their recuperative period. Lotta had gone to St. Louis, also, to be with her mother, sister, and newborn half-brother. After Lotta announced her own pregnancy, the family decided for her that she did not need to be in a rough, oil-boom town, but should remain in St. Louis where she could have the services of the best doctors. Haver and Lotta reluctantly agreed to the family-made decision of a temporary separation.

Carpenters finally completed the building of the Robinson Opera House. Root brought the Big City Company to Robinson with the show, *Isle of Spice*, to open the new facility. He hired Herb as stage manager and set designer. Root had promoted the sale of the one thousand seats in the new auditorium for ten dollars a seat for that one night. Since most opera houses furnished four standard scene curtains for their guest troupes, Herb and Haver set about painting the four standard drops the show would likely need. They worked long and hard to prepare what they considered excellent drops for the premier production. After the contracted company of fifty people arrived in town, Herb talked to the director, showing him the drops he and Haver had completed just the night before. The director told Herb to remove all the new drops; he said that he preferred the company to use its own, portable sets and drops. His decision truly upset Haver and Herb because it meant no one would see their artwork in the gala opening of the new opera house. They acquiesced; however, and both the Big City Company show and the big, new opera house opened to tremendous success.

During the performance of the Big City Company, Haver read an advertisement saying that a nearby county sheriff would offer the Williams Stock Company's furniture, costumes, props, and tent for sale to the highest bidder to pay taxes and delinquent debts. The tent measured sixty by one-hundred forty feet. Haver went to the auction where he bid $475 for the entire sale bill, and he won the bid. The tent needed only slight repairs, so Haver felt he had made a good investment. With the tent, he also got eighteen lengths of seven-inch-high backless benches called blues and bolted seats with backs called reds for a total of seven-hundred fifty seats. He was not quite ready to use his purchase, but he wanted it for when he left Robinson. Perhaps, somewhere in the back of his mind, he had begun to think of opening his own dramatic show company performing under a big top. Tent dramatic companies were becoming more numerous.[19]

3
Haverstocks Found Their Tent Show

Harvey and Carlotta Haverstock are generally typical of those show people who founded Tent Repertoire companies. They started out working in opera houses, then worked in airdomes before going into tent circus, and finally into Tent Repertoire. Their tent show was to become one of the most popular of the more than one-hundred fifty such groups performing in Oklahoma and Texas by 1925. From that number, the Haverstock show was the only standard show to survive the trials of World War I, the Roaring Twenties, the Great Depression, and World War II. Their tent did not close its doors from its founding in 1911, until 1954, after the death of its leading lady, Carlotta "Susie" Haverstock.[1]

The story of the Haverstock Comedians is the story of Tent Repertoire itself. Many of their experiences paralleled those of every other Tent Repertoire group. Some were uniquely their own. The Haverstocks stayed active in tent drama because of their love and devotion to theater for rural America. Their durability brought a kind of dignity to their company. That dignity and a clean, "Sunday school" acceptable show became their trademark. They brought joy wherever they traveled. People loved them wherever their show performed. Toby and Susie Haverstock are memorable people, and their plays are memorable theater to anyone who ever met the people or saw one of their performances.

In 1906, Lotta traveled as an actress and an acrobat with the Swift Brothers Circus and Dramatic Company,[2] a show group organized by Herb Swift, Lotta's stepfather, and his brother. Lotta had received her dramatic training while performing on the legitimate stage in New York City. She, along with her mother, Nina Mosher, also a stage actress, had come to Indiana in 1906 to visit kinfolk. They had decided to get away from the rigors of big city life, so when the Swifts offered them jobs, they took jobs as actresses in the dramatic part of their circus's dramatic show, one of the many traveling renditions of *Uncle Tom's Cabin*, referred to as a Tom show.

Soon after joining the Herb Swift show, after it split from the original Swift Brothers' Circus, Lotta and Harvey were married. Within a year after the wedding, Lotta bore their son, Rolland, their only child to survive infancy. He was born in St. Louis while the circus was in winter quarters there. Haver and Lotta again signed to travel with the Herb Swifts to Olney, Texas, in 1908. They decided to see if the business was more profitable in Texas than it had been in Arkansas. They liked Texas, and because the season was better, the troupe even decided to winter that year in Olney.

Olney was a boomtown, rapidly growing as a railroading center for the heart of north central Texas. Because of its boom, its towners had jobs, giving them more money to spend going to dramatic shows and other entertainments. The towners of a boomtown, and particularly the boomtown of Olney, longed for good entertainment; every night the Swifts opened, their circus was a sell-out. The troupers decided they could earn even greater returns by playing dramatic bills for a full winter season at the Olney opera house. That bonus season would guarantee that they would not have to worry about having enough money to live on while they learned their new repertory of plays for the coming spring and summer tent seasons. They reasoned that they could also build a following for their troupe by playing in other opera houses around the Olney area if the Olney opera house should bring in some other touring company for some performance variety.

Their reasoning was good. The winter of 1908 proved to be a lucrative one for both the Swifts and the Haverstocks. Staying the winter in Olney gave the show an advantage of an early start for their tent circus since the troupe planned to begin their new spring season from Olney. Being on location would give them the jump on other tent-circus-drama companies which had wintered in other places and had to travel into their tent areas. Many troupes of traveling shows continued to spring up overnight, it seemed. Such growth caused a great deal of competition to get at any extra money rural patrons might have to spend for theatrical entertainment, so such acting companies had to plan audience-gathering strategies well.

Since Haver loved music so much, could play any brass or woodwind instrument, and could teach all instruments but the piano and the drums, he decided to teach music in Olney. He thought that Olney needed a city band, and he could get one started by getting the local musicians together, similar to the way his childhood towns in Indiana had done, and he could reap the financial benefits by training new musicians for these bands. In advertising in the local newspaper and on placards he placed around town, Haver announced that he wanted to form a local band. He received a good response and pulled together a group of men who enjoyed playing. After just a relatively short time of polishing and with Haver's teaching skills, the group sounded good enough to play at city functions. Haver began as just one of the players, but it was not long before the band elected him as their conductor, a job that he had arranged to carry a small monetary stipend.[3]

Haver and Lotta rented a seven-room house in Olney so the Swifts' acting troupe could all live in one place to rehearse their scripts, prepare their advertising signs, and repair their travel equipment. The show had to be ready for its coming season. Haver and Herb became so adept at painting advertising signs for their show that they set up a business of painting signs on both windows and billboards for the merchants in Olney. Businesses in the boomtown started so quickly that local sign makers could not keep pace with the growth. Since every tent drama company made extra money by painting and selling signs to hang on their front curtains during performances, Haver and Herb had decided to capitalize on that activity. Before long, their work looked as good as that of the professional painters. Haver, the leg man for the team, collected sign orders from the business customers, then after both he and Herb painted them, he delivered the completed signs. Herb did most of the actual sign painting, but Haver was quite the talker and thus quite a salesman selling the businessmen the idea of having a newly painted sign. He was successful with almost any activity he pursued.

Haver had such a success in his other venture, Olney's town band, that he decided that on the days when he was not too busy working with the musicians in Olney, he could perhaps go to the nearby towns of True and Newcastle to organize bands in each of those booming places. He made arrangements with an instrument manufacturer to receive a commission on any new instruments he could sell to his prospective musicians. Business was good. Bands formed in both the smaller communities, and Haver set up lessons on brass and woodwinds for anyone who wanted to learn to play. While teaching music lessons in those cities, he could also crowd in enough time to sell sign painting jobs to their business houses, too.

As the 1909 spring show season began, Haver and Lotta decided that they loved their idyllic lifestyle in Olney so much, they would forego acting in the spring season and stay on as residents in Olney. They liked having their own house, grass, and trees. They were so involved in the affairs of the community that they felt as if they belonged to Olney. They were very well liked there, were almost accepted as town natives.

Herb and Nina decided to take the circus on the road as had been their usual custom. So, the Swift Circus began its northward trek that year without the Haverstocks among the cast. The show headed toward Colorado with bookings already set up in towns across the northwestern corner of New Mexico and the Texas panhandle, enroute toward the mountains.

Besides Haver's interest in band and drama, ever since he had been introduced to the baseball team in Indiana, he loved playing baseball. Everywhere he went in his early career travels, he joined the town's team as a first order of business. In almost every instance, it was just a matter of time before the team made him its manager. Olney was no exception. Haver joined its team as second baseman, but before he had been on the team for two weeks, they asked if he would become their team manager, setting up schedules, games, and so forth. The Olney team played Loving, Farmer, Newcastle, Archer City, Seymour, Graham, Jacksboro, Bryan, Throckmorton, and Woodson, all in Texas. Olney had a good team, according to Haver's diaries, but then, so did all the other town teams in their league, so the Olney team lost most of its games in the spring of 1909. In spite of Haver's having been the manager of a losing baseball team, the Haverstocks still felt a sense of really belonging to the community. They joined a local church so their family could be together in worship. Haver even played in the church orchestra each Sunday. Their lives in Olney were just about all for which a young family could hope.

Their comfortable life did not last as long as they had hoped it would. A wire came from Folsom, New Mexico, one of the early engagement stops on the route of the Swift Circus. Herb Swift was suddenly taken terribly ill, and though Nina telegrammed that they could replace him in the troupe with one of the orchestra men or a canvasman, they could not replace her in the cast. Nina told them that she had no choice but to stay on in Folsom to care for Herb, so the troupe needed Lotta to come to

Folsom at once to travel with them and play Nina's roles. By now Rolland had come on the scene, so Lotta and baby Rollie, as the young couple called their baby, quickly boarded the train to make their way to New Mexico for what they hoped would be just a brief stay to help Lotta's mother and stepfather keep their show on the road.

Herb's recovery took much longer than any of them expected. Haver, by the time Lotta and Rollie left, had become accustomed to having his family about him. He became very lonely, so he decided to drop all the Olney responsibilities he could and go to be with his family at Folsom. By the time he arrived, the troupe had decided it would be best not to continue their trek on into Colorado, but to try to keep the troupe active in a different area. They changed their route and headed instead toward southwestern Oklahoma. Haver talked them into this arrangement. He had strategically planned that if the troupe came back to the southern Oklahoma area, it would be close enough that he could stay in Olney most of the time. Early in each week, Haver could ride the train to the tent site and help the family with the set-up of the tent and help do the advertising signs. He could then return to Olney late in the week, keeping up his orchestra job on the weekends, and playing weekend baseball games to keep his coaching pay coming into the family coffers.

Haver actually had several things to keep his mind and his hands busy while Lotta and Rollie traveled with the Swift show that season. He was a promoter of the first order. He organized weekly Saturday night home talent shows for Olney. He also began contacting some area acting stock companies, arranging for them to come to Olney to perform in the local opera house. He acted as a commissioned booking agent for both the opera house and the troupers. The most memorable group he arranged to visit Olney that season was the King-Cole Stock Company.

By the time that he began booking for the opera house, Lotta and Rollie had ended the summer season and returned to Olney. The King-Cole show's coming to town gave the Haverstocks a chance at a further venture. Its being there offered Lotta a chance at a lead part in a bill while the company played in Olney. Mrs. King, the ingenue lead, had taken seriously ill soon after the troupe arrived in town. In order for the show to open, Lotta stepped in to play the lead role. She had no time for rehearsal in the part; however, she was a very quick study. Her acting and the fact that she was a local made her an instant hit in the show.

Mrs. King's health grew worse. Haver was persuaded to take over Mr. King's role so that King could stay at his wife's side while the show continued on its scheduled circuit. This part was Haver's first extensive foray into acting. He loved the part, and he loved acting. In fact, both Haver and Lotta grew to love working in the stock circuits while they played in the King-Cole Company there in Olney. With these roles, they both decided that what they wanted was to act as professionals on a full-time basis. They were approached to continue with the group until the Kings could rejoin their company, and they accepted the challenge with enthusiasm.

Mrs. King's illness continued to grow worse, so it was evident that she would not be able to continue with the show for the remainder of the season. Mr. and Mrs. Cole, the Kings' partners, decided it would be best to cut their losses and just close the show. Haver, however, persuaded them to allow him and Lotta to put $100 into the company to keep the show running on its course. In order to try to save the investment they had in the company, the Coles reluctantly agreed to the Haverstocks' offer. They insisted that the company change its name, however, to the Cole-Haverstock Theatre Company. They reasoned that the name change would give Haver and Lotta part of the responsibility of debt should the company not do well financially.

Just two weeks after forming the new partnership, while the company played in Roosevelt, Oklahoma, the Coles decided that they wanted to sell out. They offered to take $100 more for their share in the company. They agreed to stay on with the company for the rest of the season as paid troupers at a predetermined salary to be paid by the Haverstocks. Haver and Lotta accepted their terms, and in so doing became sole owners of a traveling theatrical company. The Haverstock Theatre Company made its debut in the opera house in Roosevelt, Oklahoma, in January 1911.[4] This was the first time that the Haverstocks had the full responsibility for a show and the first time the Haverstock name covered a theatrical banner. Haver wrote in his diary that the people in Roosevelt "were as friendly a people as I have ever met. They gave us three good days at their opera house."[5]

That first season was somewhat shortened because the troupe had not contracted a fixed route of places to play. They did perform their show in opera houses in Altus, Mangum, Olustee, Eldorado, all in Oklahoma. Additionally, they played Quannah, Motley, Crowell, and Seymour, all in Texas. While in Seymour, so near their home in Olney, the Haverstocks closed their first show company, and they traveled back to their seven-room house and their quiet life in a boomtown.

Not long after they arrived back in Olney, both of the Haverstocks realized that theater had become a necessary part of their lives. They both missed being in a show so much that they could hardly contain themselves in a sedentary home life. They were not nearly so content in Olney as they had been when they first moved there. No matter how hard they tried, the quiet life off-stage just did not offer them the challenge they sought. They thought that the "theatrical bug" would wear off, much as one could wear out a cold. They decided to do everything they could to recapture the life they had before the days of owning their own theatrical troupe. Haver joined the Olney Commercial Club, the town's Chamber of Commerce. Haver also started in a new kind of work, setting type for a local print shop. He played baseball with the local team and even got together another city band to perform on a regular basis. Again, he painted and sold business advertising signs as another moneymaker. In his spare time, he contracted jobs as a house painter and as a wallpaper hanger.

In rural north Texas, 1911 was not a good year economically. Even though Olney relied on railroad traffic and oil transporting for a big part of its income, those railroads relied on the farm economy, too. Because of a terrible drought, farmers were going broke with alarming speed. Railroad work slowed proportionately. Businesses began to advertise "Closing Out Sales." Country water wells began to go dry. Soon, even the drinking water had to be hauled into town in water wagons, and it was sold at a premium. Olney lost a big portion of its population that year, never to recapture it. Haver, finding little call for his sign-painting talents, soon found that few people could afford to have instrumental music lessons either, even if he priced his lessons at just ten cents an hour. No new students were available. No one had that extra dime.

When a house needed painting or repapering, Haver had to barter for his pay. One fellow told him that he would pay a good price to have his home painted and repaired. Haver took the job in good faith, but when it came time for the payment, the man offered Haver two city lots. Haver had to accept the lots as payment or be satisfied with no payment at all for his work.

Being quite a showman-promoter by now, and always an optimistic person, Haver thought of a scheme to raise money. He heard that the Boston Bloomer Girls' Baseball Team had plans to travel through the area. He contracted for them to come to Olney to play a team that he would organize among local folks. The Olney people cleared some pastureland for a playing field. Haver contacted one good baseball player from every city team around Olney, asking them to come join his team to take on the female baseball professionals. While he knew he would have an audience gathered for the game, Haver decided to advertise that for a small cover charge, people could attend a big dance, with his band playing, to end the day's festivities. He also persuaded Lotta to gather some local people together and as an added attraction for yet another small fee from the viewers, stage a play for a performance at the then-closed opera house. Those who did not care for baseball would surely pay to see a dramatic show.

The town virtually came to life under Haver's showmanship and promotional skills. The ticket receipts for the baseball game were over $400, of which Haver got $75 for being the agent. He and the orchestra divided the $70 they made on the ticket sales for the dance that evening. The theatrical performance played to a full house also, and gave the Haverstocks, under whose auspices the show played, a handsome profit. The reawakening of Olney turned out to be of financial benefit to Haver and Lotta.

At first, people thought about their enjoyment of the Bloomer Girls' team, the dance, and the show, but then they began thinking about all that money being taken from their town by a traveling group. They did not realize that Haver had been paid to bring the women to town. They cried out! Because of the anger of the townspeople, Lotta and Haver decided that perhaps the life they had thought so idyllic had now become tainted with reality, so they decided to leave Olney. Had the citizens known how much money the Haverstocks had actually made for themselves in those activities, the couple's decision to leave town might not have been voluntary.

The Haverstocks had a difficult time getting rid of their city lots, but finally a local physician gave them $40 cash for both lots. They let their furniture go back to the furniture store where it was mortgaged. They gave up the seven-room house and headed for St. Louis where the Swifts wintered their circus and show that year. The Haverstocks had not given up show business. On the contrary, they grew more interested in it than they had ever been before. Haver had proven himself as a show business entrepreneur. St. Louis, as a winter heart of the early-day tent dramatic activities, offered the Haverstocks a chance to find a good company to join, or even gave them an opportunity to form a second-season company of their own.

The Kings wrote asking Haver and Lotta to come back to Texas to join them in their new season. They promised to bill the show as the King-Haverstock Company, even though they did not ask Haver to buy into the show. Mollie Bailey, a show manager in St. Louis, wanted them to join her private train-car circus and dramatic company. Her company played one-night stands all over the Midwest.[6]

Bailey's offer enticed the young couple the most. She told them that she would hire Haver as the manager of her show, and both of them would have jobs as actors in the company. She also told them she wanted to retire from show business, and that if she did so, she would allow them to buy her entire operation at very good terms. That promise clinched the deal. Haver wrote the Kings to decline their Texas offer. The Kings, however, would not accept Haver's rejection. They wired Haver that if he and Lotta would just come to Texas, the company would be half theirs, with no investment. They promised that they would also buy a train-car similar to Bailey's, giving their joint company the capability of having the one-night stand programs that Bailey had promised. The prospect of half interest in a train-car company with no investment tempted Haver too much. He and Lotta decided to give the Kings a try.

After the Haverstocks and the Kings worked together for only two weeks, Haver found the reason for the Kings' generosity to him and Lotta. Mr. King had become a hopeless alcoholic. The tent show was deeply in debt, "plastered from ground to sky." Haver saw little hope of making any money during the entire season. Lotta, angry at being duped by the fancy promises of co-owning a show, confronted Mrs. King with her disgust. After King staggered through one performance, Lotta being the consummate professional actress, angrily protested. She stated that she would not allow such an action in one of the plays in which she performed, especially in one of which she was half-owner. Lotta told Mrs. King that she and Haver would leave the show because of the problems and the false promises. When only fifty people turned out for the next evening's performance, the Haverstocks packed their belongings and left.

Nearby, another tent show, the Robert Neff Theater Company, had their tent erected. Neff had an unblemished reputation. He had several years of experience as a showman. The show owned one train car to haul the company. The Haverstocks talked to the Neffs about obtaining jobs with their company. The Neffs agreed but told the Haverstocks that their time on the Neff show could be short-lived. Neff confided that he wanted to sell the show and move East to play legitimate theater. While Lotta and Haver talked of buying the Neffs' show, they did join it. Haver played in the band and in a bit part on stage. Lotta became one of the Neff Sisters, a singing vaudeville-type act which performed during the olios. She also played the soubrette in the cast. Even Rolland, then just three, had parts in their shows, *Ten Nights in a Barroom* and *East Lynne*.[7] As 1911 drew to its end, the Haverstocks had become an integral part of theater again as hired professionals in the Neffs' show.

When the Neff show reached Roosevelt, Oklahoma, the Haverstocks thought the time might be right for them to buy the company. They remembered the season before when they had bought out the Cole show in Roosevelt. They enjoyed such success with it, they thought their playing in Roosevelt might be an ownership omen for them. The Neffs jumped at the chance to sell. They gave Haver and Lotta the option of buying the show with payment at the new owners' convenience, as their profits grew. The Neffs were anxious to go East. The Haverstocks, perfectly content to stay on the prairie, completed the tour dates already set by the Neffs. Their decision to keep the route was another fateful decision for them. The Haverstocks kept that same route they bought in 1911 from the Neffs, with little variation, for the rest of their theatrical lives. They never again closed their tent show until 1954.

Haver told of the purchase of the show and some of its problems:

> Even though I had other tent designs in mind, I decided to take the Neffs' offer to sell me their tent and show. Our friends in Roosevelt would see to it that we had our first good bill under our own name, so we bought the show and placed an advertisement in *Billboard* to complete staff, filling the places that the Neffs left open with their departure. Then we set out to advertise our first Haverstock Tent Company in the Roosevelt and area newspapers. The year was 1911.[8]

The company they formed was already up on *Lena Rivers*, a tearjerker. Haver had watched Lotta play the part of the ingenue in their previous company, so he knew she would win the hearts of her audiences. That first night, they opened with only $15 in their change box. It had taken every cent of their savings, except for that $15, to buy the old Neff tent, paint their name on the front of it, run newspaper advertisements, and hire their first cast.

Everyone in the company became totally despondent when on their opening night a terrible, black cloud began moving toward Roosevelt. Lightning flashed everywhere. Cancellation of the performance appeared imminent. However, just thirty minutes before the curtain of the first

Haverstock Tent Show was to open, the cloud moved to the north, and the show proceeded right on schedule. People crowded into the tent. In fact, the hit show packed the tent for all three of the nights that it stayed in Roosevelt. The Haverstock's first season under their own canvas had begun, again in Roosevelt, Oklahoma.

From Roosevelt, Haver, as the advance man, set up dates for the tent show all over southwest Oklahoma, setting performances for Thursdays, Fridays, and Saturdays of each week. The troupe traveled in Oklahoma and North Texas until the weather became so disagreeably cold that the tent could not be kept warm enough to bring in an audience. Haver bought some charcoal-burning heaters so that the cold could be somewhat eased, but whatever they tried, the cold, north wind on the prairie proved too formidable a foe. Haver decided that the heaters could possibly work well enough in the east Texas area, where wind did not blow so fiercely, especially if the troupe could make rapid strides toward a southward route. They began working their way east and then south. They made their first stop in east Texas at a blustery and cold Longview. The more the winds blew, the more quickly the Haverstock Tent Show migrated toward Beaumont in the far southeast corner of Texas.

The Haverstocks were not the only tent show company suffering from the cold winds that season. When their show arrived in Beaumont, they met several other tent companies whose names the Haverstocks recognized. The Jennings Brothers' Two-Car Dramatic Company had already arrived and set up their tent in Beaumont before the Haverstock show arrived. The Jim Wallis Tent Company had also set up its tent to do a series of shows.

To avoid too much loss in gate revenue by having such an excessive number of companies performing simultaneously, the Haverstocks decided to move their group further into the south central Texas area. Before leaving Beaumont, they hired Carl Schuyler as their orchestra baritone player. They also added Mina Glover as a violinist and as a stock character for their stage company. Lotta played the ingenue lead in all the productions, but every company needed good, strong stock characters in the company. Mina was an excellent complement to Lotta's ingenue.

The Haverstocks had six people besides Haver in their first orchestra. The orchestra drew a crowd to the house about as rapidly as did dramatic productions. The band paraded through the town on the day the troupe arrived. The hoopla of a parade excited the towners and tempted them to buy tickets to the show. After the parade, the men in the orchestra, doubling as canvasmen, set up the tent. The ladies pressed the company's costumes and laid out the stage props for the show. The tent located near the railroad siding wherever possible, so the actors could use their train cars as dressing rooms.

During their first winter in the early part of 1912, the cold winds kept howling, so Haver decided to turn toward the very coast of Texas. He had wondered, as they got into a gulfside city, why no dramatic companies in the entire area had tents set up. He reasoned that "their loss will be our gain." Haver and the men quickly set up the canvas. The women did their chores. The tent show, apparently such a novelty in that community, pulled in such crowds that they could hardly be contained. The people crowded in so much every night that Haver added two more bills and drew crowds for two extra days of revenue.

Only after the move to the next town did Haver realize why he had seen not tent shows in the coastal area. When the canvasmen unfolded the tent at their next stop, they saw that mildew had already eaten through the canvas. The tent was a mass of holes. One small wind would tear the meshlike canvas tent to shreds.[9]

The Haverstocks completed the coastal tour rapidly with their hole-covered tent, praying that they would have no falling weather or no wind. They booked opera houses wherever they could as they traveled along the route back toward Oklahoma. The response to their plays and the camaraderie among the cast members was not nearly so good in the opera houses as it had been in the tent atmosphere. The potential customers, already apathetic to traveling stage show companies, rarely went to opera-house shows. Haver determined, after he saw the lowered gate receipts and the lowered profits, that he would buy a new canvas. He moved the show to Corpus Christi where they could call an end to their first Tent Repertoire season.

Two sets of troupes had presented shows in 1911 under the Haverstock banner; both had been organized in Roosevelt, Oklahoma. This auspicious founding gave the Haverstock Comedians a place in history that would finally cause them to be billed in 1954 as the oldest continuously running Tent Repertoire in the United States.[10]

4
The Early Years, 1911–1919

The early years of ownership of their own tent-show company were busy years of hard work for the youthful Haverstocks. They had no territory established. They had little other than distasteful experiences in tent dramatics for those beginning years. They loved the craft, but the early years tested their mettle.

Since mildew caused by the South Texas sea air had destroyed their tent in 1911, Haver decided that he should get a tent with a better design so that the stage could be seen more easily. So he designed a new type for his tent theater. The tent featured two poles, one on either corner of the stage, which eliminated the one center pole blocking the view of the center of the stage. At the close of the 1911 season, Haver ordered the prime circus tent makers, United States Tent and Awning Company of Chicago, Illinois, to build the new tent designed to fit his specifications. The troupe had closed its winter tour at the opera house in Corpus Christi, Texas, and moved to St. Louis, Missouri, their winter quarters, to await the arrival of the new tent, and to plan and rehearse its first full season, the spring tour of 1912.

The years encompassing the early period featured plays known in Tent Repertoire parlance as tearjerkers. The Haverstocks' show was no exception to the use of this traditional type of melodrama. The tearjerker play, a moralistic type of play featuring high melodrama, became the forerunner of such melodramatic theater as the soap operas of radio and television. The heroine of a tearjerker found herself getting more deeply into trouble with each passing moment of the play. Usually, the old home place had a mortgage on it. Some unscrupulous, avaricious banker or estate lawyer held the mortgage, which he had obtained under some false pretense or swindle. The ingenue, because of her naiveté, had placed her trust in the wrong person. Her affection for the handsome, but poor hero, and her call to duty, usually paying some kind of family allegiance to the dastardly, disguised villain who posed as her mentor, kept her duped or totally misled. The more embroiled the scene, the greater the sadness generated by the play. A death scene, where a child or a grandmother or a dear friend extracts from the heroine a deathbed promise of fealty, friendship, or unity almost always occurred in the play. In the real, off-the-stage world, deathbeds, all too common in these perilous years, especially in the pioneer areas where the Haverstocks took their tents, could not help but swell the flow of tears from those who attended the productions.

The Haverstocks set their tour itinerary for that first season of 1912 and basically followed the same route for most of the years they performed their tent show. They began their tour in the town of Roosevelt, the place where the friendly people helped to establish their first two Haverstock companies, both of which were initiated in the year of 1911. After Roosevelt, they usually headed their tour south to Snyder, a community that always received them graciously. They next traveled to Altus, after which they headed south toward Eldorado, Olustee, Hess, then eastward moving to Davidson, Frederick, Victory, Hollister, Loveland, Grandfield, and Devol. From Devol, where the rails ended in Oklahoma, they moved overland via dray to Randlett, Cookietown, Apheatone, then south toward the Rocky Ford and Rabbit Creek farming communities. After their dray trips, they then backtracked to Devol to reboard their Pullman car to head across the Red River into northern Texas. In Texas, their tour began in Burkburnett, then it moved to Holliday, Archer City, Throckmorton, Breckenridge, Graham, and finally to Olney, where they usually closed for the winter. They played from three nights a week up to an entire week in each town along their routes, making friends who would long remember the thrill of having seen productions of the Haverstock Dramatic Tent Show Company.

Bess Browning Pearce, in her book, *Unto a Land*, about the history of the early years of the town of Davidson, Oklahoma, recalls:

> For ten years or longer, beginning in the early Teens, the Davidson businessmen and entire community did a great service for the people by underwriting and bringing to town something entertaining and educational, the Chautauqua. Held afternoon and evening, for about a week, people looked forward to the coming of the Haverstock Tent Show which came to Davidson each summer for about thirty years. Few eyes were dry at the close of such [shows] as *East Lynne*.[1]

Early Years, 1911–1919

To these pioneer Oklahoma people, the Haverstock tent show resembled the Chautauqua many of the patrons had seen before moving West. In the true sense of the term, the tent show was not a Chautauqua. The Haverstocks offered three-act dramatic productions, whereas the Chautauqua usually featured as its fare a noted lecturer, opera singer, or a course of study. But whether it was called a Chautauqua or Tent Repertoire made little difference to the entrepreneurs. What did make a difference was that the people came to see the shows.

Rolland, the Haverstock's son, who began his acting career with their company when he was a very young child, remembered his appearance in the tearjerker *Ten Nights in a Barroom*. At four, he had not yet had a haircut. His hair was blonde and was a solid mass of ringlets covering his entire head. Lotta dressed him in the fluffy white middy-shirts worn by both genders of children six and under. He was a beautiful child, and it was difficult to tell whether he was male or female, so he could play either role. In this particular scene of *Ten Nights in a Barroom*, he played the dying daughter of the household. The audience wept pitifully as he lay propped up on many white and pale blue, lace-covered pillows. He had rehearsed the scene over and over, even though Lotta had told Haver that he was a natural in the part. He played the dying child well in each of their many rehearsals, during which he lay perfectly still and kept his eyes closed, as in death, until the curtain rang down. Lotta portrayed the dying child's distraught young mother. She had an uncanny ability to play these ultradramatic parts well, and as the scene ensued, she had built up to an especially mournful, dramatic climax while Rolland lay calmly as his mother emoted. The white makeup Rolland wore made him appear deathly pale.

As Lotta built up to the aesthetic and strongly emotional level that she desired, she began her stage weeping. She wailed. The audience was swept up in the emotion of the moment. They wept and wailed with her. She sensed their feelings. Wonderful actress that she had already become, she milked them for even more emotion. Her black eye-liner makeup ran freely from her tear-flowing eyes, leaving black rivulets on her cheeks. She kept the audience right with her. At the exact moment of her baby's death, the especially tearful young theatrical mother usually gave them a further dose of mournful pumping. The ushers had to help young mothers in the audience from their seats because they were crying so uncontrollably that no one around could even hear the play. Rolland, having not been in a performance with a live audience before, did not quite understand what was going on. He had heard Lotta crying in the rehearsals, but he had not heard the audience sobbing before, so he did not understand the dramatic milking his mother did now that they were onstage. At her most mournful moment, as both she and the audience wept so unabashedly, Rolland rose up on his theatrical deathbed, just after he supposedly had died, and said, "Don't cry, Mommy! This just a play. Rollie not really dead!" His delivery brought down the house![2]

Everywhere the Haverstocks took their tent show, people responded. Grandfield, in its weekly newspaper, *The Grandfield Enterprise*, always gave big headlines to the coming of the Haverstock shows, the favorite of the traveling troupes to play their city.[3] At least two tent companies came through the little community, the other show being one of the Brunks' Comedians troupes. Though Frank Patterson, the editor and a good friend of Haver, never slighted the Brunks in his newspaper, the Haverstock shows always got the best of his editorial comments and the best of the newspaper's advertising spaces. Boasting such a professional actress as Lotta, the Haverstocks' show was well received wherever they performed. After just a few seasons, the Haverstocks became the only Tent Repertoire group that went into the territories they selected and listed for their route. The Brunks and other competitors changed their routes so as to avoid professional conflict with the Haverstock group.

The playbills for 1912 included a classic favorite, *Rip Van Winkle*, along with *St. Elmo*, *The Sweetest Girl in Dixie*, and *Jack-O-Diamonds*.[4] On occasion, when they needed more funds than they had earned in their regular season, the Haverstocks played the winter season in South Texas opera houses instead of returning to their winter quarters in St. Louis. In Fredericksburg, Texas, they played in the Nimitz Opera House. (The son of the owner was later to become the chief of naval operations of the United States Navy.) They played any opera house they could find open from Galveston through Houston to San Antonio. Eugene Walton, a young writer, brought his new script, *The Wolf*, to Haver while the troupe played in Galveston that winter. Walton offered the heavy melodrama exclusively to the Haverstocks. It soon became one of their most successful and sought-after productions.

The Haverstocks closed their 1912 season in late March so they could travel to St. Louis for a month's rest before beginning their spring tour for 1913. It was for the tour of 1913 that Harvey Hill, a fine young actor from Marion, Indiana, joined the Haverstock show for the first time. He became a member of their troupe at Comfort, Texas, on February 20,

1912, to get up in parts so that he could be a regular in the spring tour, and he completed the few remaining weeks until the season closed.[5]

By the time that the troupe was ready to begin the 1913 tour, they found that Lotta was expecting their second child in August. As was customary for pregnant women in those years, she could hardly be seen in public, much less on stage, so she would have to miss most of the spring tour for propriety's sake. She would stay at home in St. Louis at 1402 Benton Street, in a house the Haverstocks rented so that when it came time for the new child to arrive, she could be near her sister, Elizabeth. She would miss being with Haver and the company, but since they had invested so much in the venture, Haver had to go with the company as both their advance man and as one of the characters in their productions. The show had to be successful because everything they owned was involved in its production.

On April 15, Haver took the new season's bills on the road. This was the company's first time to tour without Lotta. She was to have joined the troupe for an occasional weekend whenever Haver was able to send her enough money for her train travel, and if she felt up to the trip. She was extremely ill all the time that she carried the child, however, and did not come to meet the tour even once. In fact, in mid-July, Lotta contracted typhoid fever. Her high temperature and delirium sent her into premature labor. On August 1, 1913, the Haverstock's second son, Howard, arrived. His early delivery had brought on multiple birth problems, and as a result of these problems, he died on August 3. Lotta had Elizabeth notify Haver that the child had been born, but because of erratic train schedules in those days, Haver could not make connections to arrive in St. Louis soon enough to see his second son alive. The young couple became totally devastated. This was the first death for the young couple to have to endure, so it was very rough on them. About all they could do was to make a decision to bury their child, so they bought a plot in St. Peter's Cemetery in St. Louis, knowing that Elizabeth was a permanent resident in that city and they would always be able to come to visit her and at the same time visit the child's grave.

The tragic death of Howard closed the 1913 season early, only a little more than halfway through the tour. Lotta was in such poor spirits that Haver could not leave her alone. The trauma continued to be so great for the two of them that they could also not consider even playing the opera house circuit that winter. The doctors told Haver that Lotta was much too fragile, both physically and emotionally, for such grueling work as the tour offered. Haver decided just to close the show and take a job. He became a conductor on the St. Louis streetcar line. In that capacity, he had to arrive at work each morning at 4:00 A.M. A streetcar conductor's job was not too pleasant for one who had experienced the life of an actor and a musician, so as quickly as Haver saw an advertisement for a musician with the United Railways Company Band, he answered it. He learned that those musicians selected for the band would also be given jobs working for the railway line. Three other trombonists, all former Sousa band members, tried out for the single trombone position. Haver went to the tryouts not having any idea of the type of music the new band played. He decided to play his music at what he knew to be the normal show orchestra rhythm and sound level. As the band began playing, the conductor pounded his baton for them to stop the music. He looked over toward Haver and gave the young trombonist a terrible public bawling out, telling him that this was to be a band, not a group of soloists. Discouraged and embarrassed, Haver quickly apologized for he wanted to be the musician chosen to play. He quickly rethought the style and rhythm, playing the music. This time he realized how the conductor wanted the piece to be played. Evidently, his interpretation was exactly right with this playing, because the conductor immediately hired Haver, choosing him over the former Sousa bandsmen. Haver later recalled that the lesson taught by that conductor was the best one he had ever learned in music. He always gave the same instruction to every orchestra he organized, carefully telling the members that he wanted a unified sound from his orchestra, not solo pieces.

Once Lotta began to feel better again, she grew anxious to go back on the theatrical road. In 1914, the Haverstocks chose not to take out their own show but once again contacted the Mollie Bailey Stock Company. Mollie was seventy years old by then and was definitely ready to retire from traveling show business. Mollie hired Haver and Lotta for that season, telling them that if they took well to the job, she would happily sell them her Pullman and her equipment. She did not offer to sell them a tent for the show, since she played her shows in opera houses all year long. She told them that she had a niece who wanted to be an actress, and she promised Haver that if he would guarantee her niece a job with the show for the remainder of the 1914 season, she would sell him her business immediately. The Haverstocks could not refuse the deal she offered, so they quickly bought the Mollie Bailey railroad car, an especially built show car, which they outfitted with their own dramatic materials, including a new tent and other special equipment. They changed the company's name from Mollie Bailey's Dramatic Show to the Haverstock Dramatic Company. For their fourth season, they did, in fact, take out their own show company after all.[6]

In the 1915 season, the Haverstocks agreed to hire Mr. and Mrs. Thomas Cosgroves, providing Haver would allow his company to play in winter circuit houses owned by Cosgroves' agent. Since that arrangement gave the cast a place to try out their new season's show bills, Haver agreed to their conditions. The cast would also have a place to earn winter dollars. Al Clark, an actor, and later a famous Toby playwright, became a Haverstock cast member for 1915. Their circle stock route included St. Charles, Granite City, Edmondsville, Wood River, East St. Louis, Lebanon, and Belleville. Each night they played a different tryout show bill.

With the money earned from the circle stock venture that winter, Haver bought a second railroad car, a Pullman, which they converted into a lounge car with a dining hall. This purchase caused them to be able to boast proudly that theirs was a two-car train company! Their dining room section of the train car had collapsible tables so that the room could be turned into a rehearsal hall. Under the car, they had a 'possum belly built. The 'possum belly was a compartment, a large metal pouch distended under the train car and designed to hold the tent and much of their other theatrical equipment. The two cars were lettered with large printing covering the entire length of the car; the lettering proclaimed them as *The Haverstock Dramatic Tent Show Company*. It took the length of both cars to display properly the entire name of the company. The cars attracted a great deal of attention as they traveled to the towns on the Haverstock route.[7]

In 1916, while the two-car Haverstock Company was parked on a siding, a switch-engine hit the back car, derailing both cars. The derailment injured Lotta and six others in their crew. The railroad finally lifted the cars back on the track, but the process required several days because of the damage to the wheels of the back car. The Haverstocks had to load their show on drays for most of the remainder of that year's tour. They could not take the orchestra along because of the limited space on the drays. The instruments for the band, all stored in the 'possum belly, were badly damaged by the derailment. When the musicians looked over the damage to the car, they agreed among themselves to say that their instruments, all carefully cushioned in the storage compartment, had also suffered severe damage. They saw a chance to collect insurance and get new instruments by their bilking of the insurance company.

Early Years, 1911–1919

Lotta sustained serious injuries from the accident, so she had to leave the cast for a time. Haver hired Mina Glover Schuyler, an actress whom they had previously employed, to fill in for the rest of the run in Lotta's roles. He rented an apartment for Lotta so that she could rest well while the railroad worked on the derailment and repaired the car. The railroad company could not make the repairs to the cars where the accident had happened, so they finally had to take the Pullman into their roundhouse for repair to the damaged wheels.

The orchestra men, unable to travel on the drays with the troupe, straightened out the slight damage to their instruments. They sat around their encampment using the restored instruments to rehearse their music toward the day when they would be playing prior to the canvas's being opened each evening. One day, a friendly stranger came upon the rehearsing group. He brought along a horn and asked if he might join the group in improvising. He apparently enjoyed the company of the Haverstock players so much that he asked if he might stay around the camp with them for the next two weeks. The stranger worked his way into the confidence of the bandsmen, becoming a regular member of their group. He talked against the railroad and griped with the musicians about the alleged damage to their instruments. The Haverstock men told him everything concerning the details of the accident and its damage. They told him their instruments had not really been damaged in the accident, but they saw the accident as a good chance to get themselves new instruments via insurance payment. They added that they had seen how badly damaged the 'possum belly was, so how could anyone guess that the instruments had not also been that damaged? How could anyone doubt their story? They told how carefully they had done their work, allowing no one in the Haverstock family to see them with their hammers. Haver, who was not on the train at the time of the accident, readily believed the musicians' stories. Anyone could see how badly the wreck had mangled the brass instruments. Haver agreed with them to press for the replacement of their instruments as part of the insurance settlement, but had Haver known the full story, he would not have allowed such a deception to be attempted.

When the accident claims finally came to a court case for settlement, Lotta was able to get all her medical bills paid. The insurance paid for the rail car's repair. The friendly stranger who had become the musicians' buddy turned out to be an insurance investigator, and he was quick to expose their ruse. Not only were they caught in the lie, but each musician had to pay for the repair of his own instrument. The Haverstock Dramatic Company had many problems meeting their scheduled 1916 dates. The wreck and the subsequent hearings caused some cancellations, so Haver decided that they would just skip the remainder of that season.

For the 1917 season, since Lotta was still recovering, Haver hired the Glovers, the Schuylers, Fred Whitford, Julius Gems, Lou and Orpha Rathbone, and a Mr. Fanshawe to make up his cast. Their tent, because it was so badly damaged in the train collision the season before and was already an old one, gave Haver a chance to design a second innovative version with a totally new dramatic end. This new tent featured an A frame at the front of the stage. The whole front of the stage, using this new concept, would be totally visible to the audience, except for two tiny upper corners. The two poles, which had partially obstructed some viewing in the previous design, no longer caused such a problem. Up to that date, Haver's was the best tent design to be used for a tent show production. Other show managers widely copied it.[8]

In 1917, on October 8, the Katy Railroad caused another accident to the Haverstock's Pullman cars. The Katy engine in Olney accidentally pushed the two cars off the siding on to the main line of the Gulf, Texas and Western Railroad. Lotta's mother, Herbie Jr., and Rolland, along with the company's two chefs, were in the cars resting. Suddenly, the railroad coupled a gasoline tanker to the back of the last of the Pullman cars on the siding. As the engine moved the cars off the siding, an oil drum, hooked up for cooking onto the kitchen part of the car, came loose, spilling oil over the car and the tracks. When the engine moved the cars back to the siding, a spark from the wheels of the moving cars ignited the oil-soaked dry weeds on the rail's roadway. That fire ignited the Pullman with the leaking oil drum still partly attached.

Haver related the incident:

> We heard the fire engines several blocks away from where we were setting up our tent, but we had no idea it was our car. When someone came by to tell us of the fire, we rushed to the siding. Our car was not where we had left it. The gasoline tanker being attached to our car made the firemen afraid to try to fight the fire. A train crew, seeing our dilemma, did uncouple the tanker and pull it away. By then, however, half of our car had burned. The car, our vault, our records, our silver, Lotta's jewelry, our clothing, and all the brand new or newly repaired band instruments were totally destroyed.

Luckily, the new tent and all of the chairs were all already in place on the lot.[9]

With this second train tragedy in as many years, the troupe had to travel once again by dray to nearby Megargle, Texas, then on to Throckmorton. They traveled on to Woodson, and then to Breckenridge. Then after a stop at Breakman, the show people received notice that the show would close. For the second season, Haver had to attend a hearing over an insurance loss. In Olney, the Haverstocks stored the equipment they managed to save from the fire. Everyone thought that surely the Haverstocks had a perfect insurance case. The reason the fire did so much damage was because the Haverstock's Pullman, a passenger car, had been hooked, illegally, by the railroad to a gasoline tank car. The Haverstocks did win the case at the hearing,[10] but once again, their show closed with a short season. They did not get paid for this loss of time to their cast and crew, and since they had closed shows all along the route those two years, audiences began to question their dependability, even though their shows had always been top-notch when they had mounted them.

Rolland was in school by 1917, and he had changed schools each week since the show had been on tour. Rolland had no problems in academics in each new school he attended, but his parents wanted him to have stability. He was written up later, however, in *Ripley's Believe It or Not* as the student who had attended more schools than anyone else in the world.[11] Since he had done so much drama, he was adept at memorizing. He memorized most of his work, making him an honor student. To have a "show child," especially a bright one, in their classes thrilled most teachers. They had him share show experiences with their nontraveling students. The Haverstocks decided that since the show had to close the season early again, it would be better for Rolland if they moved the family back to St. Louis so he could attend school in the excellent system there. The family moved to 825 Madison Street in St. Louis, and Rolland enrolled in school.

When the family arrived in St. Louis, Haver immediately began looking for a new Pullman to buy. Since no Pullman was available in the St. Louis train yard, Haver headed to Chicago to look at one he had heard was available there. He had to transfer trains in the outskirts of Chicago. The depot to which he had to transfer lay thirty blocks away from his arrival point, so Haver decided to walk the distance to see some of the city. His walk proved an interesting one, leading down South State Street,

Chicago's theater district. Here Haver saw dozens of honky-tonk and burlesque theaters. Admission to the shows was ten cents, and that included a first drink. Haver carried $1,000 cash in his wallet so that he could make a down payment if he found a Pullman car to his liking. He was reluctant to venture off the street thinking about the safety of the cash, but he could not resist the shows.

He relates of the incident:

> The strangest people were in the theaters—all characters. There were but a few seats. Everyone stood for the ten minute show. I made them all and kept making them until midnight. It was 1:30 A.M. by the time I arrived at the second depot. While I was sitting there, it dawned on me what I had done. I immediately looked for my money! It was there; thank God, still intact. I really became scared as I went over the places where I had just been. It is a wonder I had not been rolled more than once.[12]

The Pullman he had heard about met their needs exactly. Nelson Lorange already had rigged it as a car for a traveling show. Haver purchased the car and had it delivered to St. Louis in time for their new season. The Haverstocks hired a new company of actors and booked a vaudeville house near their Pullman on the Frisco siding as their tryout location. As the Haverstocks gathered their cast for that year, they decided Rolland should remain in St. Louis to go to school. Nina Swift, Lotta's mother, actually made the decision that both Rolland and her son, Herbie Jr., had had enough of show business until they completed their schooling. She would stay in St. Louis to care for the boys.

Charles D. Rhea, a frequent correspondent of Haver's over the years, and a handsome, well-known leading man in Toby shows in later years, wrote Haver in 1917, after seeing his advertisement for players:

> I want you to always drop me a line when in need of a man of my size. I would be more than pleased to accept whatever lines you would offer [he had trouble in the past with his drinking]. With my wardrobe as complete as it is now, and my line of scripts, and I have a typewriter, I am in OK shape for service. Hope to hear from you at once, for I want to work for you [this season].[13]

Because Haver wanted to avoid any possibility of trouble in his cast, he did not hire Rhea. The Haverstock Dramatic Company opened in 1917, in Bourbon, Missouri, in February. They quickly moved down the Frisco line toward Oklahoma and Texas. They played in opera and vaudeville houses from February until it was warm enough to play in the tents in April.

In 1917, the Haverstock troupe was especially commended when a sponsor in Elkhart, Texas, wrote:

> The programs [the Haverstocks] present and the class are not what we ordinarily find in the transient theater. Everything is high class, clean, worthy and no cheat. They always pack a house. You can tell they are a well-coached, well-cared for troupe, and they always back local charity nicely. They did a benefit night for the local Red Cross drive.[14]

Actors usually returned to their home towns to spend the winters. Through those winters, many gave voice and elocution lessons to local children, did public script reading, and memorized their lines in anticipation for the upcoming summer season. J. F. Pennington, an actor from Cherryvale, Kansas, tried to get on with the Haverstocks. He wrote Haver in 1918, "What will you and Lotta do 'til summer? . . . I will stay here in this town until the weather gets warm and then to the tall and uncut hay for me. Please let me hear from you soon."[15] Pennington was not hired for the Haverstock cast, but they did hire Harvey Hill, a young actor who had joined the company as a novice in late 1912. They also hired old pros, Ed Coke and Lou and Orpha Rathbone. Lotta and Haver, as well as a new orchestra, rounded out the company for 1918.

For the first time ever, the Haverstocks booked into an extensive list of opera houses in Missouri. At Cassville, they nearly lost their Pullman again. It had been accidentally hooked between two empty freight cars. In that section of Missouri, where the Ozark Mountains are called hills by the natives, a long, downhill grade lay all the way from Exeter to Cassville. The engineer thought that the three joined cars were all freight cars. When a brakeman on the back of the last car signaled a hook-up, the engineer just butted the cars with the engine, playing around with the brakeman. The three cars began a freewheeling trip down the mountain to Cassville.

No one in the Pullman actually knew they were in any danger until after the cars stopped at the Cassville switch, at the bottom of the hill. The brakeman, knowing of the error, jumped from the rear speeding car up to the front car and was finally able to grind the three cars to a stop almost exactly at the place where the engine would have stopped the cars. When the troupers on the runaway Pullman found out what had happened, it was a very nervous cast of characters who walked onto the Cassville stage that night. After the show, the cast members all made absolutely sure there was an engine attached to their Pullman to move it back up the hill to Exeter, their next stop.

Haver also booked a stop at the booming mining town of Gravely, Missouri, where a new opera house had been built. The owner begged Haverstock to open the new building with its first acting company, so Haver decided to do it. When the company arrived in town, they understood why the owner had been so persuasive. Crawford's Comedians, an excellent tent show company, already had set up their tent just across the street from the new opera house. The Crawfords had the reputation of being among the best shows and musical groups on the road. The Haverstock show had also established what they considered as a reputation equal to that of the Crawfords. As the Haverstocks opened in the opera house, even though the tent across the street offered a "Ladies Free" night, the new theater drew the larger house. Neither group suffered much in attendance during the week both companies played in Gravely. The two casts became very well acquainted. When a young couple asked to be married in the tent one night, both casts held a wedding party for them. In fact, the groups were so compatible that some of the musicians, including Haver, went to the tent to swell the Crawford orchestra. The tent show people came to the concert play, a short play following the regular stage show. The Crawfords had parties with the Haverstock company each night after the concert closed.

It was on this tour that Haver initiated a long-held practice of the Haverstock players. At Quapaw, Oklahoma, where a very religious man booked the show into his opera house, Haver instructed his people to attend the owner's church on Sunday. Haver received so many compliments about his cast's being the first show people to attend church in Quapaw that he made it a rule, from that point onward, that Haverstock people attend church in every town along their route.[16] He also made a decision never to perform a play on a Sunday. The audience accepted the Haverstock players phenomenally well in Quapaw. In fact, for the first time in their history, a house manager asked that the troupe be booked for a second successive week.

Since their repertory of plays was rather limited, Haver knew he would have to repeat one of their bills during the second week. He decided they could give new names to the characters in *Lena Rivers*, and put a new title on the play.[17] As an incentive to get the new characters' names used correctly during the second performance, the cast set up a fifty cent fine for every time someone on stage used one of the original characters' names incorrectly. The cast began using the old names almost from the start during the performance. Finally, at intermission, the owner came backstage and told Haver, "Would you all just use the old names. We all know the play is *Lena Rivers*, but we are all so confused about who is who, we'd like to get it straightened out by the end of the play."[18] The audience kept the characters straight as the cast reverted to the original script names. The audience did not mind seeing *Lena Rivers* again because they loved the play with whichever set of character names. The show was a classic favorite of audiences everywhere.

The Haverstocks ended their opera house tour in Quapaw and took a week's vacation before going into the tent for the 1918 season. Rolland joined them just as soon as the school term ended in St. Louis. Everything looked bright for the company, then the Great War took its toll on the male members of the cast. The Haverstocks traveled to Roosevelt and set up their tent. Jack Worthington left the company in Roosevelt so he could join the army. Haver had to hire some older men to replace the young actors who decided to join the service.

For the 1918 tent season, Haver added the blues as the innovative seating for the tent. The blues were blue-painted risers with backless benches. These risers sat along the side walls of the tent. The owners distinguished these general-admission seats from the reserved reds by the price of admission, by the color of the tickets, and by the fact that the reds were individual red chairs bolted together sitting in front of the stage on the floor.

Later, Haver, who was 1-A for the draft, received his notice to come to St. Louis to be ready to be drafted. He stayed in St. Louis until well after the Armistice on November 11, 1918. He was never drafted into the service, but he worked at the rail yards moving the war trains for thirteen hours each day. When the soldiers returned to the States and began returning to their jobs, those men who had temporarily held those places during the war had to move out of the way. Haver's job was among the first to be reclaimed. Returning soldiers quickly bumped Haver all the way down to yard clerk on the Missouri-Pacific line.

Haver had sold his company's Pullman car in Louisiana just after he received word to come to St. Louis to be drafted. He and Lotta had stored their tent and equipment, but now they faced a big decision as to whether or not to go out on the road again. Since they did not have their own Pullman, getting one was a big problem. By this early in 1919, so soon after the war ended, the government had not diverted any rail cars from wartime use. It was difficult to find one for civilian use.

Moving pictures had come into vogue by 1919, and live dramatic companies needed something extra to keep their audiences coming. Haver knew that he needed a special show to take with him. He had never had trouble with film-house owners in the past, but he had heard horror stories, so he wanted to be prepared for any eventuality. Haver contacted a large theater in downtown St. Louis. To go on the road, he needed a blockbuster show for one-night stands in the opera houses enroute to Roosevelt, their first tent show presentation in 1919, and to use in their repertoire that season.

The biggest hit show in St. Louis then was a show called *Polly of the Circus*, starring Marie DeGaffirilla.[19] The Haverstocks saw the production several times. A tearjerker, the story involved a young girl, Polly, who wanted to go with the circus. The minister who wanted to marry Polly could not help her decide whether to go with her first love, the circus, or to remain and become his wife. Reluctantly, she decides to stay with him, but before she can tell the minister of her decision, he says, "Polly, whither thou goest, I will go!" The play ends as the wagons of the circus head off the stage with Polly and the preacher driving the last one into the theatrical sunset. Haver bought the script, and Lotta became the rage of the opera houses and the tent show circuits that year with her portrayal of Polly. The Haverstocks held the exclusive right to perform the play on the road for that entire 1919 season.

The Haverstocks met some resistance from film-house owners. Even though film-house owners generally opposed rag op'ry troupes, most of them liked the Haverstock troupe. In a letter dated 1919, E. N. Collins, the manager of the Liberty Theater and Garden Dome of Electra, Texas, wrote to Haver:

> If you had come thru [*sic*] a little earlier and played our dome, there would have been no difficulty about playing you. The way it is now makes it a hard proposition. We book our films for Liberty a month or more ahead and should you happen to want a date on which we were playing a big feature that cost us a hundred dollars or more, it would not mean any money to us to put in a show. The weather prohibits crowds from getting in for the films, and you can never

count on the clouds in this time of year on through the winter, for outdoor work.

I may enter into an agreement with the other fellow here not to play any [tent] shows this fall. He is talking of it. It would be best for both of us as both our houses are small; mine, however, is the larger. If possible, I would like to play you, though, if only for old time's sake.[20]

Haver had troubles landing contracts all along the road that year. Whatever happened, Haver remained the desirable confidant and perhaps, too easy a mark. In 1919, Clair F. Sleet of Osage, Iowa, wrote: "This town is the limit of rottenness of any place I ever saw. You know I told you I tried to sell the shotgun and couldn't. And I couldn't even raise $25 on my sax.... I will repay you as soon as I get to work, but nothing is available in Iowa."[21]

Harvey Hill rejoined the cast in 1919, and Haver decided to sell a half-interest in his company to Hill. For the next few years, the company had a new name, Harvey's Comedians. W. I. Swain, the silver-tongued leading man of the tent show circuits, also joined their cast. Harvey's Comedians opened their partnership with a show at Frisco, Texas. It was the first time since 1911 that the Haverstocks did not open their tent show in Roosevelt. They played Celina, Carrollton, St. Jo, Muenster, all in Texas; then moved to Oklahoma—Grandfield, Altus, Eldorado, Olustee, Hollis, Mangum, Erick, Sayre, Sentinel, Strong City, Harmon, Leedy, Roosevelt, and Davidson. They ended their 1919 season in March 1920, at the big boomtown of Devol, Oklahoma, just across the river from the largest oil boomtown of that era, Burkburnett, Texas.[22]

The decade from 1911 through 1919 had been a hectic one. For the Haverstocks, it featured grief, devastation, heartache, war, and sickness, but it brought them to an era of opulence, as 1920 began a boom time for tent repertoire companies. The decade had established the Haverstock tradition of working closely with the communities they visited, becoming, in effect, residents of those communities, if even for just a short time. They had established their show as being clean and family oriented. Such traditions enhanced their position as a show that claimed many friends.

5
The Good Years, 1920–1929

The 1920s roared across America in just about every way there was to roar. Money flowed in southern Oklahoma and north Texas, the area which Harvey and Lotta Haverstock had marked off for their Tent Rep route long before derricks and spewing oil darkened the skies there. By 1920, the Haverstocks had nearly a decade of show ownership experience already behind them, and Tent Repertoire show business had been good to them. The towners in their territory loved them. By the start of the decade, they were well on their way to becoming established as "The Show with a Million Friends," a motto they began using in those years on their advertising sheets and letterheads.

Lotta was a good actress who played her leading roles convincingly. One of the reasons she and Haver continued to own their own company was to assure she would continue to play lead roles. She would probably have played the soubrette in any other troupe, and did so in their own troupe by the mid-1930s when age and the popularity of the Toby and Susie motif forced her to begin playing Susie. She did not look too matronlike, but she was not the petite beauty usually hired for the ingenue leads. Her dress size was probably a comfortable fourteen, and she had large upper arms. Her features were not delicate, but as any of her friends would say, she was a totally beautiful person and audiences did not mind her not being the stereotypical leading lady type.

As the lead, Lotta had a luxurious wardrobe. Leading ladies had to dress as leading ladies should. She made many of her special garments and spent untold hours sewing individual bugle beads on a patterned cloth, so that her wardrobe would outshine that of anyone else who might join the Haverstock troupe. She lined up local seamstresses all along their route so that they could sew for her since she had to keep her wardrobe new.

Good Years, 1920–1929

All traveling actors and actresses furnished their own wardrobes unless their role called for a very special costume for a period piece. Only such costumes became theatrical properties owned by the company, and few Tent Repertoire companies played period pieces. Most of the troupers invested much of their paychecks in fine clothing so that they could get better roles. Often, if they were in competition for a role, the ones who owned the best selection of costumes would get the best parts, all other things being equal.

At the beginning of the era, Lotta had long flowing curls of dark brown hair and wore the modest dress that would be acceptable in a rural environment where their troupe traveled. But as the era progressed and their company prospered, she took on the modish styles of the flapper to suit the more contemporary scripts used by the company. She bobbed her hair or marcelled it, according to the dictates of style. She was as stylish as the city women and the leads of the larger road shows. Lotta loved jewelry and handbags. She wore good jewelry most of the time, even when she was on stage. It was always tasteful and usually diamond encrusted. Her handbag matched her dress if she had made both the dress and the bag. If she bought the garment, she chose a metallic mesh bag that could be attached to the waist of the dress as an added decoration. The painted mesh always matched one of her special dress fabrics in color, if not in pattern. Lotta favored the picture-frame, large-brimmed hats of the earlier era. They seemed to deemphasize her rather large nose, but when fashion dictated that the cloche hat, the one that hugged the skull, be worn, she wore it so that she could be a trend setter for the ladies of the rural communities along their route. They knew she wore the latest and the best.

Tent show people, especially the owners, had a responsibility to bring style and fashion to the hinterlands. Most of the rural areas on the Haverstock routes had only the local newspapers, which rarely featured photographs, and when they did, featured photographs only of locals or political figures. Those who lived on the Haverstock route relied on the Fort Worth or the Oklahoma City newspapers or the mail order catalogs or sewing magazines to tell them what fashionable people wore. But when show folk came through, the backcountry ladies could see city fashion firsthand, and they usually met the troupers upon their arrival into a town so they could get the first glimpses, requiring female troupers always to be dressed as models. The Haverstock players had come straight from St. Louis, so their women would be right at the top of fashion. Lotta often addressed ladies' groups in their towns, discussing with them the styles in St. Louis and giving lessons on how to construct such stylish items.

Though most of the men in the troupe worried about fashion also, Haver did not concern himself with looking dapper. He felt that his primary objective was to see that his show was at the top of the line with proper equipment. By the turn of the decade, Haver used a full fleet of trucks and automobiles to transport the Haverstock Comedians, their chairs, scenery, costumes, and supplies. Before they began their season, he shipped his materials and trunks on a freight car to their first stop destination where he would contract with a local freighter to transport the company for the season.

After he leased the Rock Island rail depot in Grandfield, Oklahoma, as his winter storage quarters, he hired Sterling S. Roddy, a Grandfield businessman, to transport his show. Roddy had recently returned to Grandfield from a homestead try in Colorado, after the oil boom in Burkburnett tapered off, early in the 1920s. Roddy himself wanted to establish a freight line, and Haver's contracting him to haul the show for the thirty-nine-week season gave him the borrowing clout he needed to establish the Roddy Trucking Line.[1] Roddy transported the show only one season. Then Haver bought his own fleet of trucks. Driving the trucks became one of the double duties of the canvasmen. Herbie Swift, Lotta's half-brother who had traveled with the troupe for several years as yard boss and sometime actor, had as a primary duty the maintenance of the truck fleet. Haver felt that though the arrangement tied up more of his capital in equipment, it gave him greater control of his company. Haver always had to be in total control of his show, whatever the cost.

As a general rule, actors who traveled with the Haverstocks had their own automobiles. Haver liked to hire people with nice cars. Those extra automobiles would add to the show caravan as it drove into the towns. The caravan would help draw attention to the show, and as long as the cast members were on time for the shows, rehearsals, and moves, having their own vehicles gave cast members opportunities to go on marketing trips, to travel back and forth to their lodgings, and to go to local restaurants to dine. The group could also make short sight-seeing forays. On days when their own tent was dark, they could attend competitors' shows playing in nearby communities. The only hazard of having the cast members bring their own cars was the fact that should there be a disgruntled player, that person could leave the show without notice. Haver, however, never records having had one of his cast leave his show in such a manner. Those who owned the automobiles also earned a salary bonus for the use of their vehicles, especially if they helped transport other cast members who had no personal transportation.

The Haverstock Comedians became an especially closely knit group. They spent the spring, summer, and fall on the road together. Then after a brief vacation respite away from one another, they met again in St. Louis to spend the winter together. From the earliest years after the founding of their show, St. Louis served as the Haverstocks' winter quarters. The fact that one of Lotta's sisters, Elizabeth, and her mother and stepfather, the Swifts, lived in St. Louis, helped the Haverstocks decide on that location. St. Louis was also not too far from Lotta's other sisters, both of whom lived in Danville, Illinois. St. Louis was one of the Midwest's theatrical centers, too. Most Tent Repertoire troupes wintered in either St. Louis, Kansas City, Danville, or Wichita. Each of these cities had clusters of smaller towns around them. Those smaller communities each had an opera house, making opportunities for the Haverstocks and other troupes to perform circle stock during winter months as tryouts for the upcoming Rep season's play offerings.

Haver developed an unusual approach to an even more closely knit cast of players and workers who interacted well together, and those could double as actors, scene painters, canvas riggers, or cooks. They all participated year-round for year-round pay.[2]

Haver and Lotta, with help of Lotta's sister who had been on the lookout for a special kind of real estate buy, purchased an old three story mansion in a once fashionable neighborhood of St. Louis. They did not purchase the house with any ostentatious air, but saw it as a place for their troupe to winter each year. Not only did the big home have three stories for living area, but it also had a full basement and a large carriage house for storage. The unmarried actors, canvasmen, and male concessionaires lived in the third story and in the attic rooms of the house. The married couples, according to the number of married couples in the troupe, each had a suite of rooms on the second floor, or if the troupe were inordinately large, only a single room and a shared bath for each couple. Only show owners had children who traveled or lived with the troupe, so children were never a problem for the Haverstock troupe. The single women also lived on the second floor. The living room became the cast's rehearsal hall, and the dining room doubled as their dining hall and their wing space. The basement was the prop room and scene construction area. The old mansion on Eads Avenue was made to order for wintering the Haverstock troupe.

Haver had a philosophy that if a show had a good troupe, it should keep the group happy, and to do that, the members had to be kept together. He tried to keep them together on this year-round basis. He added to the cast people with promising vaudeville acts and specialty acts. He would also encourage his regular troupers to copy a good vaudeville act they had seen on their days off while they visited a St. Louis vaudeville house.

Those who traveled with Tent Rep, perhaps even some of Haver's troupers, were as irresponsible financially as actors or caravan tent Gypsies had always had the reputation of being. They generally lived lavishly when they had money, but as the colder, bleaker days of winter approached, they had spent their money and were broke. Haver had witnessed many good actors and actresses forced to turn to pawning their belongings in the winters just to put clothes on their backs and food in their stomachs. He had seen them sell themselves as sideshow freaks, as prostitutes, or as whatever would offer them the money they needed for winter shelter or food. He had seen their frustrations with empty stomachs and cold bodies during winter months cause many an otherwise fine actor or actress to turn to drink or drugs for comfort in their despair. He determined early in his theatrical management years that his people would not feel such a need.

Soon after organizing his troupe, Haver began a financial plan agreeable to his troupers. The plan entailed withholding a portion of each actor's weekly salary in a savings account for the always-encroaching winters. His was a unique plan in the business. He acted as the depository for the funds and could have perhaps earned some interest on that money had he put it in a bank. After the initial shock of the smaller weekly salaries, the actors thought the plan a marvelous idea. They would get paid year-round, and they would not have to scrape so hard for their subsistence in the wintering months.[3]

After the Haverstocks bought the house on Eads Avenue, Haver could offer the actors and staff even more security. In the wintering, each staff member would receive weekly pay from his or her withheld salaries. Room and board was part payment for rehearsing the next season's shows and preparing the next season's costumes, sets, and so forth. Each actor could also earn extra bonus cash by performing in either the circle stock

Rolland, Lotta, and Harvey standing in front of their new car parked before the Haverstock dramatic end tent for their tent shows (ca. 1920s).

The F. G. Perry Uncle Tom's Cabin Company in 1893. Daisy Mosher (later Swift), Lotta's sister, is the third pictured. Elizabeth Mosher (Lotta's sister, Lizzie) is the fifth pictured, and next to her is Nina Mosher (later Swift), Lotta's mother. After Mrs. Mosher are two children; Carlotta (Lotta) Mosher (later Haverstock) is the second child. She made her debut in this show as the child that Eliza (Nina) carries across the ice floe trying to escape from Simon Legree.

The front entrance of the King-Haverstock Company's tent in 1911. Rolland is the second child in the row of three on the right side of the tent. Tent drama was rather primitive in 1911. After the Haverstocks bought out the Kings, this became the genesis of the Haverstock Comedians. The show was purchased from the Kings in Roosevelt, Oklahoma, in 1911.

The Haverstock Comedians' dramatic tent set up in Bluford, Illinois, in the late 1940s. Note the signs advertising Toby and Susie in a play, *At Home on the Shores of the Rio Grande*.

Rolland, Harvey, and Lotta stand ready to board their Pullman car (ca. 1917). They bought a special Pullman to haul their Tent Repertoire around their routes.

This photo shows the Haverstock Comedians' dramatic stage with all the hand-painted advertising signs hanging around the proscenium of the stage. The tent is set up in Olney, Texas, and could range any time from the early 1920s through 1954 when the Haverstocks traveled to Olney, one of their favorite towns on their route.

Harvey C. Haverstock in his first Toby costume (ca. 1919). Note that Toby has big white patches around the eyes, but Harvey's early Toby lacks the freckles, red fright wig, or quite the rube look that his later Toby developed.

Harvey is shown here in his 1930s Toby costume. He has added the dots of tears at the eyes, but he still chooses the black derby hat, with the not-so-rube tie and dress shirt.

Lotta and Harvey in their Susie and Toby costumes in the late 1940s or early 1950s. Note that by now Harvey is wearing oversized pants and suspenders pulled high, with a comic hat and tie. His makeup includes the big eyes with the tear marks and a red bulbous nose. Lotta is supposed to be a young soubrette but plays the teen with her white hair and a big red bow in it.

Lotta and Harvey as Susie and Toby play a song, often a sing-along for the audience, on their musical cow bells, Harvey's invention made exclusively for them, for an olio act between the scenes in their dramatic show in the late 1930s. Their makeup is more rube, and Harvey's Toby shows definite signs of aging and becoming more comedic.

Susie Haverstock (Lotta) and Toby Haverstock (Harvey) in their makeup and costumes during the time just prior to Lotta's death in the early 1950s. Note the trim on Lotta's dress, the big hair bow in her white hair, and Harvey's short pants pulled high with tight suspenders, his fright wig (a bright red), and his rube hat and shoes.

A serious posed sitting of Lotta and Harvey Haverstock (ca. 1950). Their makeup for Toby and Susie really changes their rather sedate appearance.

Rolland and Peggy Haverstock stand beside one of the Haverstock Entertainers' trucks from the small fleet used to transport the troupe's tent and other trappings. By the sign, the setting is in the late 1940s when magic was a big part of the Haverstock olio routines.

Rolland, Lotta, and Harvey stand before the fleet of cars used to transport the large number of players in the 1920s after they decided that the cars would attract attention to the show's coming to town. Also pictured in order are Charles D. Rhea, Toad Tharp, Sam Martin, Al Lotz, Joe Rotan, Ben Martin, and Marie and Carl Deviney. The inset shows Roddy Truck Lines vehicles out of Grandfield, Oklahoma, used to transport the Haverstocks in the early 1920s along their entire route.

Peggy with her accordion helps Rolland and Lotta "cut off" the head of an audience participant in a guillotine act from the circa 1935 magic show, a part of the Haverstock olio routine. Note Lotta's dark chestnut hair. She is still playing the leading lady, the ingenue, right after Peggy joined the troupe and prior to her Susie character roles.

The Haverstock Theatre Company's first railroad car for transporting the show (ca. 1915). They traveled in the car for a few years before adding a second car to transport their more than fifty-member cast, crew, and orchestra.

Lotta dressed stylishly to help educate the women on her Tent Repertoire route. Though she did not usually prefer the cloche hat, here she chose it to go with her mink-trimmed long coat. Note the jewels on her fingers and around her neck (ca. mid-1920s).

Some of the cast from the pre-1920s Haverstock Theatre Company's one-train car. Pictured are Roy Williams, J. Clark, Herbie Swift Jr., Rolland Haverstock, Lizzie Mosher Quick (Lotta's sister), Harvey (with the tie), Lotta, J. Wellington, and Orpha and Lou Rathbone.

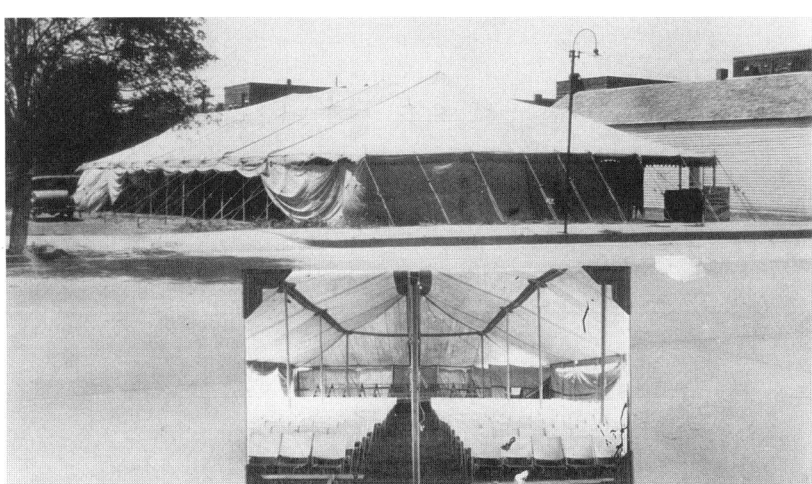

The Haverstock tent ready for use in the 1930s. The tent walls are raised so that the tent can cool off before the show crowd starts arriving. The inset shows the inside of the tent from the stage. Note the middle pole that somewhat blocks the audience's view. The "reds" are the folding wooden chairs on the floor and the "blues" are backless bleacher-type seats at the back of the tent auditorium.

The Haverstocks were proud of their automobile trailer in which they lived while on the road from the late 1930s, during which time Rolland and Peggy had bought one. The trailer homes showed the prosperity of the troupers and also gave them a chance to set up by the tent to protect it from vandals.

Lotta in a glamour pose from the 1920s. She was the typical ingenue actress of the Tent Repertoire of that era.

This 1910 photograph shows the Olney Hayseed Band, also called the Soozy Kornet Band, organized by Harvey, standing fourth from the left wearing a tie, who also taught music lessons in Olney, Texas. The men chose to be in rube attire because they did not have uniforms for parade marching or for concerts. Most of them have new horns that Harvey sold them while working as a commission salesman for the Conn Band Instrument Company.

around St. Louis or by working some winter bookings at the local legitimate theater houses which Haver had contracted with to be used as his tryout locations. He would rent or lease a route of theaters for the winter each year. Such arrangements guaranteed a well-fed, happy wintering troupe. The members were free to vacation as much as they liked because they had their withheld salaries to live on if they elected not to work. They could get all their money at once, but Haver preferred to dole it out as weekly paychecks all winter long. They could also work to keep up the kind of lifestyles they had enjoyed all the rest of the year.

Actors enjoyed showing their prosperity. Better dress and jewelry distinguished those in prosperous companies. A diamond stickpin or brooch was an investment that would be expected adornment of any prosperous thespian. Troupe members also showed the prosperity of their show company by the way they displayed their diamonds.

Whenever an actor hit upon hard times, he always had his jewels and then his expensive wardrobe to hock. This pawn revenue generally had to carry a trouper throughout the entire winter. Haverstock's company had been no exception to this rule until Lotta and Haver devised their special withholding plan. After that, the only thespians who pawned diamonds to Haver were those who worked for other companies. The Haverstock Comedians were able to wear their diamonds on a year-round basis.

Once a diamond was pawned, the owner generally just left it with a lender rather than hope to reclaim it. A large majority of lenders were the show owners. Lotta dripped diamonds, and even during the hard times of the 1930s, Lotta was not willing to part with her gems. Many times, the diamonds served as collateral when the big top needed repair, their sets or props had to be replaced, limping vehicles needed new tires, or royalties for productions had to be paid. Lotta always kept her cigar box full of diamond pawn jewelry for such emergencies.

In the 1920s, the Haverstock Comedians' cast and crew stayed in hotels or boarding houses while on the road. They preferred boarding houses in the smaller towns because boarding houses included both room and board in their charges. The cost for a week's room and board for each of the Haverstock cast was generally five dollars. This rent held true in all but the boom towns. Each actor paid his or her own road expenses, with Haver guaranteeing payment to the proprietors. Haver did make some special arrangements for his people so that they could get better lodging, less expensively. When they played Devol, Burkburnett, Olney, Electra, and Iowa Park, the big boom towns in the early twenties, Haver gave bonuses to help with the added lodging and food expenses.

Many boom towns sprung up along the Haverstock route with the Texas and Oklahoma oil play. This atmosphere created many extraordinary expenses for the troupers. In Burkburnett, for instance, in about 1920, few places existed for anyone to obtain private room and board. In fact, building owners and business owners of every kind rented out sleeping cots in their storerooms by the hour, rather than by the night. It cost as much as $5 just to have an officer stop traffic so that pedestrians could cross Burkburnett's main streets. A glass of water cost $5, but a glass of whiskey cost only $1 there. It was a typical boom town.[4] So when the troupe went to Burkburnett, Haver usually arranged for his cast members to stay in the homes of friends in the city. The canvasmen and the single actors usually stayed in the tent, to keep it from being vandalized. On nights when the oil field workers asked to rent a piece of the stage floor to sleep on, they were refused. Haver never rented the spaces, but during inclement weather, he did not run sleepers out of the tent if they came in to get out of the weather. At that point, they probably paid someone for that dry space, without Haver's knowledge of the transaction.

Haver had a fairly large tent during the early 1920s. It was not lavish. It measured seventy feet by one hundred feet and had seating for about twelve hundred people. His *reds* were folding chairs that he slip-covered in red canvas. He had twelve lengths of *blue* roosts. Children were given a space with planked seating right at the front of the stage end of the tent. The tent, then, could seat about twelve hundred and fifty crowded people. The tent measurements did not include the dramatic end of the tent, which was actually just another tent butted up against the big top. The big top was built as a circus tent was, with the poles down the center to hold up the top. The area where the poles stood was the center aisle of the tent theater. Only the very few who sat behind the poles holding up the main tent had their view obstructed. The dramatic end of the tent had poles on either side of the stage. No one in the audience had his or her view of the stage badly blocked. The big top's canvas lapped over the roof of the stage and was hooked at the front and rear of the stage area. Haver's tent design for the 1920s had been built for him in Dallas at the Fulton Bag and Cotton Mills, a company that supplied many of Haver's tents over the years.[5]

Haver carefully chose his troupers. He wanted people in his troupe who would not, for instance, be involved in any unlawful occupations or fall into frustrated drinking. He wanted to assure a squeaky-clean reputation for his troupe as they went into a community. He carefully screened those in his cast prior to hiring them. Because he chose as carefully as he did, and because he demanded so much of his cast, Haver paid his troupers what was considered at the time a respectable salary of about $50 a week per team and $30 per single. Haver wanted members of his troupe to have comfortable lifestyles.

Haver always required that each of his troupers become an active member of the community in which the troupe performed. Lotta and all the ladies joined active ladies' Bible study classes or home-demonstration clubs. The cast and crew were all required to attend local churches of their choice, and each cast member was requested to join local community clubs such as Rotary, Lions, Kiwanis, or lodges, such as the Masons and Odd Fellows. The cast and crew played in local orchestras, and the athletes played as members of local baseball teams. They all contributed to local charities. Many letters, written from happy towners where the Haverstock show performed, noted thanks for a gift of from $10 to $100 to various clubs, lodges, and churches. Haver wanted the towners to feel that their troupe was truly a part of them. That kind of public relations effort was not unique to Haverstock shows, but the Haverstock Company practiced the craft meticulously.

By the 1920s, the pioneer settlers who had opened the area where the Haverstocks traveled had become settled into their lives. They had built their homes, barns, and fences. Their world was fairly stable now that the Great War had ended. Money had begun to flow into their pockets from good commodity prices following the war, and many had received good royalty checks from the oil companies that leased their land for oil drilling. The farmers could dress up in their Sunday best and go into town to the dramatic and Chautauqua tent productions. Many had purchased automobiles, and they liked getting out in them. The 1920s were good times, prosperous for most, and towners appreciated the Haverstock Comedians' sharing their talents and lives with them.

Up until the 1920s, rural people preferred very dramatic shows. They could justify seeing tearjerkers with good lessons to be learned by youngsters or reinforced for adults. The first bill in a town was usually what was called a preacher show. This was a highly moralistic, very message-laden show. The show owners admitted ladies without charge on that night as long as the lady attended with one paid adult admission. The preacher shows they played were *Uncle Tom's Cabin, St. Elmo, Turn to the Right,*

East Lynne, Lena Rivers, Ten Nights in a Barroom, The Awakening of John Slater, or the ultimate preacher show, *Saintly Hypocrites and Honest Sinners*. Even the most devout minister or deacon could not find fault in a preacher show.

Townswomen especially liked for the show season to have *East Lynne* as one of the bills because of its being more of a period costume piece. In Herb Walters' book about his tent theater, co-authored with Velma E. Lowry, he states:

> Women in small towns were highly interested in seeing her [the heroine's] beautiful gowns, gowns with long trains on them, especially in plays like *East Lynne*. The trains on those gowns had little lead balls fastened on them so that as the actress walked, the gown would drag gracefully behind her as she swept across the floor and the stage.[6]

In the time demanding moralistic appropriateness, Tent Repertoire players had to exercise extra control so as not to smile in such a way as to suggest sexual innuendo. Haver would not allow any oath; he even used extreme care about having his company say anything questionable in a script. They even had to be careful that they did not say anything as innocuous as *durn* in the early 1920s. He somewhat relaxed that rule for *durn* at the end of the decade, but he never allowed any language more colorful or more explicit during the next thirty years the Haverstocks were in the business.

Many of his contemporary show managers allowed rougher language in the rough oil towns, but Haver held firm on his rules. He believed that those attending Haverstock shows were good, clean-thinking Christian people, and for those who were rougher, he said, "They can see some of the other show companies [naming them] if they want roughness." Neil Schaffner also said in an interview with Joe Alex Morris for a *Saturday Evening Post* article in 1955, that "there must never be an off-color word in them [the shows]" and added, "People don't come to tent shows to hear a penetrating commentary on some of the foibles of our society."[7]

Before Haver bought the Eads Avenue house in St. Louis, the troupe stayed on the road as much of the year as possible using heated tents and then moving onto vaudeville or opera house stages. They rented boarding house rooms for their family of troupers. They soon learned the futility of battling the elements of winter, even in the south central Texas area, and they faced a great deal of competition from the Brunk and Sadler shows.

Actors were not generally as loyal to owners of other Tent Repertoire shows as Haver's troupers were to him. Troupers enjoyed the kind of security offered by the Haverstocks. Many times Haver could not always offer high weekly salaries, but he kept his company together. He offered a bonus to those who stayed with the troupe throughout the season. Occasionally, a Haverstock actor might be lured away by those owners who offered better weekly salaries, but most of the time, the actors realized the value of their fringe benefits, in days when fringe benefits did not really exist. They especially appreciated the wintering salaries and the comfortable winter's lodging they were promised if they signed on as members of Haver's troupe. Haver's company prospered in the 1920s because the people to whom they played prospered. Rural Americans were entertainment hungry. Transportation and roadways lacked the sophistication to allow travel to large cities to see Broadway road-show engagements, but if culture were available to people at their doorsteps, they would readily attend a live show.

The silent film era was also at its heyday in the 1920s. People flocked to the film theaters and airdomes to see the latest releases of film idols Pola Negri, Rudolph Valentino, Theda Bara, and Ramon Novarro. Should there be a choice between film and live theatrics, however, the rural dwellers would opt for the live entertainment. The carnival atmosphere, the candy bally, the orchestra, the smell of popcorn and greasepaint drew them by the droves. Even in bad weather, they came. They would attend the shows of every troupe who came through their towns. They would travel to surrounding towns, however, to see the Haverstock shows because they knew Haver produced a good, clean, family-type entertainment.

The Haverstocks did not have to be in rural areas to get good audiences. While they wintered the troupe at the Eads Avenue house, Haver gave the company actors a chance to earn extra money by playing in circle stock. Audiences apparently flocked to the small city opera houses to take advantage of the opportunity of live theatrics there, too. Haver's circle stock enterprises were not too far behind Winn Trousdale's pioneering plan, described by Mickel, "By 1930, circle stock was the usual winter activity of the companies which played under canvas during the summer." Mickel further quotes Trousdale in 1936, "As far as I know, we were

Good Years, 1920–1929

the first [troupe] to open circle stock, circuit stock, as we called it at the time. I opened one the latter part of December, twenty-two years ago, on December 27, 1914."[8] Since Haver had no notes in his memoirs or diary entries concerning a possible friendship with Trousdale, and Haver was quick to generate ideas of his own, his circle stock idea was likely not taken from Trousdale's plan but merely coincidentally happened at about the same time.

During the height of Tent Repertoire, most actors were members of Actor's Equity. Haver did not care whether or not his troupers were members of the union. He, Lotta, Herbie Swift, Rolland and Peggy were all Equity members. It was generally accepted that if one were a professional, membership in Equity was a trademark of that professionalism. That fact is borne out as Haver recorded in his memoirs that Kansas City, the hub of Tent Repertoire, boasted some twenty-five hundred Equity members.

Kansas City offered a great deal to Tent Repertoire besides the Equity members from which owners could select their casts. Haver used Don Melrose, a playwright and theatrical agent in Kansas City as his principal contact away from St. Louis. If he needed a good play, Haver would quickly send a letter or a telegram to Melrose, who knew Haver well enough to send a script right back, and it would be suitable almost every time. If the show needed a single or a team, Haver employed the same technique, and he would take whomever Melrose recommended without so much as an interview. Melrose knew of Haver's integrity and his methods of working, so actors willing to travel the Haverstock route and live up to his standards happily took jobs with the company.

Haver hired many of his troupers because of their musical ability or specialty acts. The specialty acts he hired had unique qualities. The plays were the real drawing card for his audiences, but the specialty acts kept his audiences returning to see some of the shows repeated over the years. Haver hired fresh olio acts each year even if his actors were not new. He boasted that the Haverstock players offered good, fresh entertainment at every show.

John and Oma Brooks of Roosevelt, Oklahoma, recounted their memories of the Haverstock Comedians in an interview with the *Kiowa County Democrat* in 1975. They recalled that they saw their first Haverstock show in 1918: "The tent, put up where the high school now stands, was the scene of the action [for our town]. The grass had been mowed for safety. The grass and the wind whipped the flaps of the huge tent where the melodramas were performed."⁹ In the same interview, Don Farris of nearby Cooperton, Oklahoma, said: "That was the only time we quit pulling [cotton] bolls early. If Dad found out that the Haverstocks were in town, we piled into the car for all of the shows."¹⁰

The addition of the Toby character was the big change that made the shows more lively in the 1920s. Toby roles were in plays prior to then, but this era of prosperity allowed the people to laugh, and Toby would bring laughs with virtually every word he uttered and with every nuance that he made as he walked, talked, or even just winked on the stage.

Haver liked character roles that offered him a chance to do his ad-libbing with some legitimacy. Character actors on his troupe could get away with ad-lib with everyone except Lotta, the ultimate professional. If one played opposite her, even Haver, he had better know his lines or the post mortem after the performance each night might become the real thing. Haver's lack of exactitude in rendering lines gave another good reason for the troupe to spend their winters together at the Eads Avenue house. The more he rehearsed, the more nearly Haver rendered correctly the lines written by the author. Even in the event that Haver did ad-lib, at least those who had rehearsed together throughout the winters would be able to cover better for him and were not taken by surprise when he thought of some new way to ad-lib.

Haver's Toby character was very much like any other Toby. Each was the country bumpkin, and most wore oversized clothing, though some played their Toby characters as cowboys. Most wore the red wigs, and many used fright wigs which, when Toby pulled a hidden string, would cause the hair in the center to rise and make it look as if he were so frightened his hair stood on end. Toby makeup often used big white circles around the eyes with a tear-like line drawn through from the drawn-on, oversized eyebrows to the heavily rouged, youthfully embarrassed-looking cheeks, which bore large, pencil-eraser-sized freckles. Haver never used the white circles. He slanted his mouth with an exaggerated slant to suggest a constant aside emitting from it. Toby used as his trademark a rube hat and loose suspenders. He could hold onto the suspenders, stretch them and let them snap against his body (like a rubber band) for slapstick business to draw a special, milked laughter from his audience.

The orchestra usually played fifteen minutes of overture prior to the first curtain. Haver always played his trombone in the orchestra, and he loved playing so much that he looked for extra opportunities for the orchestra to play. If there happened to be a dance after the show, for instance, Haver would get his orchestra the gig of playing, so that they could earn extra money, and he could play some more.

Haver had time to get into his costume after the orchestra overture because the Toby character was rarely on stage immediately. Playwrights wrote in such a way that they would give the audience a chance to get to know the leading lady or the hero or the minor parts of the play prior to the Toby entrance on stage because Toby's entrance usually stopped the show for a few minutes. The writer wanted the audience to know the setting for the play, too, before Toby entered. Once Toby entered, the exposition was generally lost, because Toby's antics kept the people laughing too much to appreciate exposition or even much story line.

When Haver entered, he always stopped the show. The audience burst into applause when he came on. The audience loved Toby Haverstock, and he loved them. He would walk right out to the footlights after the applause, and do a comic curtsy bow, usually giving a big wink. That was Toby's entrance. He was the star of the Toby show just as Lotta had been the star of the dramatic shows, and Haver liked to milk the audience right from the first entry he made on the stage. They loved being milked by him. A master of those ad-libbed lines and comedic remarks, Haver would ad-lib remarks every time the show began to get too serious or began to lag for even a moment.

Between the acts of the play, Haver would come on stage so he could introduce the olio acts. He would talk casually with the audience members as if he were the best buddy of each person there. In fact, he often called towners by name as he visited with them at these moments, giving a special personal air to his Toby show. It was at such moments of ad-libbed repartee in the 1920s, that he coined one of his favorite lines, "I just thought I'd tell you, so you'd know." He used that line at every opportunity between the acts or during the play as an ad-lib, then he would hold his head askew and give a special big wink with the eye opposite the exaggerated slant of his mouth. This hilarious look would generate heavy laughter from the members of the audience. No matter how much he used the line, he got the same laughter from it every time.[11]

Toby and the tent theater were made for each other. They served their purpose in the years in which they were so popular. Tent Repertoire gave owners and actors unique challenges almost daily.

In the March 1930 edition of *Theater Magazine*, Joseph Kaye noted:

> The average troupe carries six sets of scenery, painted on both sides, which gives them settings for twelve plays. The curtains and sets are no more than ten feet high and very lightly constructed. The lighting is done by electricity, tapped from town lines. . . . The entire canvas structure can be assembled in two hours.[12]

During rain storms, Kaye also noted: "At such times, the performance is halted and the orchestra plays or the candy concessionaires operate."[13]

The interior of the tent was unique to Tent Repertoire. The owner got revenue from advertisements displayed on hand-painted signs hanging all around the proscenium, and if the ad man sold enough ads, signs also lined the side walls of the tent. The advertising man sold the ad sheets, about one by two feet, and then painted the advertisement on the sheet. The audience saw the local ad hanging for the length of time that the tent show stayed in that community. Haver had a special way of calling attention to the ads hanging in his tent. Between each of the specialty acts of the olio, he would mention a portion of the businesses advertising with him, telling people to trade with those advertising merchants. People liked the personalized sales banter almost as well as they liked the play. He would say, "Now these fine businesses are supporting your enjoyment of this evening's show. Now we people in the Haverstock Comedians go to their businesses and spend the money we've earned here in this town, and I just told you this, 'cause I thought you ought to know."[14]

The olio was extremely important in this prosperous era. Those in the plays and in the orchestra doubled in olio acts, but Haver also hired extra specialty acts that he could advertise as headliners to draw in even more people. In the 1920s, he would pay nearly as much for a team to do variety acts as he paid for actor/actress teams. He insisted on the same kind of clean olio act as he demanded in the play repertoire. His acts were always quality acts. Haver steered away from those olio people who had drinking problems. He would opt for a team rather than a single. He occasionally ran ads seeking olio acts in both *Billboard* or in *Bill Bruno's Bulletin*. He would tell in the ad where his tent would be at a given date on his route and asked for letters carefully detailing what the performers' specialties were. If he were interested, he would call or telegraph the act to join him and the company at their next route stop. Part of the salary for the new act was their transportation to wherever the show played at that time. If a contract player or specialty act left the company of his own volition, the actor was responsible for his own fare away from the company. If an actor were fired for some reason, he was given a two week severance pay as well as his fare home, usually St. Louis or Kansas City. Haver never records having fired anyone during the season.

Often, the specialty acts would sneak off from a company after having borrowed money from the show owner. On November 8, 1921, W. B. Lane wrote Haver from the Pond Hotel in Celina, Texas. His letter apparently answered Haver's letter of November 3 to him: "I do not know where you could find our friend. . . . If you find him and he has anything in his pocket, I wish that you would let me know as I would like to find him for about a hundred myself."[15] This particular friend was the owner of a badly run-down troupe, and Lane was a former actor in that show. He further explained to Haver: "The last time I saw [him] he was trying to put up the rag. I supposed he was going to play vaudeville, as he only had his wife, the violin player and one canvasman left. The outfit was sure in awful shape."[16]

In a letter of May 16, 1923, Jack Maxwell tried to get Haver to buy some new material. His letter had the flair of a 1920s writer:

> Friend "Napoleon," this am [*sic*] Friday and the gentle Zephyrs from the southland are comin' right across the peach orchard, and in my mind's eye, I can see the "old top" a flutterin' in the breeze. . . . Of course, you are hep to the situation . . . but I just thought I'd tell you, so you'd know. . . . Enclosed is latest skit. . . .[17]

Shows by Don Melrose, popular Toby plays of the 1920s, included *Love and Horseradish, The Affairs of Rosalie, When Jimmy Came to Town, The Undercurrent, Toby from Arkansas, April Fools,* and *Codfish Aristocracy.* Melrose's stationery noted that all plays were $10 each per season and that "my plays are written to suit your personality. . . . "[18] Melrose wrote from Wewoka, Oklahoma, in 1925, thanking Haver for the "one hundred dollars" in receipt of play royalties.[19] Apparently, Haver had used ten of Melrose's plays for the year.

Haver often had chances to invest in other shows and entertainments. In 1926, M. A. Moseley, who purportedly had the "Classiest Tent Theater and Company in America, the Ray Howell Players," offered to sell a partnership to Haver. He did not state his price for a half ownership, but told Haver:

> I can get along with most people.... Ray Howell and I are dissolving partnership as he is anxious to be the whole thing.... I would want you to pose as manager.... I'm out for the money, and not the glory.... There are no plasters on anything here, and I owe no one a cent—the outfit is MINE.[20]

Moseley followed this letter with a longer one three months later saying he had decided to close the show, "So it will be safe as these small towns has [*sic*] many vandals, so if you consider doing business with me, you will find me a most reasonable fellow."[21] Business was apparently tops on most routes in 1926, though rural areas were somewhat depressed economically in 1923 and 1924. But Moseley truthfully pointed out that:

> Business has been very bad all through Texas and Oklahoma because of the worst winter and spring in thirty-six years. Just now there is no money in circulation. So far this week the ticket seller on the front reports she has seen four five dollar bills. We opened to $73; Tuesday, $65; Wednesday, $69; Thursday, $95; Friday, $155, and will touch $200 Saturday maybe.... I don't give a damn for a band, as the loafers come and hear it and walk away.[22]

Moseley finally offered to sell at a "reasonable figure." It cost over $8,000.[23] Haver did not elect to join in partnership with Moseley, nor did he purchase the show outright.

In 1926, Haver advertised in *Billboard* for a variety act to fill his troupe. Lillie Cavitte who had once worked for Haver but had left the company, wrote in a letter of June 3, 1926, "I will appreciate [the position], and I will stick this time. You know my line of work. I can join you any time you say. You know my size, and I will also play any part you may cast me for that my size will allow me to play."[24]

Haver continuously looked for good new material. He often had people wanting to be a part to his show whether he had advertised or not. Zane Cobwin, a playwright from Kansas City, offered him exclusive rights for his route to *Toby's Maw*, *Preaching Molly*, and *The Devil's Doorstep*. Haver bought all three scripts for his 1927 season. George J. Crawley also wrote Haver while the show played in Detroit, Texas. Crawley offered him some good extra bills for the season.[25]

In 1928, Haver had become a member of the newly organized TRMPAA (Tent Repertoire Managers Protective Association of America) of which the secretary was Harry A. Huguenot. Harley Sadler was a board member and vice-president of the organization.[26] Huguenot had written Haver a letter inviting him to membership in the organization: "We would be more than glad to welcome you into our organization because we are confident that your experience and advice would be beneficial to our welfare and progression."[27]

In 1929, Roe Nero wrote from Rome, New York:

> I think you have about as good a show to be in as any in the country. [He had heard that Haver had sold a partnership in his show to Harley Sadler.] If your show could not make money, all others had better quit. The natives will go to the Haverstock Show if there is nothing there but Haver and his wife, and if you needed cash, you would not have to sell your show or part of it. You could get more cash than you could possibly need from friends anywhere along your route, and I do not think I exaggerated the matter either. . . . you *niza* man.[28]

In another letter written in February of 1929, a friend, Edward, hoped for a place in Haver's show. He wrote: "I always said you was [*sic*] the best man I ever worked for, and will always say that."[29]

By the end of the 1920s, Rolland had grown into adulthood. Over the years, he had attended Roosevelt High School in St. Louis until 1927, when he graduated. Rolland dreamed of playing professional baseball. Haver had pushed Rolland toward that goal, and all the Haverstock show friends knew of this goal. It was a topic to draw Haver's attention when they wrote. In Edward's letter in 1929, he added, "Hope Rolly made the grade [in getting into a baseball club] this spring."[30] Rolland had gotten an offer to join one of the teams, but he injured his ankle in the 1929 Cardinal's spring camp, and it never healed well enough to play on a professional basis, a big blow to both Rolland and his father. Rolland had never planned to be a showman. He had helped his parents in every way he could when he visited the show during holidays, but he always played baseball in St. Louis in the summers.

As a youth, Rolland just never seemed to take to theatrical work. He never claimed to be an actor. He was not a musician, as much as his father had tried to teach him brass. He was no dancer for vaudeville. He had only two ambitions for further employment. He wanted to make his living as either a ball player or a commercial artist. He loved drawing and liked to illustrate some of his poems and writings with characters he would create. After his injury, he finally had to admit he could never play baseball on a professional basis, so he joined the Harley Sadler Show. He could act, be a canvasman or whatever, and he could play on their show's exhibition baseball team. The Sadler actors and canvasmen made up a team that played exhibition baseball at every town on their route, taking on local men as their opposing team. Rolland's short-lived Cardinal stint gave Sadler a plus in advertising his tent show. His posters had a drawing of Rolland in a baseball uniform ready to play during the days the show was in town. But while with Sadler that short season, Rolland decided that if he were going to be in show business, he would just as soon be on the Haverstock stage. So after that season, he joined the Haverstock troupe as a leading man.[31]

Haver never lost faith in Tent Repertoire's success. When other shows began to fold at the end of the decade, Haver looked forward. Haver's faith in Tent Repertoire seemed apparent as he loaned money to Sam Bright in July of 1929, so that Bright could buy a defunct show company. That same month, Haver ordered a new top for his own show. He also ordered a Marmon automobile from Rich Richeson, a former actor with his troupe turned automobile salesman. The stock market crash had not yet occurred, and Haver apparently thought things were going well financially. He also contracted Arthur L. Fanshawe, a headliner, playwright, and actor, for $35 a week, to be the G-String in the plays, paint sets, and perform *Dr. Jekyll and Mr. Hyde* and *Rip Van Winkle* in the olio.[32]

If hard times were at all apparent to Haver, neither his correspondence nor his memoirs gave evidence of concern. He still traveled a route of at least thirty-nine weeks a year in the north Texas and southern Oklahoma area even as depression raged in towns along his route. The 1920s ended the prosperous era for "the show with a million friends."[33] Haver's famous line, "I told you 'cause I thought you ought to know," helped bring those friends together when hard economic times seemed to be driving friends apart.

6
The Lean Years, 1930–1939

Toby was the salvation of Tent Repertoire in the 1920s. When the rural people of southern Oklahoma and north Texas tired of the tearjerker, they wanted to laugh more and remove themselves from their labor as hardworking farmers and pioneer settlers. Toby brought them an answer. His jokes and his stage movements were near slapstick, but his perfectly timed, often ad-libbed humor brought laughter to the tent show audiences when they needed to laugh.

Rural families had automobiles; they had radios; they had movie theaters in every little town, especially toward the end of the era. This last fact, alone, set the mood for the decline of Tent Repertoire. Most blamed the Crash of 1929 and the ensuing Great Depression for the demise of tent theater. Those historical events cannot be minimized, but the moving-picture industry and people's adoration of the celluloid kings and queens were also events with which the Tent Rep owners had to deal.

In a letter to Haver on November 23, 1929, from Rich Richeson, the president of the Musicians Association, Local Number 207, of Salina, Kansas, Richeson tells of the plight of Tent Rep shows playing there:

> The Ted North Players are here all next week at the Delharce Theater, and as they play here each winter season, I imagine they will do a nice business. The Delharce is the only theater here now that runs any road shows or vaudeville. It is a new house, just opened last fall. The other two houses [film theaters] are owned by Fox, who just bought them recently, and then there is another house here, a ten-cent grind house, owned by another circuit. The Fox Company is going to build a new $450,000 [film] theater and hotel here soon, they say. I will have to see it built first before I believe it though.[1]

Lean Years, 1930–1939

A $450,000 movie theater planned by Fox for a city the size of Salina was phenomenal. But moving pictures were the rage in entertainment across America.[2] Richeson's letter shows the importance of film theater in that part of the world and indicates the lack of interest by then in live theater in the Midwest. Haver wanted to find a place to set up a winter circuit for his wintering actors so he had obviously written Richeson for information on Salina for such a center. If he were to keep his troupe together, Haver needed to widen his circle of towns with vaudeville theaters.

The same movement toward movies for entertainment was apparently nationwide. In fact, very often, moving picture theater owners tried to shut out live entertainment so they could get a greater share of their audiences' spendable money, especially as the economy worsened. They soon had an even better chance to grab the audiences' attention. Talking pictures soon opened a new interest in film entertainment. People had earlier gone to the silent films until a live show became available so they could have words with action, but with the advent of the talking picture, filmgoers would not have to read subtitles any longer. Talking pictures could offer new, unhackneyed plots with the characters orally reciting the exposition that had to be shown by pantomime in the older films. From this new situation, Rep owners sensed a hard battle to retain audiences. Movie theater owners could keep prices lower than the Rep managers could because the Rep owners had such high overhead to keep their crew and troupe on the road.

Just as Toby characters had come along at an appropriate time for the 1920s, Susie was the big innovation for Tent Rep in the 1930s. Lotta Haverstock and Caroline Schaffner led the way with the Susie character.[3] They both had mellowed into matronhood. Lotta's hair needed coloring to keep her ingenue facade; yet still, age showed. The Susie character seemed to be her answer.

On March 16, 1975, in an issue of the Des Moines *Sunday Register*'s picture magazine, Neil and Caroline Schaffner were pictured on the cover and on four inside pages with their tent show's story. Virginia Sheets, the writer of the article, wrote: "Neil Schaffner and his Schaffner Players were the Depression. . . . The Depression years [were] the death of most tent shows. . . . We [the tent owners] concentrated more on our Toby and Susie . . . to provide financial security."[4]

Susie was the female counterpart of Toby. She was Sis Hopkins, but more. She helped keep Toby in line. She was his top banana, and the butt of many of his jokes. Her lines in the olio even kept that part of the program lively. One of Lotta's favorite olio bits was:

> SUSIE: "Hey, Toby, do you want to buy some fish worms?"
> TOBY: "How much?"
> SUSIE: "All you want for a dollar."
> TOBY: "Okay, give me two dollar's worth!"
> SUSIE: "Oh, Toby, you make me so mad sometimes!"[5]

Toby's goal seemed to be to keep Susie angry. In every play, he had to be the winner, so Susie had to use her part to get Toby to the top. That was her job in the script.

Neil Schaffner, who wrote more than fifty Toby plays, has to be given a great deal of credit for Susie's development as a character. After he married Caroline in 1925, many of the shows he wrote included the Susie character. Caroline played her Susie in pigtails, freckles, and a comedy hat.[6]

Lotta's Susie was unique. In the early years, Lotta played Susie not as a bumpkin but as stylishly as she could. As to her acting style, it could be likened to that of Lucille Ball in the later years of her *Lucy* television shows. But as Lotta grew older and as her hair began turning white, she had to give Susie more depth. Susie was still lively and filled with rhubarb, but she became more rube, more stereotyped than the earlier Susie had been. The more stereotypical Susie became, the more readily identified she was with the Haverstocks. The older Susie wore a big red bow in her short, cropped white hair. She wore standard stage makeup. Lotta's Susie did not use freckles, as Caroline Schaffner's did. Lotta's dress was usually bright red with dinner-plate-sized sewing braid trim designs all around the bottom of the gathered skirt. She also wore ruffled pinafores over her straight dresses. The dress or the pinafore featured a Peter Pan collar and flouncy cap sleeves, trimmed in the multicolored trim of the skirt. She wore a wide sash tied in a huge bustle bow. Mary Jane shoes kept the audience aware that she was a youngster who could go along with Toby's little boy or juvenile role. Susie's part was technically called the soubrette role.

So Susie was the addition to Tent Rep for the 1930s, and Lotta Haverstock was the ultimate Susie. From the first time she played the role, when people saw her on the streets, she was no longer Lotta Haverstock, but was known as Susie Haverstock. In fact, from then on, Harvey and Lotta became simply Toby and Susie, except to their most intimate tent show friends and to their own families.

With the Great Depression and hard times, many changes had to take place in Tent Rep companies if they were to survive. Few did survive. By early 1930, the prosperity of the 1920s was gone. *Billboard*'s April 12, 1930, issue said: "Reps have better actors than usual because Rep actors couldn't work legitimate [theater] in winter,"[7] and even the best theatrical actors were willing to take a job with Rep, being hungry by then. By June 28, 1930, the Mary-Frank Players in Goultry, Oklahoma, reported that gates were "sixty-five percent under 1929, and with three trucks, three house-car trailers, two house-car trucks, and three sedans full of company, we can't survive that kind of a cut."[8] Also in June, the Billy Terrall Tent Company reported to *Billboard* that they had "reduced our fares to ten cents and twenty-five cents and made every night a 'Ladies Free' night, and with thirty five in our company, we can't survive with only eighty-five paid admissions."[9] *Billboard*'s editorial stated, "Many of the shows are this season cleaning house: weeding out old scripts and substituting brighter ones, and adding new novelties and specialties in an effort to please the talkie-educated natives."[10]

The Tent Reps had to meet with obstacles at every turn. The movie-house owners had resented their stealing of silent film crowds, luring them with the candy bally ("A prize in every box of candy") during intermissions and exciting specialties. After the advent of talking pictures, to pay for the cost of wiring their film houses for sound, theater owners were no longer willing to sit idly by and allow Reppers a share of local revenues. The Haverstocks did not feel the impact of this kind of problem too badly. Rolland remarked in an interview in 1973:

> Dad had the respect of the entire population of the towns where we played. If the movie-house owners knew of our [Haverstock] show arrival dates, they tried to book-in shows that would not do well. Often they'd close their house down during the tent show performance and then re-open for a midnight run. There wasn't enough business to go around in the 1930s, and we tried to keep from cutting each other's throats. If we were to survive, any of us in entertainment, we had to work together.[11]

When a tent show manager had tied up as much as $20,000 of capital in outfitting even one of the smaller shows in the late 1920s, it was difficult for him just to shut down the show and lose that investment. But in the

1930s, hundreds did that very thing. They just could not make their expenses.

In 1931, *Billboard* reported:

> The trick was to stick it out the fore part of the season or until the break comes. And the fellow with a mediocre show isn't going to be able to pull the trick. It will take a first class organization, with a set of real actors, a string of first class bills, backed up with the proper amount of exploitation and advertising to get by.[12]

Haver fit this description of a first class manager. The Haverstock Comedians opened every season in the 1930s, and his was among the few companies that never closed their runs early in those years. Salaries dropped to $25 for a team of actors and $15 for a single. That was still handsome pay, when room and board in a good boarding house was no more than $5 a week. Most of the Reppers needed only board expenses, however, because most troupers pulled their own small house-car trailers in which to sleep. Troupers, rising late, often snacked, except for one meal a day, and twenty-five cents would buy one an all-you-can-eat blue-plate special in almost any small-town cafe.

Haver stuck with his Oklahoma-Texas route as long as he could. The dust storms were a problem with which he could not easily contend. The dust became so intense that it could cut the very fiber of the tent. So after 1933, to avoid the dust, Haver's troupe began a northward trek out of St. Louis going into Illinois. They generally made a short route down into the old territory after the northern weather began to get too cold, and after the summer dust storms had abated somewhat, but they usually limited their stops to three-night stands, about all that the economy of any local community could support, anyway. Some of the good towns could still finance a week. The cities of Grandfield, Altus, Roosevelt, and Tipton, all in Oklahoma, almost always got a week's stay, especially during cotton harvest. Some of the smaller towns just could no longer draw a crowd, particularly if the patrons had to walk into town, which was often the case, since few could afford gasoline to operate their automobiles.

Gilford Miracle, who was later to play Toby in a re-creation of a Toby show in Grandfield, Oklahoma's, Harvest Theater recalled:

> We would hear that Toby and Susie were coming to town, and we would begin putting aside every cent that we could so we could take our girl friends to the show. I was in high school, and I liked the tent

shows. We never had any extra money for anything. A cow and a calf could be bought for $2.50. Even a dime for a roost seat [blue] was a real extravagance, but we always seemed to get together fifty cents for a week of Toby and Susie Haverstock.[13]

The show would give free passes to hire many teenage boys in their towns to help their then-limited canvas crews set up the tents. The advance man would sell ads for the tent show. He would gather from local merchants door prize items for the show to give away to the holder of a lucky number one could find in one of the candy bags sold during the candy bally. The saltwater taffy candy was a dime a box, and almost everyone bought a box because they wanted a chance at one of the nice prizes. Most who could scrape the extra money together would invest a dime for such a chance. Some shows tried bank nights, where a lucky number was drawn, and if your box of candy had the lucky number in it, you would win a five dollar bill, a fortune in those days when $5 would buy a nice winter coat, several pairs of shoes, or a week's supply of groceries bought from a store. Many men were thrilled with a job that paid them $5 a week. Many people worked for the county with some of the New Deal programs, building better roads in the rural areas, at $3 a week, and those government-paid workers also furnished a team of mules and a drag plow for that $3. Who would not gamble a dime on a chance for a $5 prize? Rolland told the story that someone had reported that one of their main competitors, Brunks' Comedians, had bolstered their audience attendance by giving a live baby pig as a prize one night a week. Rolland laughingly commented that Hank Brunk had probably taken in that pig as a family fare for a week of shows and had to think of some way to get rid of it.[14]

In 1933, Peggy Meador entered the Tent Repertoire scene. The Haverstock show had played in Alvord, Texas, for several years. Every young girl dreamed of entering show business; Peggy was no different. She liked the idea of becoming a star, even though as she grew up in Alvord, such a thought was likely nothing more than a fanciful dream. One day, Peggy had a group of girls over to her home to meet Lotta Haverstock, still the lead in the Toby show, which came to town every year. Peggy's mother was one of Lotta's excellent seamstresses who sewed the elegant wardrobe that was due the star of a prosperous show. As a treat for her daughter and some of her girlfriends, Mrs. Meador had prearranged that after the fitting, Lotta's son, Rolland, would meet Lotta in the family car to take her back to her home. Rolland, very handsome in 1933, just five years out of high school, had taken over playing the lead male parts in the Haverstock company. He also did romantic dramatic readings in the olios, causing every young girl's heart to throb. He was much admired, and several young ladies awaited the thrill of meeting Mrs. Haverstock's son that afternoon.

Peggy Meador was a beautiful strawberry blonde about nineteen years old. She was an extremely talented young lady, and she impressed all of the afternoon tea guests by entertaining them with her piano playing and singing. Lotta, among Peggy's impressed fans that afternoon, asked Peggy if she had ever thought of a job in theater. When Peggy admitted a special interest in having such a job, Lotta offered her a place with the Haverstock Comedians as a character actress in the shows and as the orchestra pianist. She also learned that Peggy could also play an accordion giving Lotta a third option of getting a new olio specialty for their shows.

At first, Peggy's parents were reluctant to have their daughter join show business. They were devout members of the local Church of Christ congregation. Having known the Haverstocks and the type of family shows that Lotta and Haver offered was not a problem for the Meadors, but there was a certain stigma that accompanied any connection with show business. Knowing of their concern about their daughter getting into the business, Haver helped to solve the problem by also offering a Tent Rep job to Rowe Meador, Peggy's brother. With Rowe going along with the company, he could act as Peggy's chaperone, so her parents decided to allow Peggy to join the cast. She would share a room with a single girl who was reared in nearby Wichita Falls, Texas, and who also had a speaking part in the shows. Their family knew the family of Peggy's proposed roommate, so that was an added factor in convincing Peggy's parents of the respectability of the situation.

Peggy's brother, Rowe, loved the work in theatrics, so he traveled with the show for several years during each of the summers while he completed high school and college. In fact, even after he began his teaching career, he continued to be a summer actor for the Haverstocks. Rowe's specialties included tap dancing and singing, but he also did a specialty in rope spinning, an act especially in demand after Will Rogers had made such a hit of that skill while he performed with the Ziegfeld Follies and in movies. Rowe also worked canvas, drove a truck, was sometimes an advance man, and he also, as did most of the cast members, sold ads and did the candy bally during his years in tent-show entertainment.

In the 1930s, Haver really pushed his formula guaranteeing Tent Repertoire success. He felt that plays had to be for the entire family, and that show owners had to remember that the people of small towns were not rubes. That formula was not just Haver's, being corroborated by an article in the May 7, 1932, *Billboard*: "Americans love and must have entertainment. If the show that comes to their town is not equal to the standard of amusement, then you can not expect the public to donate.... The public are not rubes anymore. There are no more sticks."[15] The family entertainment idea did not stop with the quality of show that Haver offered. It extended to the cast. They had played from the area around Alvord and Fort Worth, through Breckenridge to Throckmorton, to Vernon, all in Texas, to Altus, Tipton, and Grandfield, all in Oklahoma. This was through the early springtime. As the weather warmed or when the dust was too harsh, the company moved north into Illinois, new country for the Haverstock tent. They played the warm summer months in the northern climate, but they were certain to be back to their southern route, around Grandfield, Oklahoma, to coincide with the annual cotton harvest season there. They usually were in Tipton, Oklahoma, when truck loads of migrant harvesters were brought into the area to pull bolls (of cotton), about September 15 each year. By that time, both the harvesters and the farm owners had enough extra cash to spend on attending shows during the cotton harvest.

Peggy had not been with the troupe long until she and Rolland realized that they had fallen in love. It was September 15, 1933, that Rolland and Peggy decided not to wait until the show closed in November to get married. They would marry immediately. They talked over their plans with Haver and Lotta. The family decided that the young couple should go to Lawton, Oklahoma, about thirty miles to the east of Tipton, with Lotta accompanying them as their witness, for the wedding ceremony.[16] That afternoon, the three of them headed for Lawton. They had to have near-perfect timing because they had to be back to Tipton in time to make the curtain opening that night's show. That schedule was a challenge, but they made their connections. All three of the wedding party played the show at Tipton that evening, and their appearance gave Haver a chance to make the announcement of his son's wedding as a part of Toby's palaver that he "just thought the audience should know," prior to the show curtain's being opened.

Lotta had gone to Lawton to be a witness for the couple, but she wanted to be sure that she stayed on good relations with Peggy's family, so she decided after the long drive to Lawton that she would not attend the wedding ceremony. She said that if Peggy's mother could not attend, she did not think it was fair that she should either. She waited in the car. Lotta and Peggy had become good friends by the time of the wedding. Lotta's attitude made their friendship even more solid. They remained good friends through the twenty years they had together with the show before Lotta's death. That night after the wedding, the company had to tear down the tent so that it could be moved to Elmer, their next stop. The advance man had made a deal for Peggy and Rolland to stay at a home in Elmer for their honeymoon night. The owners of the house got to help with the tear-down and sleep with the other company stars in return for the use of their house in Elmer.[17]

Rolland and Peggy left for Elmer as quickly as the final bows were ended so they could to get to have some time together as honeymooners. But the other workers hurried with their tear-down and move, too, so they could follow as closely as possible after the newlyweds. At 5:30 A.M., Peggy heard noises outside the honeymoon house and roused Rolland. In moments, they saw the flash of car lights through the bedroom window. Everyone in the cast, the entire crew, and even the couple who had lent Rolland and Peggy their house were all outside ready to chivaree the newlyweds. The revelers made Peggy and Rolland get up and get dressed again so that all of them could drive to Wichita Falls, Texas, about eighty miles away, to hear Duke Ellington and his band who would play a matinee concert the next day at the Wichita Opera House.

Peggy relates memories of that trip:

> That was some trip. There were no paved roads in 1933. We were very, very late getting back to Elmer, and the next day we all had a call for a tent set up in time for the show that night. All Rolland and I could think of was, "Some honeymoon!" Our honeymoon night was really typical of the life on the road with a tent show.[18] If an idea occurred and we could work it in, no matter how ridiculous it might seem to others, we tried to work it into our lives. There was never a dull moment!

After the wedding some concern was voiced as to how the female fans would react to Rolland's being married. As long as he was single, the young unmarried girls treated his live appearance much as did those who were to worship the movie and rock stars of later eras. The fact that he had married apparently had little effect. Peggy said of the situation: "They still swooned when Rolland did his routines or his parts in the shows. I guess they really didn't think of him as being married. We didn't see any decline in their attendance. I think they secretly might have envied my position as the new bride of such a handsome leading man."[19]

Peggy also told the story of a woman whom she met in a church service in 1986. The woman was a native of Tipton, and when introduced to Peggy, the woman said:

> We've never met, but I feel as if I know you. I was in the audience on September 15, 1933, when Toby announced before the show that you and Rolland had gotten married that afternoon in Lawton. We girls were all green with envy, but when he walked out on the stage as the leading man, we all went back to our fantasy dreams of that handsome leading man taking us in his arms and kissing us. We forgot he was married, even when you were on stage with him. All of us always loved Rolland Haverstock.[20]

The thirties were definitely times marked by economic depression for most of the world. Rolland, in later years, had developed an interesting story for the press about how people paid their tent admission with chickens or tomatoes or other farm produce. It was a fabricated story to reflect the hard times of the era.

Peggy said of his invention:

> Rolland had a good imagination. I never knew of or saw any chickens or anything else given for show admission. I don't know about the 1920s, as that was before my time, but I doubt that it happened then either, as the 1920s were very prosperous times. Now, good friends would bring by a few tomatoes and things like that which could be eaten raw, but we never cooked. We never would have taken the time to dress and fry a chicken for certain. We wouldn't have the grease and mess in our tiny, little trailer homes.[21]

The Haverstocks and their company had no cook tent or dining car after their early years. It was much simpler just to pay the actors and the canvasmen a wage that would allow them to pay room and board. Cooks and cooking facilities were just too much trouble. Many shows did not agree with that principle, but Haver liked his method of operation.

Peggy told of their cooking:

Lean Years, 1930–1939

Occasionally, we would heat up a can of soup on a hot plate or brew a cup of hot tea or coffee, but we just took all our meals at the local cafe or boarding house. Haver felt that it was good business to have the troupe spending some of the money the show earned in a given town in support of the town's enterprises.[22]

Peggy remembered that the economic conditions of the Depression era were difficult but not disheartening:

We never closed the tent. Cash money was scarce in nearly every town we played, but everyone we knew or met was in the same boat. We never really suffered at all. Haver was a good manager. He had been especially saving during the more prosperous times. He kept a good line of equipment in good repair. He knew he had to provide proper equipment to keep a happy troupe. We even bought at least two new tents in the 1930s when not many people were buying anything. We would have liked to have had more money, of course, and our salaries did have to be cut, but as they were cut, so were the prices of things those lowered salaries would buy.[23]

The Haverstock Show always kept updated automobiles, even during the hard times. Rolland and Haver alternated years in buying a new car. Whichever couple had the new car allowed that car, which was really then a part of the show's equipment, to be used as the advance man's car. Their advance man would use the new vehicle to do the preliminary work for the show's coming to a town. Rolland, Haver, and Herb Swift always did the advance work for the troupe. Peggy told of the automobile situation: "Haver wanted our show to look prosperous. He insisted that we not look *down* in our automobiles, our clothing or our equipment. We still contributed to local charities and benevolent groups—and really, it wasn't a *front* because we just really didn't *hurt* that much."[24]

Lotta still kept and wore her diamonds during this time, and she never had to sell or pawn any of them to help pay for the show. At the end of the 1930s, she probably had not added any new diamonds, but she had not given up any either. When the banks closed, the Haverstocks lost a small amount of money, but they did not keep much money in banks.[25] They kept most of their money in grouch bags and used their cash as it came in to purchase equipment and supplies. They had not purchased the stocks and bonds on which so many other Tent Rep entrepreneurs had lost their money. The Haverstocks kept their money right with them as they traveled because without a good home base, banking was difficult, and they had no home base except the tent. Very few businesses would take checks in those years, especially from traveling groups, even when the groups had as good reputations as the Haverstocks.

Price for admission during the 1930s and for many subsequent years was ten cents for children, and thirty-five cents for adults. The opening night was always Ladies' Night and they still admitted without charge any woman accompanied by a paid adult admission. Those who desired a reserved seat paid an added ten-cent fee. If people were still out on the street when the show started, and if the tent was not full by curtain time, Haver would invite those people outside to come on in to see the show without paying a fee.[26] "Haver knew that such opportunities would only endear him to the townspeople, and that would insure their paying for the next show's admission if there were any way for them to do so," Peggy said.[27]

Incidentally, during their entire tenure in the cast, Peggy and Rolland were paid a salary just as were the other performing couples in the show's cast. Haver did expect a bit more from Rolland and Peggy for his money, but he treated the couple just as he treated other couples in his troupe. They were not thought of, nor were they ever treated, as bosses. Only Lotta and Haver had that distinction, and that was a distinction that they would never share. Rolland and Peggy took a $5 a week pay cut when they married, because couples shared a room. They earned $25 a week as a couple, while as singles, each was paid $15 a week.

Even on that salary, by 1935, Rolland and Peggy had saved enough to buy a house-car trailer. It was a trailer about fourteen feet long by six feet wide—a real luxury. It was a portable bedroom that made life on the road easier. They were so happy not to have to live out of a suitcase. Their clothing could hang in the tiny closets of their own trailer.

After Rolland and Peggy bought their trailer, Lotta and Haver decided the house-car trailer was a good idea, so that following winter, Haver had his canvas crew, hired over the wintering for tent and equipment repair, to build a house-car trailer of his own design for him and Lotta to live in as they traveled. It was larger, more bulky, and much less sleek than Peggy and Rolland's, but Haver designed it with the proper kinds of amenities that he and Lotta needed for their own personal comfort. The trailer contained a small desk, two radio chairs, a bed, two closets, a makeup area, a heater, and a rack for Haver's *Billboard*s and Lotta's movie magazines. Lotta would never be without her movie magazines, and Peggy remembered Lotta's delight in them:

Lean Years, 1930–1939

Lotta loved the movie fan magazines. She read every issue of every magazine. Besides her purses, her nice clothing, and her diamonds, her most prized luxuries were those fan magazines. One way that we could gauge how the show fared during the Great Depression is the fact that Lotta never had to do without one issue.[28]

It was prior to Rolland and Peggy's marriage that Haver sold the Eads Avenue house to Lotta's sister, Lizzie. Haver and Lotta often lived the winter months there with Lizzie, who was then widowed and glad for their company. Lizzie's home was to become the elder Haverstocks winter home until Lotta's death, and Haver stayed for a couple of winters with Lizzie even after Lotta died. After Lizzie's death, Haver moved into Rolland and Peggy's home in Wichita Falls, Texas.

Rolland and Peggy usually spent the wintering months of the 1930s at the home of Peggy's parents, the Meador family, in Alvord, Texas. Occasionally, all four of the Haverstocks stayed in Illinois and played winter circle stock near Effingham, Illinois, where Lotta's other sister and husband, Jack and Daisy Swift, lived. They also occasionally played circle stock engagements in Texas in high school auditoriums for small acts or did concert shows and magic acts to earn a little extra pocket cash. They generally stayed in the area around Alvord, Rhome, Hillsboro, and Waco, Texas. For a time, those were the southern boundaries where they opened their tent, but since Waco and Hillsboro infringed on the Brunk territory, Haver soon cut those cities from his itinerary. In later years, Haver only took his show to very carefully selected Texas communities. During the 1930s, in an effort to expand their route, the Haverstock show traveled from Texas north into Illinois. They traveled a route through Mt. Vernon, Champaign-Urbana, and the Danville area. They were so well received that they kept the Illinois towns as a part of their route from the late 1930s onward.

It was in the 1930s that a new play was making the Tent Rep rounds. It was an extremely futuristic show entitled *So This Is Television* (no copy is extant today). Ironically, the real final death knell to Tent Rep was television, but the new bill was enthusiastically received in the 1930s.[29] Television had been a novelty at the Chicago Century of Progress Exposition in 1933–34, so a writer capitalized on the idea in a script.

Candy ballies remained important throughout the 1930s. Some statistics from the 1930s *Billboard* included items purchasable for the candy bally. Packages of candy, already boxed with a prize and numbers, were

Lean Years, 1930–1939

$11.25 for two-hundred fifty packages, and $45 for one-thousand packages. *Billboard* noted the items as ten-cent sellers, and the boxes reflected the times in their decorations, with the printing on the boxes reading, "Broadway Memories," "Whoopee," "It," "Prosperity," "Hello World," "June Moon," or "Happy Days." Rep owners ordered these candies from Show People's Candy Company in Cleveland, Ohio. Those who purchased at least a thousand boxes got one-hundred extras at no cost.[30]

By the time Peggy joined the show, Haver had already stopped asking local merchants to donate front-of-the-curtain prizes. He thought it more practical to buy his candy boxes flat, then open them out and put his own candy and prizes in them. He used an occasional watch, a French doll, or an Indian blanket as the larger prize for the walk-up (those who bought candy boxes with special numbers for prizes that the winner claimed by walking up to the stage), but he placed in every box some kind of little novelty prize, similar to those in the Cracker Jack caramel corn today. Haver preferred the "gift in every box" idea as his sales gimmick so that everyone who bought candy got some kind of little gift.

Haver sold popcorn and ices prior to the show. The popcorn or the ice (snow-cone) was a nickel each. They sold only grape-flavored snow cones, which they hawked as grape ices. Lotta sold the ices. Peggy did the popcorn. The bally men sold the candy boxes. Rolland always opened the front gate. Lotta sold the reserved seats, standing near the red chairs, and took care of the popcorn until the show was ready to begin.

Peggy explained the money part of the operation in detail:

> During the 1930s, the concessions made nearly as much money as the show tickets. Rolland and Haver split the candy profits. Mother [as Peggy called Lotta] and I got the profits from the snow cones and the popcorn after we deducted all the expenses for making them were paid. Rolland and I got half of the concessions because we took care of that business, like buying the merchandise, cleaning the machines, and so forth. We were able to save all that money we made on concessions as a savings account. We ladies carried our savings accounts in our *grouch bags*. These *grouch bags* were small cloth sacks with a draw-string closing and were pinned to our undergarments, hidden in our bosoms below our dresses.[31]

Rolland and Peggy developed a big following for their magic shows, which they began in 1934. They tried to add new magic tricks often. Peggy kept a log of which acts they had played in each town so that they could wait at least five years before they would use that magic act in a given town again. Records such as this were extremely important to help assure that the Haverstock show maintained its unique integrity. The Haverstocks all exercised extreme care keeping records to assure their show would not become repetitious.

Haver kept excellent route records detailing the name of the show, its income, its cast, and changes in its bill for a given town. He tried not to repeat a show in a town within a five-year period. He also meticulously paid royalties on each performance of a show. He did not want to cheat those to whom he owed a royalty, so he always received superb treatment from those writers, giving him price breaks and writing special shows allowing Haver to premier them. Many wrote special Toby lines just for Haver.

It was in 1933 or so that Peggy took over the lead ingenue parts, and Lotta moved into the soubrette, her Susie role. The change was an easy one. Peggy and Lotta were always the best of friends, and Lotta was the one to realize that Peggy would be a perfect draw as a leading lady. In fact, a letter that year from a little girl, Della Ilee Isbell, was perhaps a big factor in making this move. The letter read:

> Dear Peggy, you are the prettiest girl I ever saw. I would not blame Toby for fainting when he saw you. You had on the prettiest dress last night that I wished I had it. I am coming tonight and see you. I am coming to see you because you were the prettiest one of all. But Toby was the funniest one. I will see you tonight. Bye. See you soon. [It was signed] Love.[32]

The 1930s were difficult days for lots of show people just as they were for many. Show folk everywhere searched for jobs. Anyone would have been happy to work for Haver and Lotta. Bess Camble wrote Lotta from Dothan, Alabama, in March 1933, telling her of the hard times in that area. She said that she had a Willys Knight and a trailer in which to haul instruments. She tried to entice Lotta to hire her orchestra for the Haverstock Show. She wrote:

> I hope you and Haver can figure some way to use us, as I would like nothing better than another season with you all. Of course, the season is different than when we were with you before, so you can arrange salaries in keeping with the times. We didn't even know

when Christmas came this year. We just knew it was the 25th and that was all.[33]

The Haverstocks did not take on Bess and her troupe based on that first inquiry, so she wrote again in June, from Old Hickory, Tennessee, asking once again to be considered for the Haverstock show:

> Old Hatchet Face, as everybody calls Mrs. Nero, is still on the job with her sarcasm and despicable ways. I know that I have a bad disposition, but if I was like her, I'd blow my brains out. . . . She tried to say Haver paid them the biggest team pay he had ever paid any couple on his show. . . . They claim he paid them $75 a week. . . . If you can use my group or just me, I would certainly like to see a good salary for a change.[34]

Haver was not too happy with the remarks about his having paid such a large salary. He never published his salaries, keeping that a confidential item between him and his employees. Haver paid fairly, in line with the salaries of the time and would, on occasion, when their talents or specialties warranted extra pay, willingly give the players a bonus, but he never talked about salaries. He also asked his employees to keep their salary information to themselves.

It was about this time that *Billboard* wrote to Haver asking him to write a special twenty-five hundred word article about his Tent Rep business. They contacted many of the successful groups who continued to operate during this harsh economic time. The article was to be a part of a special issue of the publication. The editor asked for a bust photo and a biographical sketch to be run with the article. Haver did not comply with their request because he was already bombarded with letters from theatrical friends who were almost in a condition of begging for work with his company. An article making him sound more successful, he reasoned, would make his refusing jobs to those whom he considered friends even more difficult. He was pleased that he was asked to write the article. The fact that *Billboard* had asked him to write it indicated that he was among those of Tent Rep whom the magazine considered as among the successful in the business.[35] It was in the 1930s that Haver hired his friends Alyce and Verge Lester as regulars. Alyce wrote from Fort Worth saying, "We sure would like to be with you. . . . We both do general characters and can do new specialties every week."[36] They stayed on with the show until the mid-1950s.

In the mid 1930s, Haverstock stationery had as its motto "Modern Motorized Tent Theater." The Haverstocks were the envy of the other shows. Harry Hearn wrote asking for a snapshot of Haver and Lotta's house-car trailer saying that he was tired of sleeping in rented beds. He said no one on Sadler's elite show had such a luxury as Haver had.[37]

Another 1930s specialty couple hired for the company was the King Feltons, from whom Rolland learned much magic. Felton did a magic variety act. When the Feltons left the show in 1934, Rolland and Peggy took up magic, doing three or four tricks they had learned. Their act went over very well as an olio specialty act. It was not long before they were doing a thirty-minute segment of magic prior to the opening of the regular show. Their magic would later become a mainstay for them in show business.

As the 1930s drew to a close, Audie Chapman of the Elmer, Oklahoma, community characterized the attitude of the people who supported the Haverstocks by attending their shows. The letter to Haver began, "Dear Friends," because he remembered their advertisement that this was the "show with a million friends." The letter continued:

> Each year, my family and I have looked forward to your return.... You are a part of my memories of my home town when it was more than a dying town. I realize that the small towns are doomed, and with them, the freedom and foundation of American civilization. I know, too, that as our town becomes smaller, our chances of seeing you return each year lessen. May I say in closing that you are real troupers—always the same friendly people, with few complaints to shower upon the world.[38]

This letter epitomized the fact that the hard times era was at an end for the Haverstock show. They had not suffered as some had and at times their lives had been trying for them, but an even more trying time loomed on the horizon.

7
The War Years, 1939–1945

As the Great Depression brought on an onslaught affecting Tent Repertoire, World War II brought on an even more devastating problem. The economy turned around with the talk of war and the manufacturing of war materials and weapons, but the morale of the southwestern part of Oklahoma just could not rise.

Dust had nearly decimated the population of Oklahoma as the Okies fled the winds and headed west. Stories of the Dust Bowl were more than overwhelming. Residents told tales of chickens going to roost at midday, thinking it to be dusk. Women told of scooping dust out of their homes with a wheat scoop shovel. Mothers with babies had to wet sheets and drape them over the baby crib rails so that their babies would not breathe the fine dust. Bob Glick, an Oklahoma University student in the late 1950s, quoted his grandfather, a dentist from Brooklyn, New York, as having said that on any given day in the late 1930s, a New Yorker could write his name on his furniture, removing the fine red dust that could only have come from southern and western Oklahoma topsoil, about the only place in the world with that color of red soil. Crops could not grow, and the dust and wind riddled them. It seemed as if nothing would survive.[1] Those who questioned the Oklahoma pioneers endurance just did not know those settlers and what they had already gone through.

The pioneer settlers outlasted depression and dust. So did the pioneer Tent Reppers. The Haverstock Comedians had the strength to withstand the economic problems presented to their audiences, and the show itself survived the 1930s nearly unscathed. "We were always a happy group," recalls Peggy, who had joined the show in 1933. "We were all good friends. During my more than twenty years with the show there was never any disrespect shown to anyone. Haver ran that kind of show."[2]

WAR YEARS, 1939–1945

Joseph Davenport was a canvasman with the Haverstocks during this same time period, and as he related:

> They [the Haverstocks] were such good folks to work for. I never, ever heard one bad word from or about them, and I worked for them when times were really hard and people had lots of gripes. I drove the trucks and helped set up the tent. Then, when we had to cut back on people, I also sold or took tickets. There was never one minute of trouble. Nobody had anything to gripe about when he worked for the Haverstocks. Haver was boss, and we knew it, but he didn't expect more from us than we could do.[3]

Perhaps the thing that kept the show surviving was the rapport among the members of the Haverstock company. Each of the cast and crew, whittled to a bare-bones operation because of lowered revenues, had certain jobs to do, and then when the worker finished an assigned job, he or she would pitch in to help the others complete their assigned tasks. Haver was very careful to choose people with that kind of spirit, with whom other cast and crew members could have complete camaraderie. They could not have survived without this strong ability to work together and their willingness to perform multiple tasks.

Barney McDaniels recalled his memories from the early 1940s when he was both a cast and crew member:

> We had to do some rewriting of a script, so Rolland and I were trying to make the lines funny. As one of the characters was talking and there was some alliteration of the letter "l" in the script, Rolland replied, "There are too many l's in that line." To that, I replied, "Knock the 'l out of it." We both died laughing, and worked that into the script. Haver didn't like it. He said that even that slight language innuendo did not fit the style of the Haverstock shows. We cut it without question. Haver was always right about what made a good, clean family show. Their shows were always good shows. I worked for them for two full seasons, and I loved the Haverstocks as I would have loved members of my own family.[4]

Travel presented problems for everyone during the late depression years and early war years. Peggy recalled the company's trip into Illinois for their 1939 season:

> We were on our way to open our northern season, and we had a trip I will never forget. We had two trucks to haul the chairs and sets. We

WAR YEARS, 1939–1945

had a tent trailer especially designed to haul the big top. We had at least five automobiles, each of which by then had a small house-trailer following along behind it. Those traveling with us included Mother and Dad Haverstock, Rolland and me, Herb and Rita Swift, another married couple, the two canvasmen and three extra orchestra men who doubled in canvas.

As we traveled north out of Grandfield, our winter storage place, to Illinois, we had twenty-six flat tires! Can you believe what we looked like? When one vehicle had a flat, we all parked alongside the road while that tire was repaired. We had to stay together in case one needed parts or special physical help. I'll bet those passing by the stalled caravan wondered about us. Big signs on the rolling stock said *Haverstock Comedians*, and before that trip was over, we could certainly be called *the comedic Haverstocks*. We were all near the stage of laughing hysteria after having those twenty-six flats. We were also very tired of repairing tires. In those days you patched and then patched patches. Synthetic rubber was less than satisfactory, but we had years of making do with that which we had, so we took the tire and travel troubles within our strides just as we had the other problems we had collectively faced. We didn't suffer much during the hard times, and Haver smilingly told us that we would make it through these times, too.[5]

Everyone with vehicles had those kinds of troubles with tires in the prewar years. People used tires made of synthetic rubber because the places supplying natural rubber were already under siege by Japan and the Axis governments.

Worrying about tires was not the only problem the Haverstocks' tent show faced. They had to meet their nut. They had high overhead costs. Tent Reppers sometimes had to take barter items to get people out to the shows at all. Since Haver and Lotta loved performing so much, and since they were good managers, their company had only minimal problems. Tent Rep suffered as a whole. The publishers of *Billboard*'s Rep page begged for articles about the shows:

> We solicit your cooperation in keeping the Tent Repertoire page alive and interesting. [In the 1920s, nearly the entire paper dealt with Tent Rep.] Managers, we are interested in knowing how your season business is. . . . Drop a newsy line to the Rep editor now, even if it is only a penny post card.[6]

Haver never once thought of closing. The Haverstock show had been a tradition since 1911, and Haver and Lotta could think of nothing that they would rather have done. Other tent shows had different agendas, many of which involved closing. In the early 1940s, even the Sadler Show, one of the country's largest Tent Rep shows, was about to close. In 1942, when Texans elected Harley Sadler to their state legislature, Sadler decided to cut out the extra responsibility of outfitting his tent show and laying out money for company salaries.[7]

The Great Depression had just ended when war was upon America. Most of the able-bodied young men had already joined the service by the first of January in 1942. Pearl Harbor had been bombed on December 7, 1941. Everyone wanted to get into action so that world peace could be quickly restored. But history shows that a speedy peace was not the case. The end did not come until a grueling, bloody four years had transpired.

The war machine had to be oiled, given tires and machinery, and fed. Rationing was the rule of the day. Remembering the twenty-six flats enroute to Illinois, Haver went to the War Rationing Board in Decatur, Texas, to solicit rations for extra tires and fuel so he could assure that his show could move from town to town. Several of the shows had already been forced to close because they were denied such requests. The show managers could not justify their existence to the appropriate government boards. Haver was never a pessimistic person. He was not afraid to ask for help because he knew the value of his show to the communities and areas it served. The Decatur Board had known Haver and had seen his shows for many years. The Board thought the Haverstocks were like home folks, contributing regularly to community needs, even when times were tough. The Board and Haver sat around a table and talked more than two hours about Haver's needs. Haver then left the room so that the Board members could discuss his needs in private. In just moments, the Board called him back into the room to tell him that they had granted all that he had asked. In a few days, Haver received letters from both the War Rationing Board and the War Department in Washington confirming the actions of the Decatur Board. The letter further declared that the Haverstock Comedians were as important to the home front as the military groups were to the battlefront. The Haverstocks' needs were noted as a national emergency as far as their obtaining necessary supplies, and the government cited their operation as one of America's important homefront morale builders.[8]

During the war period, the Haverstocks did change their policy of regularly purchasing new automobiles. "We had to use the same cars for the war years. There was not a great deal of choice in that. New automobiles were just not manufactured," Peggy related.[9]

For the first year of the war, Haver got a necessity exemption keeping Rolland from going into the service because he was the necessary leading man in their show. They had already established the need for the show to stay on the road. But by January of 1943, Rolland began to feel too conspicuous as he played parts on a stage to families whose sons fought and perhaps even died on the battlefields of Africa, Asia, and Europe. He just could not endure the personal pressure of knowing that he should also be a part of the military. After the Haverstocks closed the show in November of 1942, Rolland decided he had to do his part in the war effort. He left the Meadors' home in Alvord and drove to Decatur to enlist. He was inducted in early January 1943.

Herb Swift, who was Rolland's age, but physically unfit for service, took over the lead roles. Haver rewrote many of their scripts that required young men in juvenile roles, changing the roles to ones that could be played by older men. In fact, during the war years, all the scripts took on a more serious tone in rewrites from both subscribing directors and show owners as well as the original script writers. In the war years, Toby companies across the country were billing such plays as *Toby in the Service; Toby Hits Hitler; Headin' for Heaven; Too Many Soldiers; Toby, the Super Spy; Shadows and Ricochets; Flyer Toby; A Cheer for the Allies; Toby's American Sweetheart; The Girl He Left Behind; My Only Girl; Storm Over London;* and *The Spirit.* All of them propounded the superiority of the American way of life and how it was worth fighting to preserve.[10]

Peggy said of this time:

> We were interested in what was happening, especially with our friends who had loved ones overseas, and our friends were concerned over what was happening with Rolland. We tried to keep the format of our show as it always had been—entertainment. We were trying to do our part on the home-front. People liked the Haverstock show as it had always been. We were just not flag wavers for the sake of waving flags.[11]

The Haverstocks hired Bill Miller as their heavy male. Most shows by now had just five people in their casts. The three men were Haver as Toby, Herb as the lead, and Bill as the heavy. The two women were Lotta as

Susie and Peggy as the ingenue lead. If there were other parts, Haver eliminated them in script rewrites.

Setting up the tent took on a new perspective. Peggy recalled:

> We could do any play, and did do any play we wanted to do with the five of us. We eliminated the orchestra, most of whom were men in those days. We hired local boys to help set up the tent and chairs with just a boss canvasman and our show men, Bill and Herbie. Dad rarely helped because he was usually out as an advance man while the others erected the tent.[12]

Rolland served in the Army; he spent his entire tour of duty in Europe. He was in the first wave of American soldiers into Berlin and the bunkers in which Hitler stayed. Rolland shared only a very few memories of his time in Europe, but the scenes he did remember caused him to have nightmares for many years. He was a part of the troops who liberated some of the prisoner of war and concentration camps.

Rolland loved drawing, and he spent many hours writing and illustrating the special love letters and poetry which he mailed Peggy from Europe and which she subsequently framed and displayed.

Two of the poems he wrote and illustrated for Peggy read:

> To My Adorable Wife
> Just calling from across the sea
> To wish Happy Easter to you from me.
> I could write a sonnet
> About your Easter bonnet
> Instead, a word or two
> Of my sweet memories of you.
> Memory's pathway leads me back
> To days we spent together
> Always sunny—always fair
> Those days of cloudless weather.
> If things aren't just right
> And clouds obscure the blue
> I bring sunshine back again
> By just remembering you.
> My Love,
> Rolland
> Easter, 1945

> Easter greetings to my lovely wife
> Easter greetings from me to you

War Years, 1939–1945

> This, my dear, is the best I can do
> From here to distant shore
> My strength of heart and arm and brain
> I pledge to you and evermore
> While honor lives and faith endures
> Dear One of hope—My all is yours.
> Your Husband,
> Rolland
> [No Date][13]

When the war ended, Peggy and Rolland bought a home at 1412 Fillmore Street in Wichita Falls, Texas. They came to that home for the winter months each year. Peggy's father, an accomplished finish carpenter, remodeled the old house and made it a place where, in their later years, Peggy and Rolland displayed many family mementos and tent show artifacts. During the 1940s, the elder Haverstocks traveled to St. Louis to winter in the home of Lotta's sister, Elizabeth.

Peggy recalled the last part of the 1940s decade:

> The 1940s were very good to us. When Rolland left to join the service, we were all personally devastated because we loved him so, but fans accepted the changes which had to come to the show. In fact, no one ever questioned the changes. Few people living during World War II were unaffected by the war. Everyone had to live with change.[14]

Rolland returned from Europe in 1945. He took over his spot as the leading man in the show, and the troupe picked up with their scripts almost exactly where they had left off before the war.

Some of the shows of this period included the Don Melrose scripts *Night Club Nellie* and *Lightning Love*. Haver paid $5 for each script per performance. Melrose wrote Haver telling of the fact that there were not many new scripts forthcoming. He said he just did not write shows suitable for circle stock and that so many tent companies used his scripts without paying royalties that he had become discouraged: "I know I pulled a bone-head, but it's done now, and I can't help it. Regarding *Night Club Nellie* and *Lightning Love*, I wish to state that you can keep them for another season if you want them. Just shoot me a five spot for both of them for this season. Is that fair enough?"[15]

He listed in his letter several other plays he had recently written—those he thought Haver might like to use. The list included the Toby and

Susie shows: *Her Bandit Lover, Affairs of Rosalie, Playing with Love, What Sammy Brought Home* (no Susie part), *The Undercurrent, Deputy Sheriff Toby* (Susie is not Toby's girl in this one but an old maid), *One Happy Family, Love and Horseradish, Toby from Arkansas, Are You a Democrat?* (good for an election year, but no Susie), and *Sweet Papa Toby*. Melrose closed his letter by wishing Haver a successful twenty-ninth year in business. The Haverstocks used *Love and Horseradish, Sweet Papa Toby, Toby from Arkansas, Night Club Nellie,* and *Lightning Love,* but Haver did not choose Melrose's new plays. His conservative audiences just would not accept some of the new titles.[16]

Players hated to leave the business, but they had obligations they had to meet, and Haver did not have enough work for them. Many of them went into professional jobs similar to theater so that they could stay with something they knew and enjoyed. Haver received a warm letter from a former specialty act performer, Ramblin' Ray Cox, of Hopkinsville, Kentucky. Working on a radio station, doing a live show, Cox commented: "I sure do miss the show. We do have a commercial for an overall company besides our shows, and we don't give the station a percent of what we make. . . . Gib and Lillie said to tell you hello."[17]

A playwright, Kenneth Wayne, who operated a theatrical agency, just as Melrose did, wrote to Haver concerning two of his shows, *Murder by the Clock* and *On the Spot*. He gave Haver permission to use them in 1940. In his letter, he also mentions another of Haver's former employees:

> Remember Al Clark who worked with you around St. Louis [1920s]? He is in town and said to tell you "Hello." And incidentally, he has a couple of very good bills you might be interested in for next season [1941–42]. They are *Jed, The Jellybean* and *Dead Man's Letters*. [Haver used *Dead Man's Letters* for several years.][18]

While most Tent Rep companies closed down their shows, the Collier players, headed by Jack Collier of Noble, Illinois, just got into the Rep business. He had asked Haver for tips, wondering if any Repper would share secrets of the business. He and his troupe went to visit the Haverstocks while Haver's company played near Champaign-Urbana in 1941. After their visit and viewing the show, Collier wrote the Haverstocks a letter of thanks:

War Years, 1939–1945

We wish to take this opportunity of thanking you for your time and kindness in entertaining us and showing us the many clever features about your outfit.

Our visit with you was highly instructive and inspirational. If more troupers were that way [willing to share], it would make for a better Rep Show business.[19]

The Haverstocks' friends kept up with the show with a religious zeal. Charles Grassold of the newspaper *The Herrick Bulletin* of Herrick, Illinois, wrote in 1943, to reaffirm that Haver would be in Herrick on July 4, to help celebrate Independence Day: "John M. Nowlin, our mayor, will be pleased to have you come back. He likes a good show, especially when it doesn't cost him anything."[20] Among Haver's papers was also a letter from an inmate of Oklahoma State Penitentiary. Haver had ordered tooled leather purses for both Peggy and Lotta to be used as grouch bags. Haver ordered the purses in April of 1943. The bags, covered with tooled floral designs, had the women's names tooled on them in inch-high letters. By 1943, grouch bags apparently had taken on a new design. They were larger and had zippers instead of drawstrings to close them. Women no longer wore them around their necks but kept them in a bureau drawer in the house trailers or in the locked trunk of a car. The new bags measured about four by eight inches in size.[21] Peggy said, "We rarely used the bags, but the thought of the gift was nice. We thought that if the money we had were kept in a bag with our name on it, in a conspicuous place, any thief would surely recognize it right off."[22]

The war years were good for the Haverstock Comedians in spite of the fact that Rolland could not be with the family. Those years were also prosperous because the war had created a boom. Everyone had gone back to work in small and large factories or in farming to raise foodstuffs to feed the soldiers. These workers flocked to movie houses and live entertainment to break the monotony of their assembly-line jobs and work-a-day worlds. The few Tent Rep shows remaining active during and after the war offered to help wave a few flags to lift home-front morale. Many Rep companies had war bond sales as a regular part of their shows.[23] The Haverstock show did not. Peggy said, "We never sold bonds. Haver had given his son for the war effort, and he thought that was enough. Though we were personal flag-wavers and patriots, we never pushed the bond sales in our shows."[24]

The end of the war brought a sense of relief now that the fighting was over. People were ready to sit back and relax. It was shortly after the end of the war that television began to make its move to take over the role of entertaining a people ready to relax. Television stations took up where movies had formerly been, as instruments playing the doom of the traveling live theatrical show. With both the movies and television, Tent Rep owners could barely gather crowds to see their Toby and Susie shows. A time of change, at least, or perhaps a time of total demise, was rapidly approaching all Tent Rep companies. Most of the owners were older and kept at the business just because it was the thing they had always done. Even Haver and Lotta were beginning to get a little tired of the routine of the routes they had traveled since 1911.

8
The Years of Decline, 1946–1954

From the time the war ended, the decline of Tent Repertoire seemed inevitable. The script writers had to stretch their thinking to write patriotic pieces and keep them original. After all of the tragedy of war, people were not in the mood for the kind of trivial plots that the Toby shows had previously offered; yet, they also did not seem to want to see Broadway-type drama done in the Toby tents. Men had been around the world; they had seen every kind of atrocity. Many had been gone from home for four years, and when they returned from the war, they wanted to be with their families and relax. They tried to make up for lost time on the home front. They wanted to stay at home, get reacquainted, and enjoy themselves. They did not want to dress up to go to Tent Repertoire theater or anywhere else. Even movies suffered low attendance after the war. In fact, by 1948, after television was already becoming a successful medium in larger cities, Tent Rep was a rapidly dying art. A writer in California, William Lawrence Slout, collected material for a history of tent theater.[1] Histories are not usually written until years after the fact, but Slout wanted to preserve it while some of the history makers were still available for interviews.

Slout wrote to Haver at Alvord in 1948:

> I am working on a book about tent shows which have held my keen interest ever since I was a small boy [his father owned a Tent Rep company].... Though I know managers are incessantly bothered by ambitious, would-be writers, I would like to ask you for a little help. ... I am interested in Tent Rep shows and in their history. If you should be inclined, I should like to write you several letters asking specific questions about your experiences. At the moment, however,

Years of Decline, 1946–1954

> I am most interested in one point, whether those shows still on the road are attracting as many people as they did before the war.[2]

The towners along the Haverstock routes were still friends of the show people. Those friends would come out to the shows, but even the old reliable towns did not participate as fully as they had in the past. Why? Towns where the Tent Reppers had their greatest following, the small towns, had little entertainment other than the occasional tent shows or local school programs; they had grown even smaller as a result of the move to cities during the war years of much of their population. Young couples, and even those too old to enter the service, but still not too old to get a good job in a factory, had moved to the manufacturing centers to do their bit for the war effort. For the most part, they stayed in the urban areas, having become accustomed to their new life styles. The technologies of the war had brought easier harvesting capabilities, requiring farmers to hire fewer harvesters to come into a community around harvest season to bring in a crop. The war had allowed farmers to produce an overabundance of commodities so that produce could be shipped overseas. But in 1948, one of America's chief problems was overproduction.

The scarcity of cash was another factor which forced the returning soldiers, now more sophisticated and cosmopolitan, to seek the kind of life offered in urban environments. The world just was not the same after World War II as it had been before. Hiroshima had brought the birth of the Atomic Age, and Tent Rep simply was not a part of that age—it seemed an anachronism. It was a rapidly disappearing dinosaur; only those who liked to preserve relics kept it alive. Even that preservation was not the same kind of exuberance and love that had preserved it as a tradition up until the time just prior to the war.

Haver still booked and played full seasons with his show. Business was not *that* bad for the Haverstock Comedians' show. It had survived many situations that were just as bad. After Rolland's return, the company played its old routes to big audiences who seemed to want to welcome Rolland home by attending the show and giving special applause for him. Even though many of the good towns of the 1920s and 1930s had begun to decline in the war years, they still supported the Haverstock shows. To the handful of active show companies still around by 1948, a three-night stand with good houses was a phenomenal event.

Schools also took on a larger role in community life with athletics becoming more important. Little Leagues and summer camps kept the children occupied. Once the youths were busy, Mom and Pop, now both wage earners, would opt for an evening at home rather than having to dress to go out to a tent show. They just did not want to go out, even to a show with which they had been friends for so many years. With this kind of atmosphere, even the Haverstocks had to work hard to maintain any profitable existence. With Rolland's return from Europe to become, once again, the Haverstock Comedians' leading man, the troupe was eager to try to keep their customers. It seemed that their efforts paid off. For 1945, Haver had booked six plays. Among his titles were *Headin' for Heaven* and *Crash Landin'*, as well as the old standards.[3]

Where *Billboard* had once been filled with Tent Rep news, it was during this decade that it practically discontinued Tent Rep articles, with one showing up only very rarely. On April 6, 1946, Marion McKennon ran an advertisement in *Billboard* seeking both actors and specialty acts for the McKennon Tent Repertoire show. Their show played the South in those years, headquartering in Paris, Tennessee. Their ad concluded each time with the words, "State your lowest salary and send along a photo."[4]

In 1946, the list held nearly all old standards, adding only one new bill, *A Cheerful Liar*.[5] The small-town Haverstock audiences were happy with the return of Toby and Susie and Rolland for a while. In 1947, Haver billed *The Awakening of John Slater*, *Girl Shy*, *Sputters*, *Steppin' on the Gas*, *Just Plain Folks*, *Because She Loves Him So*, and *Whose Gal Are You?*[6]

Haver seemed to have to work overtime at thinking of things to grab his audiences. One example of this kind of work resulted in a monologue written by Haver as a part of his specialty number between the acts. The piece, corny by most standards, is dated 1946, and is titled, "What Is It All About?" It is subtitled, "Written especially for Rolland Haverstock by the Famous Comedian, Mr. Harvey Haverstockskynczxqstwen [*sic*]":

> (Enter and raise hand to audience.) Shhhh. . . . .Don't make no noise! (Pause.) My foot's asleep!
> You know, the funniest thing just happened to me. I was standing out there on the corner and a fellow asked me to hold his dog a while, so I did until I got tired, then I tied the dog to a Ford. A policeman saw me do it, and he arrested me for tying a tin can to a dog's tail.
> You know, I've been so mean lately that Paw made me go to Sunday school, so I was out to a Sunday school picnic last week with a

lot of kids and my teacher, and we all went out boat riding. A big storm came up and the boat began to sink and the teacher said, "All of you kids pray, or you'll all be drowned." So all the kids started to pray but me, and the teacher said, "Toby, you better pray or you'll get drowned." I said, "Teacher, I can't pray." She said, "Then do something religious!" So I just took up a collection.

A fellow asked me if I had lived here all my life, and I told him, "Not yet!"

(Start looking around floor. Pick up spit and wipe it on pants.) Some durn fool spit like a nickel.

You know, I used to be the smartest boy in our family, until my brother, Bud, started to drinking beer. That made Bud Wiser!

I saw a boy standing on the corner today, and I asked him what was the matter. He said, "I got a new baby brother down to our house." I said, "What is that to cry about?" He said, "Paw ain't home yet." I said, "What difference does that make?" He said, "When Paw gets home, I'll get a lickin'!" I asked him why, and he said, "Everything that happens at home is always blamed on me."

(Wipe nose.) Stay up there, durn you, or I'll lick you!

Gosh, I feel so unnecessary. I went into the restaurant this morning and said to the lady waitress, "How's the chicken today?" And she said, "I'm feeling fine. How are you?" I said, "Have you frog legs?" And she said, "No, rheumatism makes me walk this way." I then asked for a bowl of soup and she brought me it. And I asked what kind it was, and she said, "Bean soup." I said, "It might have *been* soup, but it shore ain't now." I went to pay the bill, and she said, "One dollar!" She made me pay it, and I started out. I happened to notice a little ribbon she wore around her neck. I said, "By the way, what is that around your neck?" She said, "That's my ribbon, of course. What business is that of yours?" I said, "Well, everything else is so high here, I thought maybe it was your garter."[7]

This monologue is a corny rube routine designed to make an audience laugh. People who attended Haverstock shows expected this kind of humor. As Toby, Haver often used the piece as his act in the olio, even though the piece was written especially for Rolland, but Rolland never did it. He preferred his magic or his artwork act for his olio number.

In 1948, among the shows Haver chose to produce were *Trail of the Lonesome Pine* (a call back from the 1920s, a tearjerker) by Neil Schaffner, *The Westerner* (another 1920s rerun), and *Tenderfoot*.[8] Rowe Meador remembers that when he returned from the war, he, too, was asked to take a part in the shows. He played two full seasons, 1947 and 1948. Rowe said of that experience, "I did a number of parts during that time, but they must not have been too dynamic, since I don't remember what they were."[9]

Most of the parts by then were not too memorable. The individual parts were even less memorable than the plays themselves. The Haverstocks' show was still doing fairly well in drawing audiences. The crowds were pleased to see the family all together again. Peggy recalled: "The 1940s, after Rolland returned from the war, were okay for the Haverstock show, even though there was a slight attendance decline. We didn't suffer for anything."[10]

During the 1940s, Haver added some one-season performers who joined the Haverstocks because their shows were closing and they were not ready to stop acting. Actors in those times took whatever parts they could get. Herb and Rita Swift separated and left the Haverstock show. Ted and Paul Thardo did short stints with the Haverstock tent, though both were Harley Sadler regulars. Billy Dean, a Western singer brother of another Western singer, Jimmy Dean, had a vaudeville spot and sometimes took bits in the shows. Players were thankful for a guarantee of just a few weeks of specialty billings. Haver and Lotta tried to oblige their friends' requests by giving them concert billings. It was not the money that these seasoned actors craved; it was to have a place again in a live show. In fact, these Tent Rep players wished just to hold on to their past happy life for a moment longer before they had to let it go. It seemed as if they all knew the end was in sight for Tent Repertoire.

By the 1940s, Haver and Lotta were both in their sixties. They wanted to give their characters as much vibrancy as they always had, but age had begun to tell on them. The tenor of the show changed, the players doing what they could to create their theatrical magic. The pressures of the time grew heavier. Many of their standard viewers had moved away from the farms; many had died. For instance, Grandfield had always been at least a week-long show town, but in the 1950s, their old friend Frank Patterson was elected to the state legislature, and publicity was not quite as vivid as it had been earlier when Frank edited the Grandfield newspaper, *The Enterprise*. After Patterson moved to the capital and quit writing stirring advertisements for the newspaper, Grandfield became just a three-day stop for the Haverstock show. When before Grandfield had been the opening slot on their routes, they did the Grandfield productions just prior to their quartering the show for the winter months. Rolland, never fully the showman that his father was, and Peggy, now happily just Mrs. Rolland Haverstock, were always content to be at their small home in Wichita Falls, Texas. Lotta and Haver spent some of their time visiting at the younger Haverstocks' home, and the rest of their time they spent with Elizabeth in St. Louis.[11]

In 1949, the Toby comedies became more predominant again. Haver booked *I'm from Missouri, Rosie of the Rancho* (with Susie as the leading part), *End of the Trail,* and *Sputters.*[12] In 1950, the route book lists among the Haverstock bills *Steppin' on the Gas* and *Sensible Heart.*[13] It must be noted that it was in 1951 that the first drop in total number of shows on the bill occurred. Haver chose to do only four shows that season: *The Victorious Romeo, The Sheriff, Romance in the Valley,* and *The Westerner.* He decided to give more exposure to Rolland and Peggy's magic show, very popular and polished in the olios, rather than playing longer Toby shows or dramatic shows.[14] In 1952, the list of titles included *Henpecked Toby* (a very old Toby, updated), *Clouds and Sunshine* (another 1920s hit feature), *Under Arizona Skies* (an early 1940s revival), and *Circus Day.*[15] In 1953, Haver cut to only three shows: *Toby Takes Over, Back Home in Tennessee,* and *Cowboy Toby.*[16]

The Haverstock Show was also beginning to feel the effects of television. By the 1950s, many rural people had television sets, even though they had to use thirty-foot-tall antennas so they could receive the signals from distant metropolitan stations. They could enjoy shows right in their own living rooms on their six-or eight-inch round picture sets. Both Pete Humphrey's and Fuqua's Mid-Continent Hardware stores in Grandfield put television sets in their store windows by 1949, using the window displays as sales gimmicks. They had the sound transmitted out on the streets for passers-by to enjoy. In 1955, Wichita Falls opened two televisions stations, and soon afterward, one opened in Lawton, Oklahoma. Television was no longer just for the city folk and the wealthy.[17]

By the mid-1950s everything was in a state of change. Stores stopped staying open after 8:00 P.M., even on Saturday evenings. Up until the late 1940s, stores had been open until at least ten o'clock every night and until midnight on Saturday nights so people could shop or relax after working hours. Because people typically did not spend their time in town in the evenings anymore, places of local entertainment, such as the movie houses, reduced their programs to one feature an evening and only added a midnight feature on Saturday to entice teen-age patrons. The younger set of moviegoers began driving to the larger cities to go to an area first-run theater rather than seeing the very old features that rural town theaters could afford to book. The Grandfield theater, the Rio, got its first run of *Gone with the Wind* in 1946, and that was seven years after it had swept the Oscar race in 1939. (The movie had been rereleased in 1942.)[18] The 1950s actually saw the sporadic closing and reopening of the small-town movie houses.

By the 1950s, stores began closing for the day at 5:00 P.M., with only the grocery markets staying open until 7:00 P.M. to try to capture late grocery shoppers. Stores could not operate without customers, and with the growing strength of television and the advent of summer/winter air-conditioning, people enjoyed sitting at home. In fact, even home-town athletic events and programs at the schools saw diminishing crowds. The more liberal churches began canceling first their midweek prayer services and then decided that small crowds at their Sunday evening services were not large enough to warrant the added costs of overhead for utilities. Times, they were a-changing.

The Haverstock Show suffered a crushing blow as they wintered in Wichita Falls in 1952. On December 10, Lotta died while she and Haver were visiting in Rolland and Peggy's home. "We were absolutely heart-broken," Peggy recalled. "We didn't work at all that winter. Her death just about stopped us all. We were such a closely knit group, having been hardly apart in the twenty years since I'd joined the show as Rolland's wife."[19]

Many friends came to say their final good byes to Carlotta Mosher Haverstock when her funeral services were held at her church, the 23rd and Grace Church of Christ in Wichita Falls. The services were held on December 12, 1952. They buried Lotta in Crestview Memorial Cemetery in Wichita Falls. Lotta's death totally devastated Haver, then sixty-six. He had lived for his Susie, and she, for him. They had been separated only during those brief times when she was ill and the show had to go on, or when Harvey had to take a job away from home to support his family in its early years. Harvey and Lotta had become Toby and Susie to every one of their "million friends," and to themselves as well.

Peggy remembered about the importance of keeping the tent open to keep Haver going. She said:

> We couldn't keep the tent closed, though. We realized that Haver had to keep busy if he were to survive the deep depression that came over him when Lotta died. Since show business had been his entire life, we decided that the next spring we would go out on the road

once again. We hired the Dale Maddens. Lois did the leads. Dale did the heavies. I did Susie. Dad did Toby, and Rolland did male leads. The show was good, but it just never was the same without the real Susie, Lotta.[20]

Dale Madden related his memories of playing on the Haverstock show in those days following Lotta's death:

> I loved working with Haver. I could see that the life had gone out of his Toby part. Lotta had been the perfect ploy for him, and she just wasn't any longer there. People of theater knew, but Haver never let his audiences know. He told them that he missed Lotta, as he was sure they did, too, but he always told them, "The show must go on, and I just told you how much we miss Lotta 'cause I thought you ought to know."
>
> He had me play my organ in place of using an orchestra before the show's curtain. I also played it as a part of the olios.
>
> In my years of theater (and they number more than 62)[21] I had heard of the Haverstocks, but I'd never performed with them. I'm delighted I got that opportunity. Haver, Rolland, and Peggy truly should have had the reputation of the show with a million friends. They were great to work with. I never heard one word of criticism of their show in all the places we stopped. Once one became accustomed to Haver's ad libs, he was a dramatic teacher, right there on stage, even for those of us who thought we were old pros.[22]

During the winter months, Haver booked Rolland and Peggy's magic show into the area schools. Haver did not work in the show but acted as the booking agent, making arrangements with the school officials. Peggy related his involvement:

> He actually never saw us work. He was always just ahead of us on the road. We were on a tight schedule, playing as many as four schools in a day. We charged the children ten cents for tickets to the shows, then we split the revenues with the sponsoring schools. The schools were never disappointed with our performances. We could have continued doing that for a long time, but it was very tiring, even if it was a profitable venture.[23]

By 1953, when Omar Ranney noted in "Forever Toby," in August's *Theater Arts* magazine, recounting the reminiscences of Toby and his impact on American theater, Toby was virtually merely a remembrance that deserved some notice. Ranney said:

Years of Decline, 1946–1954

Down through the rural Southwest and Middle West, the Toby tent show's troupe, one of the oddest character types in American comedy is hanging on by a corn tassel. Movies, radio, and television have cramped the old style of the Toby shows, but they have not beaten them into oblivion. There are still on the road this season at least a dozen Tent Repertoire troupes that pitch canvas in the cool cover of village parks and county fairgrounds, keeping alive the tradition of the freckled-faced, slow-witted, boisterous boob.[24]

In fact, Ranney said in the same article that people were still getting to see the Toby character, but that they were now watching him on television in the person of Milton Berle, the father of television comics. "Berle frequently borrows his [Toby's] characteristic red wig, freckles, and blackened-out front teeth."[25] He added, "Lou Costello has found a fortune playing him [Toby] in burlesque version. . . . Charlie Chaplin didn't wear the wig, but his wistful little man in the baggy pants is probably the most profound of Tobys."[26]

Ranney cited several from the ranks of the famous who began their careers in Toby shows:

> The late Jeanne Eagles got her start in show business with the old Dubinsky Brothers' tent out of Kansas City. Jennifer Jones, when she was Phyllis Iseley, played in Toby shows through the Texas Panhandle. Clark Gable, Wally Ford, Warner Baxter, and Charles Winniger all had seasons in Tent Rep.[27]

It was in 1954, after they had closed the season, that Peggy's mother, Nelle Meador, read with interest an advertisement in the Wichita Falls *Times and Record News* advertising an opening with the Post Office Department. In November, Rolland applied for the position. The post office needed men to work two months to deliver mail. Rolland had a veteran's preference, and he did well enough on the test to become a postman, so the post office hired Rolland. He liked the work, so when the tent show closed permanently, Rolland took the required civil service examination hoping that he could get on permanently with the post office. He became a full-time employee in the winter of 1955, and he kept that job until he retired from it in 1979, after the equivalent of twenty-five years of postal service.

"Even though business was not too bad when we closed at the end of the 1954 season in November, the advent of night-time high school football, television, and Lotta's death had taken its toll," Peggy recalled.[28]

Years of Decline, 1946-1954

Haver had always been a smart businessman. In 1954, the show tent would seat four hundred people. The show was still a viable business operation, but Haver talked over the situation with Rolland and Peggy. He told them he wanted them to quit while people still loved the show, not to quit because they had to. The Haverstock Comedians decided to close their tent at Peggy's hometown of Alvord, Texas, at the end of the season in November 1954. At towns along their route, the performances were billed as the final season for the show.

That final season drew lots of attention from media people along their route. A story in the Centralia, Illinois, newspaper, *The Sentinel*, nostalgically recalled how people felt about the Haverstock show and what was to be their final appearance in Centralia. An article by Pete Brown, entitled, "Tent Show Players, A Breath from the Past," related:

> "You say you played in the picture, *Birth of a Nation*?"
> "Tha's right. I sure did."
> "And what part did you play in *Birth of a Nation*?"
> "I went for the doctor."
>
> A breath of the sweet past has come to Walnut Hill for the last three nights. The Haverstock Company has relied on one tried and true formula to stay in business year after year: "Play for the entire family, and remember, small townspeople are not rubes."
>
> Sticking to this gentle principle, Toby and Susie have outlived all but four other touring shows in the entire country. . . .
>
> Inside, roughly half the folding chairs were filled with men, women, teenagers, and children waiting curtain time . . . to see *Sundown at Honeymoon Ranch*.
>
> The grape ice [snow cone] stand was doing good business. We got out tickets for thirty-eight cents for adults; fourteen cents for children. . . .
>
> He [Toby] said the Haverstock Company was so old, they can no longer buy the type plays they like, so they get what they can, then re-write them to suit their own folksy tastes. . . .
>
> Between the acts, Rolland entertains by painting a reverse picture behind a transparent glass. When he's through, he turns it over and flicks a yellow light on, revealing a beautiful picture of a ranch with purple hills in the distance. . . .
>
> The evening was one of the best spent we can remember in a long time. The humor was as refreshing as a draught of sarsaparilla. . . . The Haverstock players close-out tonight with another playlet, *Uncle Edward's Circus*. No animals, as Toby told the audience, because

Years of Decline, 1946–1954

there weren't enough children around Walnut Hill to water the elephants.[29]

Those words painted a true picture of what the show still meant to those who bade it the final good-bye later that year in Alvord, Texas.

After the show closed, the ensuing years for Haver were not particularly happy. He had no permanent home, no roots. The Haverstocks had been traveling people. He was happy enough when he stayed with Rolland and Peggy, but even there, he seemed lost without Lotta. He visited his brother-in-law, Herb Swift, in Colorado. He stayed on the road visiting friends as much as he could, but he tired of that. Wherever he went, he found little contentment. Old age encroached upon him. Near his final year, he would wander off and not be able to get back to his home. He never was harmful to others or himself, but he was lost in the past tent show glories, and neither the present nor the future really existed for him.

Finally in 1969, when he was past eighty-three, he went to live in a retirement care home. He died just two weeks short of his eighty-fourth birthday, on February 7, 1970. His funeral service was held at the 23rd and Grace Church of Christ, in Wichita Falls, Texas, and the family buried him beside his beloved Lotta, his Susie, in Crestview Memorial Cemetery.[30] Because of bad weather, very few of the old show folks were able to attend his service.

Rolland and Peggy carved a new life for themselves after the show closed. Rolland loved his new work with the postal system. He had made dozens of new friends as he worked the special delivery route in the Wichita Falls Post Office. His postal peers elected Rolland the secretary for the local unit of the National Association of Letter Carriers, Branch 1227. He served in that office for fifteen years. He also served on the board of directors for the Postal Credit Union in Wichita Falls for twenty-two years. Rolland and Peggy had mementos all around their home of their days with Tent Rep. The mementos gave them many nostalgic moments, but they truly loved their new, more sedentary life on Fillmore Street.

Rolland and Peggy still traveled some. During Rolland's times off, they took vacations every time they could. They traveled some with Rowe (Peggy's brother who had traveled with the show in the 1930s and 1940s) and Margie Meador and enjoyed that fellowship. Rolland still loved baseball, and whenever he could, he would watch a game on television. He loved it better live, though, so he and Peggy frequently traveled to the

Astrodome to watch the Houston team in action. He liked the Rangers in Arlington, Texas, and he and Peggy missed few of their home games.[31] Rolland was also an ardent golfer. He tried to teach the game to Peggy, but she begged off, thinking that Rolland needed time to relax away from her. The times on the road had offered them a great deal of time together. Peggy often did not have the same hours off from her work as Rolland did. She worked for ten years at the Marchman Hotel as the hotel's coffee shop hostess and cashier. She also worked for seven more years as a clerk at the Patricia Shoppe, an exclusive shoe store in Wichita Falls. "I really didn't have to work for livelihood, but I had worked all our show years, and I just didn't think I'd feel content sitting at home," Peggy said.

Peggy became ill with a malignancy and had to have several intense treatments. The doctors were optimistic about the surgeries, though, and she was soon out of the hospital and able to resume a normal life as a housewife. She did not work for the public after that, but she attended meetings of the Postal Union with Rolland and always attended plays when Broadway touring companies stopped at the Wichita Falls Municipal Auditorium or at the State Fair Music Hall productions in Dallas.

Peggy and Rolland were also very active in their church life. They were members of the 23rd and Grace Church of Christ congregation. Rolland served communion each Sunday at their church-owned nursing home facility. Peggy volunteered weekly at the home. They involved themselves in that ministry and in taking some of their elderly neighbors to church services and on shopping trips.

Rolland retired from the post office in 1979. After that, he and Peggy traveled even more. They more often accompanied Rowe and Margie on their excursions, especially after Rowe retired from the University of North Texas (then North Texas State University) Marketing Department. Rolland enjoyed more and more hours of golfing after his retirement.

In fact, when he was taken ill with his fatal heart attack, Rolland was playing a round of golf at the Weeks Municipal Course in Wichita Falls. He died before arriving at the hospital, on October 29, 1980.[32] His funeral was two days later at the same church where his mother's and father's services had been held. Very few of the show folks were at this service. There were such a few left, and many who were still alive could not travel easily at their advanced ages. Hundreds of friends were present, however. Many had to stand outside the building. They came to comfort Peggy and to say their final farewells to Rolland. Those present were young and old. They were well and infirm. Rolland was a much-loved member of the entire community. Peggy chose for his bier a beautiful silver-gray coffin, and on it she laid one long-stemmed American Beauty rose. The single rose was symbolic of the one red rose that Rolland had given her on each of their forty-seven wedding anniversaries.

In 1975, when Texas Technological University in Lubbock, Texas, set up a Bicentennial project producing some Toby shows, Rolland and Peggy had gone as guests of the college for several interviews with Dr. Clifford Ashby of Tech's drama department. Ashby used the interviews as data for a book about a contemporary of the Haverstock Comedians, and perhaps their greatest area-wide business rival, Harley Sadler.[33] Ashby's Bicentennial effort was to get as much information gathered about the rapidly passing history of Tent Repertoire as he could. In connection with that effort and with a grant from the government, Tech produced a big tent show, *The Awakening of John Slater*, on their campus and in some other important Sadler route towns. The university also established a popular culture museum in the library on their campus.

After Rolland's death, Peggy contacted Tech and gave them most of the Haverstock Comedians' memorabilia to become a part of the museum's permanent display. In a brochure published by Tech, they list the Haverstock collection as having 3734 leaves and five rolls of microfilmed bits of theatrical history in word and pictures filed on the Haverstock shows in their Southwest collection. The university also has several of Rolland's magic pieces, Lotta's beaded gowns, the musical cowbells, Haver's trombone, and his band uniform from his Swift Circus days. These items periodically go on display in glass cases within the archives area of the university's museum.[34]

Dozens of people have interviewed Peggy for projects on Tent Rep history. She was readily accessible and had a wonderful memory of the touring days. As recently as December of 1991, she was among a small group of old-time performers who gathered in Granbury, Texas, to talk over tent show days and see a production of a rewrite of *The Awakening of John Slater* at Granbury Opera House. Magazines and newspaper journalists have interviewed her for nostalgia pieces. Several groups and individuals have made videotape series concerning the show for educational television. Judi Sprague, one of the drama students of Ashby at Texas Tech, in 1989 completed a dissertation on the Haverstock shows.[35]

In 1984, Peggy fell in her kitchen and broke her hip. After almost a year of staying in and being very careful, she was able to resume her regular routine. In 1991, she broke an ankle and had to wear a cast for some time, but soon overcame that situation. She gave up her volunteer work at the nursing home facility but goes there occasionally to visit friends. In November of 1992, she had major surgery, but came through it well. Until very recently, when she fell once again and injured her arm, she still enjoyed having several friends ride to church with her. Except for the last few months of therapy, which required her to stay in a nursing care facility, she visited almost daily with her elder brother, James, who lives in Wichita Falls. She also enjoyed trips to visit her brother, Rowe, and his wife Margie in the Dallas area. Among her kin, she has two nieces and their families whom she sees regularly, and especially on holidays. In 1995, Peggy entered a nursing facility near Plano, Texas.

In my last visit with her, Peggy told of her life:

> Until just very recently, when a good tour came up, or when Rowe and Margie invited me to go on a trip with them, about all I had to do was ask how long I had to pack my bags. I still knew how to travel lightly from those days of packing during the show season. I don't get to travel much now, but I still enjoy life. I enjoy my wonderful memories. My home is still crowded with personal memorabilia, and I love it all. I have marked it all and listed each piece in a book as to whom it should go when I am finished with it. Even though he has been gone from me for really a short time, I still miss Rolland, of course, but I will always do that. We had a beautiful, full life together.[36]

Today Tent Repertoire is virtually gone from the American scene. There is just a fragmentary amount of activity for Tent Rep people except perhaps at meetings such as their annual convention in Mount Pleasant, Iowa, each year in April where society members read prepared papers on the various Tent Rep troupes or on the kinds of entertainments they did. Every once in a while, someone does a nostalgic presentation on the memories of the Tent Rep past in an article for a newspaper or a magazine. Occasionally, there will be a new book on one of the companies that traveled through the good times, and often about as rarely there will be a production of an old Tent Rep play. Through reading these occasional stories and perhaps seeing one of these Tent Repertoire plays re-created on stage, one can see how a group might easily develop such a motto as "the show with a million friends," as the Haverstock Comedians did.

Notes

Glossary

Bibliography

Index

Notes

Preface

1. George Carmack, "Entertaining Texans Under the Big Top," *The News* (San Antonio, TX), June 11, 1981, p. 4-e.
2. George Carmack, "Entertaining Texans," p. 4-e.
3. Barney McDaniels, Telephone interview, Ada, OK, June 6, 1992, notes. Author's personal collection.
4. Barney McDaniels, Interview, June 6, 1992.
5. E. N. Collins, Letterhead: "Liberty Theater and Garden Airdome," Sept. 22, 1919, Electra, TX.
6. Charles D. Rhea, Letterhead: "Leads and Directs; Large Repertoire of Small Cast Bills," Sept. 17, 1917, Faye, OK, address, unpublished letter. Author's personal collection.
7. Dale Madden, Telephone interview, Ada, OK, July 14, 1992, notes. Author's personal collection.
8. Howard King, Telephone interview, Ada, OK, July 14, 1992, notes. Author's personal collection.
9. William L. Slout, Telephone interview, Ada, OK, Apr. 7, 1992, notes. Author's personal collection.
10. Caroline Schaffner, Personal interview, Mount Pleasant, IA, Aug. 6, 1992, notes. Author's personal collection.
11. Peggy Haverstock, Personal letter, Wichita Falls, TX, Apr. 10, 1992. Author's personal collection.
12. Peggy Haverstock, Telephone interview, Ada, OK, Apr. 12, 1992, notes. Author's personal collection.

1. Tent Repertoire's Place in Rural American Culture

1. W. L. Slout, *Theater in a Tent: The Development of a Provincial Entertainment* (Bowling Green, OH: Bowling Green Univ. Popular Press, 1972), p. x.
2. Slout, *Theater in a Tent*, p. 22.

3. Slout, *Theater in a Tent*, p. 14.
4. Slout, *Theater in a Tent*, p. 20.
5. Slout, *Theater in a Tent*, p. 23.
6. Slout, *Theater in a Tent*, p. 27.
7. Slout, *Theater in a Tent*, p. 39.
8. Bess Browning Pearce, *Unto a Land* (San Antonio, TX: Naylor, 1968), p. 203.
9. *Billboard*, "Tent Drama," May 27, 1910, p. 6.
10. *Billboard*, "Tent Repertoire Pages," May 29, 1930, p. 30.
11. *Billboard*, "Tent Repertoire Pages," Apr. 12, 1930, p. 32.
12. *Billboard*, "Tent Repertoire Pages," Apr. 12, 1930, p. 32.
13. *Billboard*, "Tent Repertoire Pages," Apr. 12, 1930, p. 32.
14. Cornelia Otis Skinner, *Madame Sarah* (New York: Dell, 1966), p. 288.
15. Skinner, *Madame Sarah*, p. 290.
16. Slout, *Theater in a Tent*, p. 73.
17. Neil Schaffner, with Vance Johnson, *The Fabulous Toby and Me* (Englewood Cliffs, NJ: Prentice-Hall, 1968), p. 5.
18. Schaffner, *Fabulous Toby*, p. 5.
19. Schaffner, *Fabulous Toby*, p. 5.
20. Schaffner, *Fabulous Toby*, p. 5.
21. *Billboard*, "Tent Repertoire Pages," July 25, 1942.
22. Deloris Dorn-Heft, "The Twilight of a Tradition." *Theater Arts*, Aug. 1958, pp. 52, 58, 80.
23. Virginia Sheets, "It's Still Show Time for Toby and Susie." *Des Moines (IA) Sunday Register*, Mar. 16, 1975, pp. 6–9.
24. Charles McRaven, "Toby Show." Brochure for Branson, MO, Wilderness Settlement, 1981.
25. Paula Dittrick, "Ex-Tent Show Troupers Won't Let the World Forget." *Houston Chronicle*, Nov. 9, 1983, Southwest Section, p. 1.
26. "Grandfield Residents Revive 1912 Tent Show Tradition," *Texas Letter Carrier*, June 1973, p. 12.
27. "Depot Seeks National Register Status," *Big Pasture News* (Grandfield, OK), Aug. 1996, p. 1.
28. Program. "Too Poor to Paint—Too Proud to Whitewash," an adaptation of *The Awakening of John Slater*," Granbury Opera House, Granbury, TX, Jo Ann Miller, director, Nov. 8–Dec. 1, 1991. Special program honoring many of the old-time Toby Show players at Matinee, Nov. 30, 1991. Peggy Haverstock and her brother, Rowe Meador, as well as Dale Madden, a member of the Haverstock cast in the 1950s after Lotta's death, were all present at the special show and were recognized and allowed to speak of nostalgic memories.

2. Harvey and Carlotta Haverstock Before Tent Repertoire

1. Truett Wilson, "They Kept 'Show on the Road' for Nearly 50 Years," *Wichita Falls (TX) Times*, Mar. 12, 1961.
2. Harvey C. Haverstock, Diaries, 1893–1970, unpublished, undated. Author's personal collection.

3. Harvey C. Haverstock, Diaries, 1893–1970.
4. Harvey C. Haverstock, Diaries, 1893–1970.
5. Wilson, "They Kept 'Show on the Road.' "
6. Harvey C. Haverstock, Diaries, 1893–1970.
7. Contract dated Apr. 20, 1903, signed H. Swift, unpublished. Author's personal collection.
8. Harvey C. Haverstock, Diaries, 1893–1970.
9. Neil Schaffner, with Vance Johnson, *The Fabulous Toby and Me* (Englewood Cliffs, NJ: Prentice-Hall, 1968).
10. Harvey C. Haverstock, Diaries, 1893–1970.
11. Harvey C. Haverstock, Diaries, 1893–1970.
12. Harvey C. Haverstock, Diaries, 1893–1970.
13. Advertisement from St. Louis World's Fair, Swift and Mosher, "The Maid and the Dummy," 1903. Author's personal collection.
14. Harvey C. Haverstock, Diaries, 1893–1970.
15. Original photographs for the two *Uncle Tom* shows; 1893 photograph has names of all cast members listed on reverse of photograph. Among those listed are Daisy Mosher, Lizzie (Elizabeth) Mosher, Mrs. Nina Mosher, and Little Carlotta. Author's personal collection.
16. Trudi Perkins, "Grandfield Residents Revive 1912 Tent Show Traditions." *Frederick (OK) Daily Leader*, May 6, 1973, p. 8.
17. Kathleen J. Sprague, "The Haverstock Family Tent Show," Ph.D. Diss., Texas Tech Univ., 1989, discusses this story and notes that Robert Windeler confirms in his book, *Sweetheart: The Story of Mary Pickford* (New York: Praeger Publishers, 1974), p. 30, that Pickford was playing Little Eva during the 1890s, p. 21.
18. John Clark, "Haverstock Brought Fun to Town," *Wichita Falls (TX) Times*, Feb. 29, 1976.
19. Harvey C. Haverstock, Diaries, 1893–1970.

3. Haverstocks Found Their Tent Show

1. *Chicago Herald Tribune* (Obituary Section) Dec. 19, 1952.
2. Swift Brothers Advertisement, dated 1907. Author's personal collection.
3. Dave Allred, "Early Tent Show Star, Owner Dies," *Wichita Falls (TX) Times*, Feb. 8, 1970, pp. 1, 2.
4. John Clark, "Haverstock Brought Fun to Town," *Wichita Falls (TX) Times*, Feb. 29, 1976.
5. Glen Shelton, "Fate Launched Haverstock Shows on a 35-Year Run," *Wichita Falls (TX) Times*, May 3, 1964.
6. Olga Bailey, *Mollie Bailey: The Circus Queen of the Southwest* (Dallas: Thomas, 1943), p. 184.
7. Tanner Laine, "Visiting Couple Talk of Tent Show Days," Texas Tech College Newspaper, circa. 1976, Title page along with date and page number not on photocopy. Author's personal collection.
8. Harvey C. Haverstock, Diaries, 1893–1970, unpublished, undated. Author's personal collection.
9. Harvey C. Haverstock, Diaries, 1893–1970.

10. Truett Wilson, "They Kept 'Show on the Road' for Nearly 50 Years," *Wichita Falls (TX) Times*, Mar. 12, 1961.

4. THE EARLY YEARS, 1911–1919

1. Bess Browning Pearce, *Unto a Land* (San Antonio, TX: Naylor, 1968), p. 203.
2. Rolland Haverstock, Interview, Nov. 14, 1972, Wichita Falls, TX, audiotape. Author's personal collection.
3. F. G. Patterson, "Toby and Susie Coming," *Grandfield (OK) Enterprise*, undated, from Haverstock scrapbook. Author's personal collection.
4. Harvey C. Haverstock, Diaries, 1893–1970, unpublished, undated. Author's personal collection.
5. Harvey C. Haverstock, Diaries, 1893–1970.
6. Harvey C. Haverstock, Diaries, 1893–1970.
7. Photograph of Pullman cars with slogan painted on the side, dated circa 1915. Author's personal collection.
8. Harvey C. Haverstock, Diaries, 1893–1970.
9. Harvey C. Haverstock, Diaries, 1893–1970.
10. Harvey C. Haverstock, Diaries, 1893–1970.
11. Trudi Perkins, "Grandfield Residents Revive 1912 Tent Show Traditions," *Frederick (OK) Daily Leader*, May 6, 1973, p. 8.
12. Harvey C. Haverstock, Diaries, 1893–1970.
13. Charles D. Rhea, Letterhead: "Leads and Directs; Large Repertoire of Small Cast Bills," Sept. 17, 1917, Faye, OK address, unpublished letter. Author's personal collection.
14. Dr. Charles Cromwell, Elkhart, TX, Dec. 23, 1917, unpublished letter. Author's personal collection.
15. J. F. Pennington, Cherryvale, KS, Jan. 19, 1919, unpublished letter. Author's personal collection.
16. Harvey C. Haverstock, Diaries, 1893–1970.
17. Ned Albert, *Lena Rivers* acting script (New York: French, 1941).
18. Harvey C. Haverstock, Diaries, 1893–1970.
19. Harvey C. Haverstock, Diaries, 1893–1970.
20. E. N. Collins, Letterhead: "Liberty Theater and Garden Airdome," Sept. 22, 1919, Electra, TX. Author's personal collection.
21. Clair F. Sleet, Osage, IA, Jan. 30, 1921, unpublished letter. Author's personal collection.
22. Minnie King Benton, *Boomtown: A Portrait of Burkburnett* (Wichita Falls, TX: Nortex, 1972), p. 15.

5. THE GOOD YEARS, 1920–1929

1. Sterling S. Roddy, Interview, Grandfield, OK, undated notes. Author's personal collection.
2. Harvey C. Haverstock, Diaries, 1893–1970, unpublished, undated. Author's personal collection.
3. Harvey C. Haverstock, Diaries, 1893–1970.

4. Minnie King Benton, *Boomtown: A Portrait of Burkburnett* (Wichita Falls, TX: Nortex, 1972), p. 15.
5. F. A. Fowler, Letterhead: "Fulton Bag and Cotton Mills," Dallas, TX, July 25, 1929, unpublished letter. Author's personal collection.
6. Herb Walters, with V. E. Lowry, *Fifty Years Under Canvas* (Hugo, OK: Achme, 1962), p. 68.
7. Joe Alex Morris, "Corniest Show on the Road," *The Saturday Evening Post*, Sept. 17, 1955, p. 61.
8. Jere C. Mickel, *Footlights on the Prairie* (St. Cloud, MN: North Star, 1974), p. 24.
9. Jimmy Jones, "Haverstock Script Brings Memories," *Kiowa County Democrat* (Snyder, OK), Dec. 18, 1975), p. 1.
10. Jones, "Haverstock Script Brings Memories."
11. Rolland Haverstock, Interview, Nov. 14, 1974, Wichita Falls, TX, audiotape. Author's personal collection.
12. Joseph Kaye, "Drama under the Big Top," *Theater Magazine*, Mar. 1930, p. 31.
13. Kaye, "Drama under the Big Top."
14. Rolland Haverstock, Interview, 1974.
15. W. B. Lane, Nov. 8, 1921, Celina, TX, unpublished letter. Author's personal collection.
16. Lane, Letter, 1921.
17. Jack Maxwell, May 11, 1923, Arlington, TX, unpublished letter. Author's personal collection.
18. Don Melrose, Feb. 7, 1925, Wewoka, OK, unpublished letter. Author's personal collection.
19. Melrose, Letter, 1925.
20. M. A. Moseley, Letterhead: "The Ray Howell Players," Apr. 16, 1926, Minco, OK, unpublished letter. Author's personal collection.
21. Moseley, Letter, 1926.
22. Moseley, Letter, 1926.
23. Moseley, Letter, 1926.
24. Lillie Cavitte, Letterhead: "Doc Holland's American Amusement Enterprises," June 3, 1926, Fort Worth, TX, unpublished letter. Author's personal collection.
25. George J. Crawley, Sept. 10, 1927, Clarksville, TX, unpublished letter. Author's personal collection.
26. Harry A. Huguenot, Letterhead: "Tent Repertoire Managers Protective Association of America, Inc." (TRMPAA), Oct. 2, 1928, Dixie, LA, unpublished letter. Author's personal collection.
27. Huguenot, Letter, 1928.
28. Roe Nero, Jan. 28, 1929, Rome, NY, unpublished letter. Author's personal collection.
29. Edward, Feb. 17, 1929, undetermined last name or place of origination, unpublished letter. Author's personal collection.
30. Edward, Letter, 1929.
31. Sadler baseball advertisement noting on it, "Haverstock, the kid wonder who is under option to a Major league club will play with Carnegie, Sunday, August 8," circa 1928. Author's personal collection.

32. Arthur L. Fanshawe, Cincinnati, OH, May 31, 1929, unpublished letter. Author's personal collection.

33. Rolland Haverstock, Interview, 1974.

6. The Lean Years, 1930–1939

1. Rich Richeson, Letterhead: "Salina Musicians Ass'n, Local No. 207," Nov. 23, 1929, Salina, KS, unpublished letter. Author's personal collection.

2. Confirmed by a conversation with Salina City Library, July 12, 1992. Construction was completed in 1931.

3. Larry Eckholt, "Theater Comes to Iowa," *Des Moines Sunday Register*, Mar. 16, 1975, p. 6.

4. Eckholt, "Theater Comes to Iowa," p. 6.

5. Rolland Haverstock, Interview, 1974.

6. Eckholt, "Theater Comes to Iowa," p. 7.

7. *Billboard*, "Tent Repertoire Pages," Apr. 12, 1930, p. 32.

8. *Billboard*, "Tent Repertoire Pages," June 28, 1930, p. 30.

9. *Billboard*, "Tent Repertoire Pages," June 14, 1930, p. 30

10. *Billboard*, "Tent Repertoire Pages," Mar. 30, 1930, p. 30.

11. Rolland Haverstock, Interview, Mar. 10, 1973, Wichita Falls, TX, notes. Author's personal collection.

12. *Billboard*, "Tent Repertoire Pages," Feb. 21, 1931, p. 26.

13. Gilford Miracle, Interview, Dec. 12, 1975, Grandfield, OK, notes. Author's personal collection.

14. Rolland Haverstock, Interview, 1973.

15. *Billboard*, "Tent Repertoire Pages," May 7, 1932, p. 26.

16. Peggy Haverstock, Interview, Mar. 12, 1984, Wichita Falls, TX, notes. Author's personal collection.

17. Peggy Haverstock, Interview, 1984.

18. Peggy Haverstock, Interview, 1984.

19. Peggy Haverstock, Interview, 1984.

20. Peggy Haverstock, Interview, July 7, 1988, Wichita Falls, TX, notes. Author's personal collection.

21. Peggy Haverstock, Interview, 1988.

22. Peggy Haverstock, Interview, 1988.

23. Peggy Haverstock, Interview, 1988.

24. Peggy Haverstock, Interview, 1988.

25. Peggy Haverstock, Interview, 1988.

26. Peggy Haverstock, Interview, 1988.

27. Peggy Haverstock, Interview, 1988.

28. Peggy Haverstock, Interview, 1984.

29. There is no extant copy of this play. The material relative to it is from Haver's route book where he kept a list of plays for each year.

30. *Billboard*, "Tent Repertoire Pages," Mar. 28, 1931, p. 43.

31. Peggy Haverstock, Interview, 1988.

32. Della Ilee Isbell, Letter, undated (but soon after Peggy joined the company in 1933), unpublished. Author's personal collection.

33. Bess Camble, Dothan, AL, Mar. 7, 1933, unpublished letter. Author's personal collection.

34. Bess Camble, Old Hickory, TN, June 17, 1933, unpublished letter. Author's personal collection.
35. William Sachs, Letterhead: "The Billboard," Cincinnati, OH, Jan. 20, 1930, unpublished letter. Author's personal collection.
36. Alyce Lester, Fort Worth, TX, Apr. 18, 1930, unpublished letter. Author's personal collection.
37. Harry Hearn, Spearman, TX, Aug. 30, 1930, unpublished letter. Author's personal collection.
38. Audie Chapman, Letterhead: "Elmer-Hess Public Schools," Elmer, OK, Nov. 26, 1937, unpublished letter. Author's personal collection.

7. THE WAR YEARS, 1939–1945

1. Robert Glick, Interview, Norman, OK, Mar. 1, 1988, notes. Author's personal collection.
2. Peggy Haverstock, Interview, 1984.
3. Joseph Davenport, Telephone interview, Ada, OK, Aug. 3, 1992, notes. Author's personal collection.
4. Barney McDaniels, Telephone interview, Ada, OK, Aug. 3, 1992, notes. Author's personal collection.
5. Peggy Haverstock, Interview, 1984.
6. *Billboard*, "Rep Ripples," Aug. 22, 1942, p. 27.
7. Clifford Ashby and Suzanne DePauw May, *Trooping Through Texas: Harley Sadler and His Tent Show* (Bowling Green, OH: Bowling Green Univ. Popular Press, 1982), p. 151.
8. Harvey C. Haverstock, Diaries, 1893–1970, unpublished, undated. Author's personal collection.
9. Peggy Haverstock, Interview, 1984.
10. Harvey C. Haverstock, Route Book lists, 1929–1954, unpublished. Author's personal collection.
11. Peggy Haverstock, Interview, 1984.
12. Peggy Haverstock, Interview, 1984.
13. Peggy Haverstock, Interview, 1984.
14. Peggy Haverstock, Interview, 1984.
15. Don Melrose, Kansas City, MO, Feb. 10, 1940, unpublished letter. Author's personal collection.
16. Melrose, Letter, 1940.
17. Ramblin' Ray Cox, Letterhead: "Paducah Broadcasting Company," Hopkinsville, KY, June 23, 1940, unpublished letter. Author's personal collection.
18. Kenneth Wayne, Letterhead: "Wayne's Theatrical Agency," Kansas City, MO, Oct. 29, 1940, unpublished letter. Author's personal collection.
19. Jack Collier, Letterhead: "The Collier Players," Noble, IL, Aug. 23, 1941, unpublished letter. Author's personal collection.
20. Charles J. Grassold, Letterhead: "The Herrick Bulletin," Herrick, IL, May 17, 1942, unpublished letter. Author's personal collection.
21. Robert Duffy, Letterhead: "Oklahoma State Penitentiary," McAlester, OK, Apr. 10, 1943, unpublished letter. Author's personal collection.
22. Peggy Haverstock, Interview, 1984.

23. Harvey C. Haverstock, Diaries, 1893–1970, unpublished, undated. Author's personal collection.
24. Peggy Haverstock, Interview, 1984.

8. The Years of Decline, 1946–1954

1. William Lawrence Slout, *Theater in a Tent: The Development of a Provincial Entertainment* (Bowling Green, OH: Bowling Green Univ. Popular Press, 1972).
2. William Lawrence Slout, Letterhead: "*San Francisco Chronicle*," San Francisco, CA, Oct. 4, 1948, unpublished letter. Author's personal collection.
3. Harvey C. Haverstock, Route Book lists, 1929–1954, unpublished. Author's personal collection.
4. Marian McKennon, Advertisement for actors and specialties., *Billboard*, Apr. 6, 1946.
5. Harvey C. Haverstock, Route Book lists, 1929–1954.
6. Harvey C. Haverstock, Route Book lists, 1929–1954.
7. Harvey C. Haverstock, "What Is It All About?" unpublished monologue, 1946. Author's personal collection.
8. Harvey C. Haverstock, Route Book lists, 1929–1954.
9. Rowe Meador, Garland, TX, 1986, unpublished letter. Author's personal collection.
10. Peggy Haverstock, Interview, Mar. 12, 1984, Wichita Falls, TX, notes. Author's personal collection.
11. Rolland Haverstock, Interview, Mar. 10, 1973, Wichita Falls, TX, audiotape. Author's personal collection.
12. Harvey C. Haverstock, Route Book lists, 1929–1954.
13. Harvey C. Haverstock, Route Book lists, 1929–1954.
14. Harvey C. Haverstock, Route Book lists, 1929–1954.
15. Harvey C. Haverstock, Route Book lists, 1929–1954.
16. Harvey C. Haverstock, Route Book lists, 1929–1954.
17. Robert Lee Wyatt III, *Grandfield: Hub of the Big Pasture, II* (Marceline, MO: Walsworth, 1975), p. 408.
18. Wyatt, *Grandfield*, p. 361.
19. Peggy Haverstock, Interview, 1984.
20. Peggy Haverstock, Interview, 1984.
21. Dale Madden, Telephone interview, Ada, OK, Aug. 3, 1992, notes. Author's personal collection.
22. Madden, Interview, 1992.
23. Peggy Haverstock, Interview, 1984.
24. Omar Ranney, "Forever Toby," *Theater Arts*, Aug. 1953, p. 8.
25. Ranney, "Forever Toby," p. 9.
26. Ranney, "Forever Toby," p. 9.
27. Ranney, "Forever Toby," p. 9.
28. Peggy Haverstock, Interview, 1984.
29. Pete Brown, "Tent Show Players, A Breath from the Past, Perform at Walnut Hill," *Centralia (IL) Sentinel*, June 7, 1952, p. 1.
30. Dave Allred, "Early Tent Show Star, Owner Dies," *Wichita Falls (TX) Times*, Feb. 8, 1970, p. 1.
31. Peggy Haverstock, Interview, 1984.

32. "Rolland Haverstock," Obituary, *Wichita Falls (TX) Times*, Oct. 20, 1980. p. 2.

33. Clifford Ashby and Suzanne DePauw May, *Trooping Through Texas: Harley Sadler and His Tent Show* (Bowling Green, OH: Bowling Green Univ. Popular Press, 1982).

34. Cindy L. Martin and Rebecca J. Herring, "Music and Entertainment: Bibliography of Collections in Southwest Collection, Texas Tech University," Lubbock, TX, Oct. 1983. (Haverstock Collection noted on page 3.)

35. Kathleen Judith Sprague, "The Haverstock Family Tent Show," Ph.D. diss., Texas Tech University, 1989.

36. Peggy Haverstock, Interview, 1984.

Glossary

For one to understand fully about Tent Repertoire, I offer this small glossary of terms unique to that genre of theater.

Airdome: an open-air theater surrounded by some kind of wall, either of canvas, metal, wood, or mounded earth, in which live theatrics or films were presented.
Bally: show-talk expression for advertising.
Bill: the show piece to be played by the acting troupe.
Blues: bleachers made of wood and painted blue to designate them as general-admission seats. These seats were usually the back rows or the side areas of the tent.
Candy pitch: the sale (pitch) of the candy boxes with prizes and a few pieces of salt-water taffy candy in them. These pitches were made during the intermissions and provided the owner, the concessionaires, and the cast a chance to earn extra money.
Canvasmen: crew members who were in charge of setting up the tent and getting the stage, the lights, and the audience seats ready for the show. They usually loaded and unloaded the materials for the show and were often the drivers of the trucks used to transport the show. They usually slept in the tents to protect them against intruders and the curious.
Circle stock: a circle of towns around a home base that provided theaters in which actors and troupes could try out the shows they were rehearsing to take on the road during the regular summer season. This gave employment to the acting companies for the winter months during which the tents could not be kept warm enough to perform in. The troupe could play in a given part of the circle for from one day to a week, providing a small theater with a repertory of different plays.
Concert: a short musical set played for audience entertainment or a short (often one-act) play performed after the evening's main attraction. Those who attended the concert play paid an additional ticket rate causing the theater owners and tent owners to earn a better gate for that evening in which concerts were played.
Doubling: this could be a doubling in brass or a doubling in canvas. One of the workmen could do two different jobs, and tent show owners sought people

GLOSSARY

who could double, requiring them to hire fewer people to complete their companies.

Dramatic end: the end of the tent in which the poles to hold up the big top were arranged to give a full view of the stage. Each Tent Repertoire entrepreneur claimed the distinction of having designed the perfect dramatic end tent. Haver claimed that he designed several dramatic ends, each progressively giving more viewing range for his audiences.

Dray: a wagon used to haul heavy cargo, often tent show companies, from a railhead to an area to which the rail lines did not travel. It was a large wagon pulled by several mules or horses. It sometimes took several dray wagons to haul the entire company setup.

Gate: the receipts from ticket sales on a given evening.

Grouch bag: a small leather or cloth bag on a drawstring worn around the neck or pinned to the undergarment of the actor. Actors kept their money and other valuables in their grouch bags to keep them from possibly being stolen while the actor performed on-stage.

G-string: a comedic part wherein an actor dons a beard or a goatee which is held in place by a string (hence the name). It usually refers specifically to the part of the wise sage in the script who would have a beard to denote his age.

Heavy: the character who is the serious role or the villainous role. It is designated as to gender as in *male heavy* or *female heavy*.

House: the audience or the theater itself. One could determine gate receipts by counting the house.

Ingenue: a young, sweet, and innocent woman. The show often revolved around this character's needs.

Lead: the role that stands out as the leading character in the script. Usually, the role is designated as to its gender, as *male lead* or *female lead*.

Nut: the amount of money required by a company to meet its expenses for the evening's performance, its operating expense.

Olio: the official name of the masking curtain pulled or dropped to hide the main stage for a change of scenes. Since that curtain is pulled or dropped, vaudevillians often performed an act while new sets were gotten ready, and the act became known as an *olio*. The acts were performed to hide the sounds of the set rearrangement going on behind the olio curtains. The acts are often called *olio acts* or merely *olios*.

Opera house: a theater, usually found in small towns, in which traveling troupes performed. It is often a flat-floored, large room on the second story of another business.

Possum belly: a receptacle built onto the bottom of a baggage car for storage of extra equipment needed by a theatrical troupe.

Reds: the chair-type seating that was set up on the main floor of the tent and was sold as reserved. These seats cost the viewer ten cents extra, often a real luxury, especially during the days of the Great Depression.

Repertoire: a series of plays presented in repertory fashion. This is the spelling designated for tent-show repertoire groups. Casts in a repertoire group usually consisted of three women and five men. Casts were later reduced to two and three to cut back on costs during hard times. These casts often played a different show each night for a five-night run. Repertoire is synonymous with Tent Rep.

Soubrette: the female foil or straight character, off which the comedian plays his

GLOSSARY

sarcastic or ironic humor. The soubrette was often called Susie in the old-time Toby shows. Caroline Schaffner and Lotta Haverstock had predominant Susie roles, taken from the old Sis Hopkins-type comedic character.

Susie: The soubrette, often the rural counterpart of the Toby character.

Toby: The silly kid, country-bumpkin-type character whose antics kept the audience in laughter and who often saved the day by his antics. Harvey Haverstock and Neil Schaffner were early Toby character actors, but Fred Wilson is most often credited with originating the role for Tent Repertoire.

Towners: those inhabitants of towns along the Tent Repertoire routes. A term used by show people to separate themselves from the people who dwelled in a community. Some companies called the locals hicks and rubes but did not necessarily mean these as derogatory terms.

Troupers: Those people who acted in or worked for a theatrical troupe.

Bibliography

Interviews

Davenport, Joseph. Telephone interview, Ada, OK, Aug. 3, 1992, with author.
Glick, Robert. Norman, OK, Mar. 1, 1988, with author.
Haverstock, Peggy. Wichita Falls, TX, Mar. 12, 1984, with author.
———. Wichita Falls, TX, July 7, 1988, with author.
———. Telephone interview, Ada, OK, Apr. 12, 1992, with author.
Haverstock, Rolland. Wichita Falls, TX, Mar. 10, 1973, with author.
———. Wichita Falls, TX, Nov. 14, 1974, with author.
Hill, Audrey. Conversation while setting up first Grandfield production, 1973.
King, Howard. Telephone interview, Ada, OK, July 14, 1992, with author.
McDaniels, Barney. Telephone interview, Ada, OK, June 6, 1992, with author.
———. Telephone interview, Ada, OK, Aug. 3, 1992, with author.
Madden, Dale. Telephone interview, Ada, OK, July 14, 1992, with author.
———. Telephone interview, Ada, OK, Aug. 3, 1992, with author.
Miracle, Gilford. Grandfield, OK, Dec. 12, 1975, with author.
Roddy, Sterling S. Grandfield, OK, undated, with author.
Schaffner, Caroline. Interview, Mt. Pleasant, IA, Aug. 6, 1992, with author.
Slout, William L. Telephone interview, Ada, OK, Apr. 7, 1992, with author.

Unpublished Materials

Edwards, Lee. "Adjudicator's Comments." Oklahoma Community Theater Association Festival, Mar. 8, 1975. Audiotape in author's collection.
"Expense List" for *Trail of the Lonesome Pine* at Altus, OK, Oct., 1975.
Haverstock, Harvey C. Diaries, 1893–1970. Author's collection.
———. Route Books lists, 1929–1954. Author's collection.
Melrose, Don. *Dead Man's Letter*, a three-act play, ca. 1920.
———. *Sweet Papa Toby*, a three-act play, ca. 1925.
———. *Toby from Arkansas*, a three-act play, ca. 1940.
Schaffner, Neil. *Toby Goes to Washington*, a three-act play, ca. 1943.
———. *Trail of the Lonesome Pine*, a three-act play, ca. 1925.

Bibliography

Books

Albert, Ned. *Lena Rivers*. New York: Samuel French, 1941.
Ashby, Clifford, and Suzanne DePauw May, *Trooping Through Texas: Harley Sadler and His Tent Show*. Bowling Green, OH: Bowling Green Univ. Popular Press, 1982.
Bailey, Olga. *Mollie Bailey: The Circus Queen of the Southwest*. Dallas: Thomas, 1943.
Benton, Minnie King. *Boomtown: A Portrait of Burkburnett*. Wichita Falls, TX: Nortex, 1972.
Blum, Daniel. *A Pictorial History of American Theater, 1900–1950*. New York: Greenwood, 1950.
Calkins, Ernest Elmo. *They Broke the Prairie*. New York: Scribner's, 1937.
Churchill, Allen. *The Theatrical Twenties*. New York: McGraw-Hill, 1975.
Downer, Alan S. *Fifty Years of American Drama*. Chicago: Regnery, 1951.
Fox, John, Jr. *Trail of the Lonesome Pine*. New York: Scribner, 1908.
Gallegly, Joseph. *Footlights on the Border*. The Hague: Mouton, 1962.
Hall, Stuart, and Paddy Whannel. *The Popular Arts*. New York: Pantheon, 1960.
Houghton, Norris. *Advance from Broadway*. New York: Harcourt, 1941.
Lewis, Phillip C. *Trouping: How the Show Came to Town*. New York: Harper, 1973.
Martin, Jerry L. *Henry L. Brunk and Brunk's Comedians: Tent Repertoire Empire of the Southwest*. Bowling Green, OH: Bowling Green Univ. Popular Press, 1984.
McKennon, Marian L. *Tent Show*. New York: Exposition, 1964.
Mickel, Jere C. *Footlights on the Prairie*. St. Cloud, MN: North Star, 1974.
Pearce, Bess Browning. *Unto a Land*. San Antonio, TX: Naylor, 1968.
Schaffner, Neil, with Vance Johnson. *The Fabulous Toby and Me*. Englewood Cliffs, NJ: Prentice-Hall, 1968.
Skinner, Cornelia Otis. *Madame Sarah*. New York: Dell, 1966.
Slout, William L. *Theater in a Tent: The Development of a Provincial Entertainment*. Bowling Green, OH: Bowling Green Univ. Popular Press, 1972.
Walters, Herb, with V. E. Lowry. *Fifty Years Under Canvas*. Hugo, OK: Achme, 1962.
Ware, Harlan, and James Prindle. *Rag Opera*. Indianapolis: Bobbs-Merrill, 1929.
Wyatt, Robert Lee, III. *Grandfield: Hub of the Big Pasture, I*. Marceline, MO: Walsworth, 1974.
———. *Grandfield: Hub of the Big Pasture, II*. Marceline, MO: Walsworth, 1975.

Articles from Newspapers, Magazines, and Journals

Allred, Dave. "Early Tent Show Star, Owner Dies." *Wichita Falls (TX) Times*, Feb. 8, 1970, pp. 1, 2.
Bicd, Dan. "Toby and Susies Aren't About to Fold Their Tent." *Hawkeye Gazette* (Burlington, IA), Sept. 28, 1958.
Billboard. 1896–1964.
Bill Bruno's Bulletin. 1928–30, 1935–42.

Bibliography

Brown, Pete. "Tent Show Players, A Breath from the Past, Perform at Walnut Hill." *Centralia (IL) Sentinel*, June 7, 1952, p. 1.
Carmack, George. "Entertaining Texans Under the Big Top." *The News* (San Antonio, TX), June 11, 1981.
Chicago Herald Tribune. "Obituary Section," Dec. 19, 1952.
Clark, John. "Haverstock Brought Fun to Town." *Wichita Falls (TX) Times*, Feb. 29, 1976.
Crawford, Bill. "Grandfield Takes 'Tent Show' to Washington: Toby and Susie at Capital?" *Lawton (OK) Morning Press and Constitution*, Feb. 8, 1976.
"Depot Seeks National Register Status." *Big Pasture News* (Grandfield, OK), Aug. 1996.
Dittrick, Paula. "Ex-Tent Show Troupers Won't Let the World Forget." *Houston Chronicle*, Nov. 9, 1983, Southwest Section, p. 1.
Dorn-Heft, Deloris. "The Twilight of a Tradition." *Theater Arts*, Aug. 1958, pp. 52, 58, 80.
Eckholt, Larry. "Theater Comes to Iowa." *Des Moines Sunday Register*, Mar. 16, 1975, p. 6.
Gillette, Don Carle. "Toby Thrives in the Tents." *New York Times*, Apr. 10, 1954, p. 3.
"Grandfield Players to Revive Tent Show Days in Production in Altus." *Lawton (OK) Morning Press and Constitution*, Oct. 15, 1975.
"Grandfield Residents Revive 1912 Tent Show Tradition." *Texas Letter Carrier*, June 1973, p. 12.
"Harvest Playhouse Slates Pair of 'Toby-Suzy' Plays." *Lawton (OK) Morning Press and Constitution*, Feb. 12, 1976, p. 2.
Jones, Jimmy. "Haverstock Script Brings Memories." *Kiowa County Democrat* (Snyder, OK), Dec. 18, 1975, p. 1.
Kaye, Joseph. "Drama under the Big Top." *Theater Magazine*, Mar. 1930, p. 31.
Laine, Tanner. "Visiting Couple Talk of Tent Show Days," *Texas Tech University Newspaper*, circa. 1976.
"Last Tent Show." *Variety*, Apr. 11, 1962.
Martin, Cindy L., and Rebecca J. Herring. "Music and Entertainment: Bibliography of Collections in Southwest Collection, Texas Tech University" (Lubbock, TX), Oct. 1983.
May, Earl Chaplin. "Our Canvas Broadway." *Country Gentleman*, May 1931, pp. 16, 17, 95.
McRaven, Charles. "Toby Show." Brochure for Branson, MO, Wilderness Settlement, 1981.
Morris, Joe Alex. "Corniest Show on the Road." *Saturday Evening Post*, Sept. 17, 1955, p. 61.
Neal, Clara. "Haverstock Show Returns to Roosevelt." *Daily Oklahoman* (Oklahoma City, OK), Dec. 18, 1975.
"Old Time Tent Show Slated." *Altus (OK) Times-Democrat*, Sept. 30, 1975, p. 1.
Patterson, F. G. "Toby and Susie Coming." *Grandfield (OK) Enterprise*, undated.
Perkins, Trudi. "Grandfield Residents Revive 1912 Tent Show Traditions." *Frederick (OK) Daily Leader*, May 6, 1973, p. 8.
Ranney, Omar. "Forever Toby." *Theater Arts*, Aug. 1953, p. 8.
Sharrock, Tom. "Choice of Harvest Playhouse for Event in D.C. Reinforced.: *Lawton (OK) Morning Press and Constitution*, Feb. 18, 1976, p. 1.

Bibliography

Sheets, Virginia. "It's Still Show Time for Toby and Susie." *Des Moines (IA) Sunday Register*, Mar. 16, 1975, pp. 6–9.

Shelton, Glenn. "Disaster Played Big Role in Haverstock Tent Shows." *Wichita Falls (TX) Times*, May 3, 1964, p. 1.

———. "Fate Launched Haverstock Shows on a 35 Year Run." *Wichita Falls (TX) Times*, May 31, 1964, p. 1.

———. "Haverstock Troupers, Audience Had Mutual Admiration Society." *Wichita Falls (TX) Times*, May 17, 1964, p. 1.

———. "Real Drama Took Place During Haverstock Shows." *Wichita Falls (TX) Times*, May 24, 1968.

"Toby Thrives in Tents." *New York Times*, Apr. 25, 1954, Section II, p. 3.

"Too Poor to Paint—Too Proud to Whitewash." Granbury (TX) Opera House Program. Nov.–Dec. 1991.

Triplett, William. "David Tent Show vs. Goliath Picture Trust." *Equity*, Sept. 1930, pp. 24, 26, 28.

Wallace, Irving. "Everybody Loves a Tent Show." *Service*, Apr. 1965, p. 19.

Warman, Lisa. "As Actor or Mailman, He Believes in Delivery." *Wichita Falls (TX) Times*, Apr. 30, 1978.

White, Perry. "Chattanooga Seniors to Sponsor Oklahoma Toby." *Big Pasture News* (Grandfield, OK), Mar. 29, 1976, p. 1.

———. "First Season's Show at Harvest Playhouse." *Big Pasture News* (Grandfield, OK), Feb. 12, 1975, p. 1.

———. "Oklahoma Toby Goes to Olustee." *Big Pasture News* (Grandfield, OK), Oct. 1, 1975, p. 1.

Wilson, Truett. "They Kept 'Show on Road' for Nearly 50 Years." *Wichita Falls (TX) Times*, Mar. 12, 1961.

Dissertations and Theses

Clark, Larry Dale. "Toby Shows: A Form of American Popular Theater." Ph.D. diss., Univ. of Illinois, 1963.

Kittle, Russell Dale. "Toby and Susie." Ph.D. diss., Ohio State Univ., 1969.

Klassen, Robert Dean. "The Tent Repertoire Theater: A Rural American Institution." Ph.D. diss., Michigan State Univ., 1969.

Prince, Jane E. "Treatment of Female Characters in Selected Tent Show Dramas." Master's thesis, Texas Tech Univ., 1977.

Richer, Suzanne DePauw. "Harley Sadler and His Own Company," Master's thesis, Texas Tech Univ., 1973.

Snyder, Sherwood III. "The Toby Shows." Ph.D. diss., Univ. of Minnesota, 1966.

Sprague, Kathleen Judith. "The Haverstock Family Tent Show." Ph.D. diss., Texas Tech Univ., 1989.

Index

Abbott and Costello, 13, 125
Affairs of Rosalie, 86, 114
Altus, OK, 33, 41, 55, 94, 97
Alvord, TX, 95, 97, 102, 117, 126, 127
Apheatone, OK, 41
April Fools, 86
Archer City, TX, 31, 41
Are You a Democrat?, 114
Arlington, TX, 128
Ashby, Clifford, 8, 129
Awakening of John Slater, The, 13, 80, 119, 129

Back Home in Tennessee, 122
Bailey, Mollie, 36, 45
Bailey Dramatic Stock Co., 45, 46
Ball, Lucille, 13, 92
Bara, Theda, 81
Batch Royal Show, 24
Baxter, Warner, 125
Beaumont, TX, 38
Because She Loves Him So, 119
Belleville, IL, 46
Berle, Milton, 13, 125
Bernhardt, Sarah, 8, 9
Big City Co., 27
Billboard, 7, 8, 12, 24, 85, 87, 93, 94, 97, 101, 102, 103, 105, 109, 119
Bill Bruno's Bulletin, 85
Birth of a Nation, 126
Boston Bloomer Girls' Baseball Team, 34
Bourbon, MO, 50

Branson, MO, 13
Breakman, TX, 49
Breckenridge, TX, 41, 49, 97
Bristol, IN, 15
Brooklyn, NY, 23
Brooks, John, 82
Brooks, Oma, 82
Brown, Pete, 126
Brunk, Hank, 95
Brunks' Comedians, 43, 81, 95
Bryan, TX, 31
Bryan, William Jennings, 6, 15
Burkburnett, TX, 41, 55, 58, 77
Burlington, IL, 21
Byers, Alex, 11

Camble, Bess, 104
Carrollton, TX, 55
Cassville, MO, 51, 52
Cavitte, Lillie, 87
C. Charleston Guy Rep Co., 10
Celina, TX, 55, 86
Centralia, IL, 126
C. G. Conn Band Instruments, 16
C. G. Phillips Touring Co., 23
Champaign-Urbana, IL, 102
Chaplin, Charlie, 125
Chapman, Audie, 106
Cheer for the Allies, A, 111
Cheerful Liar, A, 119
Cherryvale, KS, 51
Chicago, IL, 9, 40, 49, 50
Circus Day, 122

Index

Clarendon, AR, 25
Clarendon Opera House, 25
Clark, Al, 46, 114
Cleveland, OH, 103
Clouds and Sunshine, 10, 122
Cobwin, Zane, 87
Codfish Aristocracy, 86
Coke, Ed, 51
Cole-Haverstock Theater Co., 33
Collier, Jack, 114
Collins, E. N., 54
Comfort, TX, 43
Cookietown, OK, 41
Cooperton, OK, 83
Corn Crib Theater, 13
Corpus Christi, TX, 39, 40
Cosgroves, Thomas, 46
Cowboy Toby, 122
Cox, Ramblin' Ray, 114
Crash Landin', 119
Crawford's Comedians, 52
Crawley, George J., 87
Crestview Memorial Cemetery, 123, 127
Crowell, TX, 33

Dallas, TX, 9, 78, 128, 130
Daniel Boone Show, The, 22
Danville, IL, 59, 102
Davenport, Joseph, 108
Davidson, OK, 41, 55
Dead Man's Letters, 114
Dean, Billy, 121
Dean, Jimmy, 121
Decatur, TX, 110, 111
DeGaffirilla, Marie, 54
Delharce Playhouse, 90
Deputy Sheriff Toby, 114
Detroit, TX, 87
Devil's Doorstep, The, 87
Devol, OK, 41, 55, 77
Dothan, AL, 104
Driver, Walter, 7
Driver's Improved Theatrical Tent, 7
Dr. Jekyll and Mr. Hyde, 89
Dubinsky Brothers, 125

Eagles, Jeanne, 125
East Lynne, 8, 37, 41, 80
Edmondsville, MO, 46
Effingham, IL, 102

Eldorado, OK, 33, 41, 55
Electra, TX, 54, 77
Elkhart, IN, 14, 15, 16, 17
Elkhart, TX, 51
Ellington, Duke, 98
Elmer, OK, 98, 106
End of the Trail, 122
Erick, OK, 55
Evening Shade, AR, 26
Exeter, MO, 51, 52

Fanshawe, Arthur L., 48, 89
Farmer, TX, 31
Farris, Don, 83
F. C. Perry Co., 23
Felton, King, 106
First-of-May, 19, 20
Flyer Toby, 111
Folsom, NM, 31
Ford, Wallace, 125
Fort Worth, TX, 57, 97
Fox, John, Jr., 10
Frederick, OK, 41
Fredericksburg, TX, 43
Frisco, TX, 55
Ft. Dodge, IA, 10

Gable, Clark, 125
Galveston, TX, 43
Gems, Julius, 48
Girl He Left Behind, The, 111
Girl Shy, 119
Glick, Bob, 107
Glover, Mina, 38, 47, 48
Gone with the Wind, 123
Goultry, OK, 93
Grace Church of Christ, 123, 127, 128
Graham, TX, 31, 41
Granbury, TX, 13, 129
Grandfield, OK, 13, 41, 43, 55, 58, 94, 97, 109, 121, 123
Granite City, MO, 46
Grassold, Charles, 115
Gravely, MO, 52
Green, Harvey, 20, 21
Griffith, D. W., 24
Guin, Lorin H., 10

Harley Sadler Show, 13, 121
Harmon, OK, 55

INDEX

Harveys' Comedians, 55
Haverstock, Carlotta Mosher (Lotta): birth and early family, 23; buys first tent show, 33; buys Mollie Bailey show, 45, 46; children, 32, 42, 43, 44; death, 28, 123; first Haverstock Comedians, 55; first home in Olney, TX, 31, 32, 33, 34; with King-Cole show, 32, 33; King-Haverstock show, 36; luxury wardrobe, 56, 77, 95; marriage, 26; meets Harvey, 18; preacher shows, 79; as Susie, 92, 93, 94, 123; Swift shows, 28, 29, 30; tearjerker ingenue, 41, 42; theater debut, 23; trailer home, 99, 101; train accidents, 47, 48; vaudeville star, 21; World's Fair, 21, 22
Haverstock, Harvey (Haver): baseball, 17, 18, 31, 32, 34; birth and early family, 14, 15, 16; buys first tent show, 38; buys Mollie Bailey show, 45, 46; candy bally, 95, 102, 103; children, 32, 44, 48; circle stock, 82; comedy writer, 119; death, 127; ends show, 126; enters show business, 20, 21, 24, 25; first Haverstock Comedians, 28; first home in Olney, TX, 31, 33, 34, 37; first job, 15; Harvey's Comedians, 55; IL routes, 102, 109; with King-Cole show, 32, 33; King-Haverstock show, 36; marriage, 26; meets Lotta, 18; "million friends" motto, 56, 89, 130; music, 18, 20, 21, 22, 25, 26, 35; railroad jobs, 21, 22, 45; routebooks, 104; St. Louis home, 49, 53, 60; Swift shows, 25, 26, 30; tearjerker years, 40, 41; tent ads, 85; Toby, 83, 84, 99, 129; trailer, 101; train accidents, 46, 48, 49; trucks and autos, 58, 100, 111; withholding system, xiv, 60, 81
Haverstock, Peggy Meador: community volunteer, 130; enters show, 96; illness, 128, 129, 130; magic act, 103, 122, 124; marriage, 97, 98, 99; places artifacts, 129; salary, 101; salesclerk, 128; Susie role, 124; trailer, xviii, xix, 99, 101; Wichita Falls home, 113, 122, 127
Haverstock, Rolland: army days, 111, 112, 115, 118; artist and poet, 112, 113, 126; baseball, 88, 89, 128; birth, 27; death, 128; enters show business, 42; joins Sadler show/team, 89; magic, 103, 122, 124; post office work, 125, 127; salary, 101; schooling, 49, 88; trailer, 101
Haxton, Toby, 11
Headin' for Heaven, 111, 119
Hearn, Harry, 106
Henpecked Toby, 122
Her Bandit Lover, 114
Herman, W. C., 10
Herrick, IL, 115
Hess, OK, 41
Hill, Harvey, 43, 51, 55
Hillsboro, TX, 102
Holliday, TX, 41
Hollis, OK, 55
Houston, TX, 43
Howell Players, 86, 87
Huguenot, Harry A., 88

I'm from Missouri, 122
Iowa Park, TX, 78
Isbell, Della Ilee, 104
Iseley, Phyllis. *See* Jones, Jennifer
Isle of Spice, 27

Jack-O-Diamonds, 43
Jacksboro, TX, 31
Jack Swift Show, 25
Jed, The Jellybean, 114
Jennings Brothers' Two-Car Dramatic Co., 38
Jones, Jennifer (Phyllis Iseley), 125
Just Plain Folks, 119

Kansas City, MO, 59, 82, 86, 87
Kaye, Joseph, 84
King, Howard, xvi
King, Katherine, xvi
King-Cole Stock Co., 32, 33
King-Haverstock Co., 36

Lane, W. B., 86
Lawton, OK, 97, 98, 99, 122
Lebanon, IL, 46
Lee, Pinky, 13
Leedy, OK, 55

Index

Lena Rivers, 8, 37, 53, 80
Lester, Alyce, 105
Lester, Varge, 105
Levy, Jules, 16
Lightning Love, 113, 114
Logan Point, IN, 22
Longview, TX, 38
Lorange, Nelson, 50
Love and Horseradish, 86, 114
Loveland, OK, 41
Loving, TX, 31
Lowry, Velma E., 80
Lubbock, TX, xvii, xviii, 129

Madden, Dale, xvi, 124
Madden, Lois, 124
"Maid and the Dummy, The," 21
Majestic Vaudeville Circuit, 21, 22, 25
Mangum, OK, 33, 55
Marchman Hotel, 128
Marion, IN, 43
Mary-Frank Players, 93
Maxwell, Jack, 86
McDaniels, Barney, xiv, xv, 108
McKennon, Marian, 119
McKennon Tent Repertoire, 119
Meador, James, 113
Meador, Margie, 127, 130
Meador, Nelle, 102, 125
Meador, Rowe, 96, 120, 127, 128, 130
Megargle, TX, 49
Melrose, Don, 82, 86, 113
Mickel, Jere C., 81
Milikin Glass Co., 24, 25
Miller, Bill, 111
Miracle, Gilford, 94
Morris, Joe Alex, 80
Moseley, M. A., 86, 87
Motley, TX, 33
Mt. Pleasant, IA, xvii, 130
Mt. Vernon, IL, 102
Mt. Vernon, OH, 24
Muenster, TX, 55
Murphy, Horace, 11
Murphy's Comedians, 11
My Only Girl, 111

Neff Theater Co., 36, 37
Negri, Pola, 81

Nero, Roe, 88
Newcastle, TX, 30, 31
New York City, NY, 21, 23, 24, 28
Night Club Nellie, 114
Nimitz Opera House, 43
Noble, IL, 114
North Judson, IN, 17, 18, 21, 24
Novarro, Ramon, 81
Nowlin, John M., 115

Okeene, OK, xvi
Oklahoma City, OK, 8, 57
Old Hickory, TN, 105
Olney, TX, 29, 30, 31, 32, 33, 34, 35, 41, 49, 77
Olney Opera House, 29
Olustee, OK, xvi, 33, 41, 55
One Happy Family, 114
On the Spot, 114
Osage, IA, 55
Out of the Fold, 10

Paris, TN, 119
Patricia Shoppe, 128
Patterson, Frank, 43, 121
Pearce, Bess Browning, 41
Pennington, J. F., 51
Pickford, Mary (Gladys Smith), 24
Plano, TX, 130
Playing with Love, 114
Polly of the Circus, 54
Preaching Molly, 87
Pryer, Arthur, 17

Quannah, TX, 33
Quapaw, OK, 52, 53
Quick, Elizabeth Mosher (Lotta's sister), 23, 26, 44, 59, 102, 113

Rabbit Creek, OK, 41
Randlett, OK, 41
Ranney, Omar, 124, 125
Rathbone, Lou, 48, 51
Rathbone, Orpha, 48, 51
Rhea, Charles D., 50
Rhome, TX, 102
Richeson, Rich, 90, 91
Ripley's Believe It or Not, 49
Rip Van Winkle, 43, 89

Index

Robinson, IL, 26, 27
Robinson Opera House, 26, 27
Roddy, Sterling S., 58
Roddy Trucking Line, 58
Romance in the Valley, 122
Rome, NY, 88
Roosevelt, OK, 33, 37, 38, 39, 41, 53, 55, 82, 94
Roosevelt High School, 88
Rosie of the Rancho, 122

Sadler, Harley, 8, 11, 13, 81, 88, 89, 121, 129
Saintly Hypocrites and Honest Sinners, 80
Salina, KS, 90, 91
San Francisco, CA, 9
Saturday Evening Post, 80
Sayre, OK, 55
Schaffner, Caroline, xvii, 10, 91, 92
Schaffner, Neil, 10, 11, 13, 80, 91, 92
Schaffner Players, 10, 13
Schricker, Henry, 18
Schricker Hall, 18, 21
Schuyler, Carl, 38, 48
Sensible Heart, 122
Sentinel, OK, 55
Seymour, TX, 31, 33
Shadows and Ricochets, 111
Sheets, Virginia, 91
Sheriff, The, 122
Show People's Candy Co., 103
Silver Dollar City, 13
Sis Hopkins, 10, 91
Sleet, Clair, 55
Slout, William, 4, 5
Smith, George, 16, 17, 18
Smith, Gladys. *See* Pickford, Mary
Sollen and Needles New South Showboat, 21
So This Is Television, 102
Sousa, John Phillip, 16, 45
Spirit, The, 111
Sprague, Judi, 129
Sputters, 119, 122
St. Charles, MO, 46
St. Elmo, 43, 79
Steppin' on the Gas, 119, 122
St. Louis, MO, 21, 23, 25, 26, 29, 35, 40, 43, 44, 45, 49, 50, 53, 54, 57, 58, 59, 60, 77, 80, 86, 88, 94, 113, 114
Storm Over London, 111
Strong City, OK, 55
Sundown at Honeymoon Ranch, 126
Swain, W. I., 55
Sweetest Girl in Dixie, The, 43
Sweet Papa Toby, 114
Swift, Daisy, 18, 23, 24, 25, 102
Swift, Herb, 18, 24, 25, 28, 29, 30, 31, 127
Swift, Herbie, Jr., 48, 50, 58, 100, 109, 111, 121
Swift, Jack, 18, 19, 25, 102
Swift, Nina Mosher, 18, 23, 24, 25, 26, 28, 31, 48, 50
Swift, Rita, 109, 121
Swift Brothers' Circus, 18, 20, 22, 28, 30, 31, 129

Tenderfoot, 120
Ten Nights in a Barroom, 20, 37, 42, 80
Tent Repertoire Museum, xvii
Terrall Tent Co., 93
Terre Haute, IN, 22
Texas Tech University, xvii, 13, 129
Thardo, Paul, 121
Thardo, Ted, 121
Theater Arts, 124
Theater Magazine, 84
Throckmorton, TX, 31, 41, 49, 97
Tipton, OK, 94, 97, 99
Toby from Arkansas, 86, 114
Toby Hits Hitler, 111
Toby in the Service, 111
Toby's American Sweetheart, 111
Toby's Maw, 87
Toby Takes Over, 122
Toby, the Super Spy, 111
Trail of the Lonesome Pine, 10, 120
Trousdale, Winn, 81
Tufts, M. B., 23
Turn to the Right, 79

Uncle Edward's Circus, 126
Uncle Tom's Cabin, 8, 20, 23, 29, 79
Undercurrent, The, 86, 114
Unto a Land, 41

INDEX

Valentino, Rudolph, 81
Victorious Romeo, The, 122
Victory, OK, 41
Violin Maker of Cremona, The, 24

Waco, TX, 9, 102
Wallis Tent Co., 38
Walnut Hill, IL, 126, 127
Walters, Herb, 80
Walton, Eugene, 43
Wayne, Kenneth, 114
Westerner, The, 120, 122
Wewoka, OK, 86
What Sammy Brought Home, 114

When Jimmy Came to Town, 86
Whitford, Fred, 48
Whose Gal Are You?, 119
Wichita, KS, 59
Wichita Falls, TX, 96, 98, 102, 122, 123, 125, 127, 128, 130
Wichita Opera House, 98
Williams Stock Co., 27
Wilson, Fred, 11, 12
Winniger, Charles, 125
Wolf, The, 43
Wood River, MO, 46
Woodson, TX, 49
Worthington, Jack, 53

Robert Lee Wyatt III is an associate professor of education at East Central University in Ada, Oklahoma. His specialty is elementary and secondary language arts education. He has taught at the University of Oklahoma from which he holds his baccalaureate, master's, and doctor of philosophy degrees. He was head of the Department of Journalism at Tarrant County Junior College in Fort Worth, Texas, in 1970. Wyatt was a motion picture writer and director as an industrial engineer with General Dynamics in the 1960s. He owned and published a weekly newspaper in Grandfield, Oklahoma, from 1976 to 1986. He taught secondary school in Iowa Park, Texas, Las Cruces, New Mexico, and Grandfield, Oklahoma for more than twenty-five years. He has published three books of area history and has seen performed both a one-act play and a high school musical that he wrote. He has been directly involved in founding two community theaters, and in seventeen years, he directed more than a hundred plays at Harvest Theater in Grandfield, Oklahoma. He is also a watercolor artist and has had numerous one-man public showings of his work. As a fiction writer, he has completed three novels.

PN2297.H38 W93 1997
Wyatt, Robert Lee, 1940-
The history of the
Haverstock Tent Show : "the
show with a million friends

OHIO UNIVERSITY LIBRARY
Please return this book as soon as you have finished with it. In order to avoid a fine it must be returned by the latest date stamped below. All books are subject to recall after two weeks or immediately if needed for reserve.

TOBY AND THE

In a New 3-Act Come...

With Sensational F...

★ MUSICAL M...
★ LIGHT...
★

EXTRA! AT...

ROLLA...